LIVE LIKE YOUR HEAD'S ON FIRE

GW00728072

Sally-Anne Lomas

To the CH girls for the blessing of lifelong friendship

Flame on!
Live like your head's on fire
Sally-Anne Lomas

Contents

Prologue: The Dancing Seed   9

Part 1: Trial by Fire   15

Part 2: Trial by Water   121

Part 3: Trial by Cheese Grater   275

"She burns but she is not consumed."

- Scott Cairns

Prologue:
The Dancing Seed

I'd never thought about being a dancer until the morning I went crazy in dance class. If I'd known that would lead to me running away from home then I wouldn't have dared take a single step. But maybe there's a seed inside each of us that's going to grow the way it grows, whatever, like a daffodil bulb is destined to be a daffodil and can't ever be a primrose. My name's Pen Flowers. People say stupid things like – *what kind of flower are you?* Maybe there was always a dancer inside me just waiting for the right conditions to shoot out.

Some seeds in Australia need to be burnt alive in forest fires *in order* to grow, others want drowning in cold, dark water for months. There's a rose in our garden called Penelope, same name as me, with squishy, pale peach flowers. I love to push my face into the petals and hoover up the lush smell. Rose seeds have to be scoured and flayed for them to germinate. Maybe that's what it takes to be a dancer; fire, water and a giant cheese grater scraped over your skin. Maybe the betrayal, the shame, the overwhelming fear, had to happen – to test if I was tough enough. How else do you learn to live like your head's on fire?

Part 1:
Trial by Fire

1

We always had dance last class before lunch on Tuesdays. It wasn't ballroom or anything awful like that, it was modern dance, you know, making up moves to music. The trouble was I really liked dancing but my best friend, Tamasin, thought it was stupid. She took dance as the soft option for PE like most of the other girls.

'Begin.' Mrs Hadley shouted and a high haunting bassoon solo drifted into the silence. Everyone was spread around the edges of the school hall. We were starting a new piece called *First Day*. The idea was that we were curled up like embryos inside eggs and Mrs Hadley wanted us to break out of our shells as if we were seeing the world for the first time.

The music was quiet and tender so I came up onto my knees, keeping my head down and rocking gently. Safe inside my shell I waited. Through the screen of my hair I watched what the others were doing. Next to me, Vivienne Cooper, with her mouth open and eyes popping, was dazzled with wonder by the sight of the school chairs stacked into piles on the opposite side of the room. Tamasin was already on her feet. She'd pulled her gym shirt over her head, and with her hands out in front of her was staggering around like a zombie. The girls near her were sniggering. She was looking my way expecting me to join in but I didn't want to.

The music was strange, like nothing I'd ever heard before. There was a jagged edge to the notes and I liked how fierce it was. The wooden floor felt rough beneath my hands and knees. I pushed up into the middle of my back, arching as high as I could. The music was seeping into me, filling me right to the skin. As long as the chords remained slow and drawn out, I was going to keep stretching, pushing my muscles to their limit.

The tempo changed suddenly and there was an explosion of noise as the whole orchestra roared out together. I tucked my head under and rolled forwards so fast that I came up into a crouched standing position. I didn't stop to consider what anyone else would think I just went for it. The music was harsh and fast and full of fury. I started lashing out with my arms and legs and jerking my head as I ran, leaping and slashing through the air. The music had grabbed hold of my will and I had no choice but to run and jump and punch and kick until it let me go. The school hall was barely big enough to contain me.

When the music finally slowed into a mournful, messed up lullaby, I sank down onto my knees, rolled over onto my back, and then lay on the floor twitching. My heart was crashing so hard against my ribs I thought it might burst through. Staring up at the vaulted ceiling, I imagined the night sky, galaxy upon galaxy stretching above me. Keeping my head and shoulders on the floor, I turned myself in a circle, using just my feet, as if the world were turning under me and I was floating away into the soft, cool, darkness of outer space.

I was out at the far edge of the known Universe when the bell went for the end of lesson. The music stopped and suddenly I was lying in the middle of the school hall with everyone staring at me.

What had I done? I stayed on my back and closed my eyes. I wished I could vanish, puff, gone.

Tamasin said, 'I think Pen's must have been a dragon's egg.'

And Sadie Thompson, the class bitch and my vowed enemy, answered, 'Yeh, right, some kind of reptile.'

Tamasin, annoyingly, laughed.

The room filled with chattering voices and a draft came in through the doors as the class filed out of the hall. I sat up and crawled over to the place where I'd left my bag. Vivienne was waiting there, grinning at me. I avoided looking at her.

'That was really good, like, what you did.'

'Yeh,' I picked up my bag and moved away but she walked after me.

'No – honestly, it was amazing, like freaky, but amazing. Everyone stopped dancing and watched you.' Vivienne was dark haired, dark eyed, heavy, and clueless. She really did arrive at school every day as if she were new born. I knew I was in for trouble.

'Penny,' Mrs Hadley was calling me. She always

wore the most ridiculous outfits. Today she was blinding in a neon pink playsuit. I don't know where she got her bras from but her breasts protruded like two traffic cones. She turned and they pointed straight at me.

'You put your heart into that Penny, well done.'

My shoulders rose up my neck and I stepped away but she moved in after me.

'What made you respond so energetically?'

'Don't know,' I managed, as she stood there with her hands on her hips smiling at me in a determined way, 'the music?'

I tried to squeeze past her but she wasn't going to let me go until I delivered. 'I was thinking about how it would feel to be in your body for the first time.'

'Oooh,' she cooed, her mouth a little round donut, 'I like that, I like that very much. We could work that into a solo for the dance show.'

A screeching chord crashed through my head. She had to be joking. Mrs Hadley carried on smiling as if she'd given me a present. I stared at her face. The mole on her chin had three white hairs coming out of it. Her lipstick frayed at the edges, drifting up the tiny channels that feathered out from her lips. Being in the dance show was one thing - but a solo? The idea was terrifying. Me, on my own on stage in front of hundreds of people; impossible, crazy, total insanity. I had to say 'no' quickly.

Mrs Hadley was watching me; waiting. The problem was, a part of me had been enchanted by that strange, angry, music. A wave was swelling up inside me and surging forward to break over Mrs Hadley's conical breasts.

'Okay,' I said. And that was that, from then on, I was doomed.

2

Why had I danced like that? What had come over me? I walked slowly down the oak panelled corridor towards the changing rooms. We wore our gym kit for dance so I needed to put my uniform back on. The dinner ladies were clattering steel trays in the kitchen and the rank smell of fried mince caught in my throat. The thought of facing Sadie Thompson made me feel sick. I could wait until the lunch bell rang when the changing room would be empty but why should I have to lurk about getting cold? I carried on through the cloakrooms towards the extension where the showers were.

Kings - that's my school - was originally a boys' school but about a hundred years ago they added a girls' school next door. The boys had the old building but ours was nicer with pale coloured wood and huge windows looking out over the playing fields. It's supposedly one of the best schools in Birmingham. We used to be a grammar school but now you had to pass a special exam to get here and pay fees. Most of the girls' parents are lawyers or doctors or company directors; posh types.

There are only four girls in our class with free places. Julia Worth who lives miles away and is unbelievably clever and comes top in everything. Then there's Vivienne and Sadie. They're both from Kings Heath. I think the school has to take some local girls. Vivienne's Dad is a window cleaner and her Mum works at the chocolate factory. Sadie's Dad's the foreman at the car manufacturers in Rubery. If our class were a wolf pack, Sadie would be the leader and Vivienne the runt. Poor Vivienne, Sadie is always picking on her. I don't know why Sadie is so powerful. Tamasin's pretty and clever and funny, so of course she's popular, but with Sadie it's just the force of her personality. I don't like the way she dominates so I try to stand up to her.

And finally there's me, Penelope Flowers, most people call me Pen. We're not really poor but without the free place we couldn't afford this school. My Dad works for an insurance company and he's an area manager now. I have no idea how I got the scholarship. Dad practically died of happiness. He goes around saying 'my daughter at Kings' until I want to tape his mouth shut.

As I reached the changing room the door closed. Inside I could hear shouting and loud guffaws of laughter. The door was painted a pale butter colour. Julia Worth came out, not a hair of her blonde bob out of place. She kept her eyes down as she passed me. Even though she was super clever Julia never opened her mouth in class. She had such a magical capacity for invisibility, sometimes I forgot she existed. Her instinct was to stay out of trouble. Unfortunately I had the opposite instinct. Trouble tracked me down. I caught the door with my foot before it swung shut and looked through.

Daisy and Flick were getting dressed at the far end of the room. When I walked in everyone went quiet and then Sadie and her gang burst into smothered giggles. They'd obviously been talking about me. I ignored them and walked over to my peg and started getting changed. A shout of laughter bounced around the tiled room and I turned. Sadie was hanging out her tongue and shaking all over. She started twitching as if she were having a fit and collapsed on the floor. People were darting sneaky looks at me. I should have ignored them but I couldn't stop myself.

'Aww, Sadie, I didn't know you were epileptic - don't bite your tongue off,' I said.

She kept jerking about on the floor imitating the way I'd spun myself at the end of my dance. Her chorus of supporters were falling about laughing. I turned back to the wall and started to pull my tights on, putting a fingernail through the nylon and laddering them. I hated the way the shower room smelt of wet mouldy towels.

Sadie kept wriggling on the floor enjoying the reaction she was getting. Tamasin was grinning and seemed amused. Even before the dance class I'd felt wound up but now the whole of me was seething like molten lava.

'Give over Sadie, stop that,' I said. She twitched even more, moaning as if she was having an orgasm. I went and stood over her.

'Stop it,' I shouted and when she didn't I just lost it and kicked her. I didn't really hurt her – just tapped her leg. She stopped moving and glared at me.

'You're a right bitch,' she said,' your dance was mental and you're mental.' The whole room was silent now their eyes on me and Sadie.

I was shocked at what I'd done. This sharp vicious feeling had flared up inside me filling my mind and I'd just lashed out. My legs felt shaky and I stumbled back over to my peg and sat down quickly. Sadie deserved to be kicked but I still shouldn't have done it. My emotions were in a whirl. I was angry and upset and ashamed at once. But I wasn't going to cry. I clenched my jaw hard and stared at Sadie until she looked away. She muttered 'Bitch' again and then picked up her bag and walked out. The rest of her lot followed.

I looked towards Tamasin who'd been keeping quiet at the other side of the room. She pulled a freaked out face as if it was all a joke. She didn't wait for me to finish changing, saying that she needed to get in the lunch queue. She had school dinners but I brought my own sandwiches because it was cheaper.

Sitting on the bench, in just my tights and shirt, I took as long as I could to tie the laces of my brogues. I bit the inside of my cheek.

Vivienne was the last to leave. She hovered by the door.

'You ok?' she asked.

'Fine,' The lunch bell was ringing. I stood up to put my skirt on, turning away from her. I heard the door close. It was kind of Vivienne to care but school was hard enough already without being associated with her.

When classes finished I couldn't face the bus queue so I raced out and sprinted up to the High Street to get on the bus before the others. Being on the High Street is a sixth form privilege but I don't see how they can enforce that. There's no law that says I can't walk up Kings Heath High Street. As a privilege it's not up to much. There's a Poundland, a WH Smith and a Boots and that's about it, not even a McDonalds.

There were two sixth formers eating donuts at the bus stop. They ignored me and before long the bus came. I helped an old lady struggling with a heavy shopping bag get onboard and then sat down next to her. She must have bought leeks because their oniony stink was stronger than the smell of diesel. My phoned bleeped. A text from Tamasin wanting to know why I'd rushed off. I didn't reply.

Outside the street lamps had come on and the sky was turning inky. The bus pulled up at the stop opposite the school gates and I watched the fight to get on. Girls pushed and shoved their way onto the bus squealing like gulls circling a bag of old chips. The noise bulged into the downstairs silence and then trailed up to the top deck. No one noticed me.

When the bus reached Bourneville, and the last of the Kings' girls got off, I went upstairs and sat on the front seat. There were miles to go before my stop but I liked looking down on the dark streets, watching people shuffling along wrapped in their stories. When we pulled into Harborne High Street a girl about my age, maybe a bit older, was leaning against the bus stop. In the light of the street lamp her auburn hair blazed against the black sky. She was pretty with a soft dreamy look. What if I had a best friend like her, someone I could talk to, and who understood how I felt? Maybe I wouldn't feel so lonely.

I leant against the window thinking about how stupid I'd been to do that mad dance, exposing myself to Sadie's scorn and Tamasin's laughter. What had made me do it? The music had matched a feeling trapped inside me. Perhaps I really was 'mental' like Sadie said. Like mother like daughter - was madness genetic? Since Dad's promotion he'd been working in Leicester for half the week and Mum's nervous problems had gotten worse. She'd been getting regular panic attacks. The one last night had been the worst yet. I'd calmed her down but somehow I'd got jangled up.

Maybe that was why I'd danced like that? I must have looked ridiculous leaping about going crazy. I expected to feel ashamed but I didn't, not deep down. Instead the music rushed back into my head and a ball of fire began glowing in my chest. I wanted to get up, right there on the bus, and start dancing again. I'd do the dance solo even if that meant fighting Sadie Thompson every day for the rest of term.

3

Mum and Thomas were cuddled up on the sofa watching telly when I got in. Thomas still had his pyjamas on and his hair was sticking up in clumps. Had he managed to skive off school again? Mum's left hand was on the go, repeatedly stroking the arm of the sofa. Her hand was like a little creature with a mind of its own and from the way her hand moved I could tell what kind of state she was in.

'Hi.' I announced. The local news was on, something about workers being laid off at the car factory.

'You're home at last,' Mum said. With Mum she's either like the gas fire turned up too high or else she's when it's about to go out, spluttering and popping.

The gas was way up in Mum's voice.

'Normal time. I'm starving. Have you started tea?' I asked. She obviously hadn't.

'We're having fish fingers.'

'Ok, I'll put them on.'

'No,' she shouted too loudly and jumped up, flinging the blanket off her knees. 'You've got homework.'

I went upstairs to change out of my uniform. I'd just pulled on my favourite jeans and was struggling into my baggy black jumper when Mum screamed in the kitchen below.

Thomas was there before me, reaching up to put his arms round her.

'It's ok Mum,' he kept saying. Her hand was bleeding.

'Stupid knife,' she looked at me as if I'd stabbed her, 'just slipped out of my hand.'

'Do you need a bandage?' I asked.

'No I'm fine,' she was cuddling Thomas. 'You go back and keep warm darling,' she told him. She'd been peeling potatoes in the sink.

'I'll finish these,' I said, 'you get the fish fingers

on.'

Mum fiddled with the gas grill, her hands trembling, snapping matches as she tried to get one to light. The automatic ignition had stopped working ages ago. The gas was escaping and would explode with a massive bang when she lit it. I worried that one day she'd burn her face off and I'd have to get her to hospital with her skin hanging in strips and the bones showing through. What if I couldn't handle it? Why did she make everything so difficult?

There was a square table in the kitchen and we each had a favourite chair. Even though Dad didn't come home on Tuesdays, we kept to our usual places. There was no ketchup because Mum had forgotten to put it on the table. I got up.

'Sit down Penny, you're always jumping about.'

'Ketchup,' I got it out of the cupboard and sat down again.

'How was school?' Mum asked. I pushed butter into the potatoes with my fork. She used to make proper mashed potatoes but now she didn't even do that.

'Alright,'

Mum clattered her fork against her plate.

'You used to be full of stories - never shut up.'

'Had dance today and Mrs Hadley wants me to…'

'Thomas,' Mum shouted, 'don't put your knife in your mouth,' cutting me off.

I didn't bother carrying on. She was looking away as if someone else was going to walk into the room and then she started.

'I could've been a professional dancer, after Blackpool. There was an agent wanted to take me on.' Mum was always going on about her ballroom triumphs.

I took a bite of fish finger. It was still frozen in the middle. I spat it out.

'These aren't cooked,' I said and Mum looked at me then.

'Mine are fine,' she said, like I was a liar. Thomas was shovelling in peas.

'We shouldn't eat them. I'll put them back under the grill for a bit longer,' I said. Mum threw down her cutlery so her knife bounced off the table smearing tomato sauce across the floor.

'Nothing I ever do is good enough for you,' she

cried in full on drama mode then ran out of the kitchen.

I picked up the knife and wiped away the ketchup. Upstairs the bedroom door slammed. I put everyone's fish fingers back under the grill. When they were golden brown on both sides I knew they were cooked. Thomas had gone back into the living room, so I put a plate over Mum's dinner to keep it warm, and took mine and his through.

'What's the matter with Mum?' He asked. Maybe she made him feel jumpy too.

'She's nervous, you know, scared.'

'But what about?'

'It's just her. She's poorly.' I didn't know how to explain when I didn't really understand.

'When will she be better?'

'I don't know.'

'When is Dad coming back?' Thomas asked.

'Thursday as usual I think.'

'He said he'd take me to watch City play.'

Do you want pudding?' I asked.

There was only a bit of ice cream left in the tub so I gave it to Thomas then went upstairs to see Mum.

Standing outside her bedroom door I could

hear her crying. I knocked and she said to come in. She was in bed in the dark with the blankets pulled up to her chin. The curtains were open so a glow of orange light came in from the street lamp. I sat down next to her and put my arm round her even though I couldn't bear the way her body twitched. She pushed her head into my shoulder.

'I'm sorry I upset you Mum,' I got the words out but felt as if a bit of frozen fish finger was stuck in my throat.

'No,' her crazy hand clawed at my arm, 'it's me. I'm useless. I make a mess of everything.'

'You're nervous that's all.' I tried to be sympathetic but part of me couldn't help agreeing with her. Why did I always end up looking after her? Why couldn't she look after me and Thomas properly like other Mums?

'I hate it here, I've never liked this house. We should never have moved.' Mum was always miserable. I spent a lot of time worrying about how awful her life was but nothing I did made her better. She had agoraphobia which meant she was scared of going outside on her own. She wanted to go out but thought she'd die if she did. Apart from the back garden, Mum hadn't been out on her own since Thomas was born, not once, and he was going to be ten in July.

'Come on Mum, come down and watch television with us. Maybe you should take one of your Valium.'

'OK,' she gave me a hug, 'you're a good girl Penny.'

Only I wasn't. She really annoyed me.

4

We had to write an essay on the slave trade for homework. I worked in the living room to keep Mum company. She was going through her ballroom dancing scrap book, pouring over the photos, and press cuttings. I decided I'd write as if I was an African living happily in my village, but then captured by slave traders, and taken on a terrifying journey chained up in a giant smelly ship. It wasn't the proper way of doing a history essay but I enjoyed writing it. When Mum said she was going to bed I was surprised that the time had vanished.

We always kept the landing light on because Thomas got scared. Well no, I want to be honest, it was me - I had a problem with the dark. I wasn't scared of burglars or rapists or anything like that, not things

I could fight. But what about supernatural creatures, ghosts of the dead or alien invaders who could harvest your organs while you slept? How did you deal with them?

I ran across the landing to my bedroom and dived into bed, squeezing my eyes shut and willing myself to go to sleep. But it was no good, the bad colours started. When I closed my eyes at night, weird lights - I called them the bad colours - attacked me so I had to keep my eyes open.

A branch knocked against the window. There was an ancient lilac tree right outside my bedroom which I loved. In spring the blossom made my room smell like heaven. I opened the window and cold night poured over me. A small round moon was tangled in the bare branches of the tree. I felt as if I could lean over and untie it, set it free to float across the sky. There were billions of stars, the obvious bright ones, then behind them splatters of minute dots. Looking up at the huge sparkling stretch of space I felt tiny in comparison. I had an idea – this was obviously my day for doing mad stuff - and pulled my clothes on over my pyjamas. Our kitchen extension had a flat roof where I sunbathed in the summer. I jumped down onto it.

Walking to the edge of the roof I climbed into the heart of the lilac tree, cradling my arms around the trunk. Standing in the main fork of the tree, the dark was no longer full of horrors. This night was gentle. I laid my cheek against the knobbly bark and looked up. Now I was in the tree the moon had slid across the sky and I wanted to follow. I thought about the essay I'd written describing the slaves chained up and unable to move. Our house was so full of Mum, with her energy pinging off the walls and bouncing around, that I felt as if there was no room to breathe, that in some way I was trapped, too.

Out here was different, out here I could fill my lungs with galaxies of space. A breeze whooshed through the lilac branches making them sway. I needed to get moving, the wind was calling me. I climbed out of the tree onto to the garden wall then scrambled over into the alley.

The moonlight gave everything a strange gleam. It must have been collection day because the bins were lined up outside the back gates like an alien army. I couldn't believe how bright the moon was; just crazy beautiful. I ran along the path as fast as I could, my shadow raced beside me, flying along the back fences. If only I could soar up into the blue-black velvet sky, not a bird but a winged horse, galloping the heavens. I sprinted then jumped, dashed then exploded, pushing myself to go faster, higher. I wanted to get back the buzz I'd had in dance class. The sense that I could be and do whatever I wanted without worrying about what other people thought.

I ran all the way down the alley from the back of our house to where it comes out just before the Lordswood Road. There was absolutely no one else around, every house was in darkness. There was just me owning everywhere. I felt so free, as if I could do anything.

When I got to the junction with Lordswood I stopped. A girl was walking along the pavement on the other side of the main road singing to herself. She was the one with auburn hair that I'd seen at the bus stop earlier. I'd never noticed her before and now she'd appeared twice in one day.

Stepping onto the main road out of the estate felt risky. I didn't want to go any further. Instead I twirled back down the middle of our street, arms stretched out making circular leaps one after the other, until I was back at our house. Behind the closed curtains, in the upstairs front bedroom, Mum was sleeping. She'd wanted to be a professional ballroom dancer but she'd given up. I didn't want to end up like her. What if I agreed to do the solo for the dance show and then I wasn't any good?

5

Rain battered against the classroom window on the day I started rehearsals. I was watching two drops have a zigzag race down the glass when the desks banged. Mr Richards, our form teacher, was already out of the door, off for his break-time fag, round the back of the staff room.

The usual crowd had gathered around Vivienne's desk. She brought in reject Creme Eggs from the chocolate factory shop that she sold at half price. For ten minutes every day, before the eggs ran out, she was the most popular girl in the class.

Sadie and Razi emerged first, peeling the foil off their eggs. At the back of the room, on Tamasin's desk, a group had started playing cards. Tamasin and

I usually sat together because our surnames followed alphabetically. This term Mr Richards had decided to change the desks around. Now I was near the window, miles away from Tamasin who was at the back on the other side of the room. Everyone loved Tamasin, with her curly blonde hair and funky green framed glasses, she was the coolest girl in the class. Effortlessly clever, she could mess around in lessons and still do well. I was about to go over but when Sadie and Razi joined her game I changed my mind.

Vivienne had sold her stock and was counting the cash. I didn't like Crème Eggs; the sticky white and yellow gunk felt disgusting coating my teeth. Vivienne looked up and seeing me watching her, put the coins into her purse, and walked over. She had long thick dark hair which she tied into neat pigtails. Her head was shaped like a potato with a pointed chin that seemed to have been borrowed from another face. Most people showed some of their top teeth when they smiled, but Vivienne showed all of her teeth and most of her gums too. Her square hands fiddled up and down the cord of her school purse which she wore the official way, over the shoulder and across her body. No one apart from year sevens did that. Everyone broke the cord and kept the purse in their pocket. I didn't understand how she hadn't noticed.

'I've saved one for you,' she took an egg out of her pocket. 'You don't have to pay.'

'Thanks Viv, but I don't like them.'

'Me neither, I've like eaten so many they make me feel sick now.' She sat on the window ledge in front of my desk looking at the rain. 'We'll have to stay in lunchtime. We could go to the library if you like?'

'Can't,' I said, opening my desk to avoid looking at her and moving stuff around. 'I've got a dance rehearsal.'

'Are you going to be in the dance show?' She shrieked, so everyone could hear.

'Shhhhh.' I tried to stop her.

'I said you were good, didn't I? Can I watch?' She gushed in the loudest whisper I'd ever heard. As the bell went, she leant forward and gave me a super gummy grin. 'Better get back to my desk, speak laters.'

I let out a long slow breath. All through the centre of me I'd contracted, a wave drawing away to sea that could now flow back over the shore. I couldn't bear the idea of anyone watching me. I'd have to sneak away quickly at lunch time or Vivienne might follow. I hadn't even told Tamasin I was doing the show.

Miss McBride, the history teacher, arrived and everyone went quiet instantly. She was one of the best teachers so no one played her up and everyone had their essay ready to hand in. We were doing the road to universal suffrage. We'd finished slavery and were onto working men getting the vote

She put up an illustration - crowds of working men marching towards Birmingham Town Hall surrounded by troops with guns. There was a quote. *'It was not Grey or Althorp who carried The Reform Act but the brave and determined men of Birmingham.'* As I copied the words in my notebook I could feel tears bubbling up. For some reason anything heroic sent me watery. I wanted to find a great cause to fight for, something that really mattered.

When the bell went I raced out of the classroom first so that no one would see where I was going. Tamasin would tease me if she knew and I couldn't handle that. Dancing mattered to me in a way I couldn't explain. But I needn't have worried she was already laughing at something on Sadie's phone. She didn't even glance in my direction.

The dance studio was at the back of the main school building. There were glass windows down one side, but as no one was using the playground in the rain I felt safe from view.

Mrs Hadley had given me a CD of *Rites of Spring* by Stravinsky, the music that had sent me wild in class. The piece was written for a ballet about a young girl being chosen as a sacrifice and how she danced to her death. How cool was that! As soon as the music began - I was off. The sound was like a socket with me as the plug, and once we were connected, energy charged through my body. I could have powered a train or the city centre Christmas lights. I was just getting into my groove when Mrs Hadley stopped the music.

'Let's pause there, Penny, the intensity is good but you need more control. You can't just flail about – it's got to grow.'

I felt embarrassed and stupid. This was exactly what I'd feared. I wasn't any good. I was going to make a complete twat of myself. I should walk out now. I didn't want to do the show anymore.

Mrs Hadley broke the music down into short sections and made me plan a series of moves and repeat the sequence until I remembered. I started to get what she was after. We were building up a pattern, like telling a story line by line. We took a simple punching movement which Mrs Hadley said was a 'motif' and we improvised ways of changing and adapting the move using different parts of my body. When the bell went for the end of lunch I didn't want to stop. I was too busy having fun to worry about whether I was good or not. This was the best thing I'd done since I came to Kings by a hundred million miles.

The chords were still playing in my head as I ran back to the classroom. I had to stop myself twirling down the corridor. There was a game of volleyball going on in the classroom, using someone's jumper tied in a ball. I dodged round to my desk. My hands were shaking as I pulled the tinfoil off my sandwiches. I was so hungry I crammed almost a whole sandwich in my mouth. Vivienne bounced over squatting down beside me, behind my open desk lid.

'Tamasin asked where you'd gone,' she whispered, 'she wanted to play table tennis.' My mouth was full of bread and cheese and the white pulp stuck to my palette. I felt so vulnerable about the solo and with Tamasin you had to laugh at everything. Not caring was cool. My courage was like a tiny snowdrop and if Tamasin trod on me I might not bounce back.

'I said I didn't know,' Vivienne continued.

I managed to swallow the giant mouthful of sandwich.

'Thanks Viv,' I said.

'I thought perhaps, you didn't want her to know?'

Maybe Vivienne wasn't as clueless as I thought.

'I just feel a bit embarrassed, you know, about the show.'

'Oh I get that – it's like really scary what you're doing,' she gave me her biggest gummy smile, 'but you'll smash it. Mum said come to tea tomorrow, if you want?'

I felt a rush of gratitude and found myself saying without thinking,

'Yeh, that'd be great.'

But the moment I agreed I regretted it. If the cool crowd saw me hanging out with Vivienne Cooper they'd drop me. If I wasn't careful I'd end up being outside the pack just like Viv was.

6

The next day I played table tennis with Tamasin as usual. We were both pretty good and neither of us liked losing.

'You know my birthday's next month?' She said as I served.

'Uh huh.' No way was she distracting me. I knew her tricks. At Kings we were divided into forms by date of birth. Our class were the spring babies born between February and May. The fee paying girls competed to have the best birthday party. Tamasin always won. Last year she'd had a disco with a real DJ and a glitter ball. She smashed the ball back but missed the table.

'Mum's says instead of a party I can take some friends to London. See a Show,' she said as I served.

She sliced the ball back into the far right corner and my back hand return went wide.

'Wow! That would be so cool .Your serve, 2-3,' I'd never been to London and was desperate to go. 'What about that new Westside story? The bit I saw on telly looked awesome.'

'I'll discuss with the Mater. She says I can take three friends,' Tamasin fired a serve down the middle of the table which I lobbed back. She played a neat forehand into the corner but it bounced up high and I slammed it so hard she didn't stand a chance.

'2, 4,' I called the score.

'Who else do you think we should take?' Tamasin served into the net.

'How about Vivienne?'

'Not potato head! There wouldn't be room in the car!'

'That's harsh. She's just curvy.'

'Yeh, and so's the Taj Mahal!' Tamasin expected me to laugh but I didn't. 'I thought about Sadie,' Tamasin continued, giving me a sneaky look. Was she trying to wind me up? She knew me and Sadie hated each other. What was going on? The hairs on the back of my hand prickled like they did when I felt frightened.

'3, 5,' I said without responding.

Tamasin hit the net with her return and carried on talking.

'Sadie goes to a youth club in Kings Heath and guess who else goes?' I waited for her to tell me. 'Only GB!' GB was Grant Barker, from the boy's school, Tamasin's latest crush. That explained why she was suddenly so interested in Sadie. 'I'm going with her on Friday. You might like to tag along.'

As if I was some pathetic sidekick! As if I'd go anywhere with Sadie.

'No thanks, 6, 4, my serve,' I said and she tossed me the ball. "By the way I'm in the dance show so I'll be rehearsing most lunchtimes.' I tried a fast slice serve and missed the table by a mile.

Tamasin made her eyes wide in mock surprise and tilted her chin up.

'Whatever does it for you darling, I'd rather die than be seen in public in a leotard, but it's your funeral.' She smashed my next serve straight back at me. I blocked and my return rolled over the net and died.

'My point,' I said.

I didn't mention about going to tea with Vivienne. Usually I told her everything.

The next day I hung back after school hoping that if we left late enough no one would see me going home with Vivienne. The drive had emptied by the time we emerged and I thought I was in the clear, but then Tamasin, of all people, was still standing at the gate waiting for her Mum to pick her up.

Vivienne said really loudly, for no reason, because she'd already told me,

'My house's just over the road.' Tamasin raised her eyebrows in a sarcastic way. Vivienne had walked ahead of me, so I grabbed a section of my hair and mimed being pulled along. Tamasin snorted and Vivienne turned round. I hoped she hadn't seen. I didn't want to hurt Vivienne's feelings but I didn't want Tamasin to be put out either.

I hadn't been to Vivienne's house before. She lived in a small red brick terrace that seemed to have too much furniture for the size of the rooms.

Mrs Cooper gave us chocolate cake as we sat

scrunched up at a sort of breakfast bar in the tiny kitchen. The cake was amazing, soft and fluffy with chocolate icing on top. I let each mouthful sit on my tongue and then moved the sweet mush around before I swallowed. Vivienne shovelled in a massive wedge. If I had the possibility of cake like that every day I'd probably be as plump as she was. Looking at the kitchen clock I couldn't believe it was only four twenty. Most days I'd still be at the bus stop fighting to get on a number eleven.

Vivienne's Mum looked just like her, same potato head, but with brown hair that curled up at the bottom, in a weird hair spray u-bend. You could have used her hair as a tray to serve nibbles on. The main problem with the kitchen, apart from its size, was that wherever you looked something bright leapt out at you. The walls were painted the yellow you get in a kid's painting set and the curtains had giant red poppies on them. Even Mrs Cooper was a visual challenge with an orange flowery apron over a maroon dress. All the colours banging together were making me feel sick, though that may have been the cake. I'd eaten a huge slice.

Mrs Cooper said I could borrow her bike if we fancied going for a cycle ride, but Vivienne wanted to show me her room. If I'd felt sick before, I had a problem not vomiting when she opened the door. The curtains, carpet, bedspread even the woodwork, were different shades of purple. It was like falling into a blueberry pie. As if the colour wasn't bad enough, the pop singer Dominic Sawyer leered down at me from every wall. Maybe I'd liked him when I was twelve but you'd have to torture me to admit it now.

'Purple's my favourite colour,' Vivienne felt it necessary to say. I couldn't speak. 'But you probably guessed that.' She laughed and sat down at a pretty kidney shaped dressing table with a three way mirror.

Vivienne opened the top drawer.

'Look,' she took out a black and white photo. Written in black felt pen was 'to Vivienne with love Dominic'. 'We went to London to see him in *Oliver*. The show was fantastic.' I didn't reply not wanting to be rude.

'Do you have a boyfriend?' She asked - out of nowhere. From the way she said it - I could tell that she had. How a girl who looked like Vivienne had managed to get a boyfriend was a mystery that even Sherlock Holmes couldn't solve. He must be some spotty wimp with sweaty hands hoping for a chance to paw at her enormous breasts. There was no way I was telling Viv that I'd never had a boyfriend. How was I going to meet any boys? By the time I'd got the bus home, looked after Mum and Thomas, and done my homework, I'd have to meet one in the middle of the night. I remembered the bikes.

'Let's go for a ride before it gets dark,' I suggested. Vivienne looked disappointed, cheated of her big love story revelation. I made for the door.

Mrs Cooper said we should fetch Viv's Dad back for tea, so we cycled down to the allotments. It was as if a slice of countryside had been dropped into the city. A soft peacefulness hung over the place. The allotments smelt of newly mown grass and wood smoke; two of my all-time favourite smells. They reminded me of Dad being home and the whole family outside in the garden. Mr Cooper was in his shed. When he saw Vivienne his face brightened like the sun had come out. He gave her a huge bear hug and promised to follow us in ten minutes.

There was just a line of pale peachy light left over the dark roof tops as we cycled back. Without the sunlight the temperature had dropped and as I stood on the pedals to get up the hill, I could see my breath reaching out in front of me. I tried to remember the last time my Dad had cuddled me.

There was steak and kidney pie for tea with chips and peas, plus homemade rice pudding with raspberry jam to ripple through. We sat in the living room with trays on our knees, and ate in front of the telly. Thomas would have loved it.

Vivienne and I cleared away the dirty plates. It was her job to wash up.

'Tamasin seems to be hanging out with Sadie now?' Vivienne said clattering a load of crockery into the water. I was drying up.

'Where shall I put the plates?' I asked.

'On the table. You wanna watch out for Sadie, she's like, well, she's got problems.'

I couldn't believe that Vivienne Cooper was giving me advice - *Here's how to become really unpopular like me.*

'You know her Mum died when Sadie was only ten?' Viv went on.

'No, how awful.'

'Yeh, it was breast cancer, very sad. We were like best friends at primary school and she was round here the whole time. But when we both got into Kings she started bullying me. I feel sorry for her but I don't like her anymore. Shall I tell you a secret?'

'What?'

'Promise not to tell anyone – not even Tamasin?'

'Ok.'

'Mum and Dad complained to the Head about Sadie and that's why we've all moved desks.'

So that was Vivienne's fault.

'You need to watch out. I think she's picking on you now.'

'It's ok Viv, I can look after myself,' I told her.

She'd made a mass of bubbles and flicked some at me.

'You sure? Anyway I'm really glad I've like ended up sitting near you.'

I did that trick where you crack the tea towel like a whip and swiped Vivienne's back.

'Oi!' she squeaked laughing.

Maybe there was more to Vivienne than I'd realised. She'd given me loads to think about. If Tamasin was hanging out with Sadie and Vivienne was right about me being Sadie's latest target where did that put Tamasin?

7

Mr Cooper gave me a lift home. There was only room for one passenger in his window cleaning van so Vivienne didn't come with us. I felt shy sitting on my own in the front with Mr Cooper.

'Viv says you're going to be in the dance show- is that right? I don't know much about contemporary dance – is it like break dancing?'

I explained how you had to make up your own moves, and that my idea was about being in your body for the first time. How I'd start with ugly moves but gradually turn them into something beautiful. Mr Cooper was listening and asking questions. He was really easy to talk to. When we got to the traffic lights in Selly Oak I realised I'd been jabbering on for ages.

'Well that's ace,' he said,' now I'll understand when I come and watch. We go to all the school shows. Viv loves them. She wants to be an actress, you know, goes to this Youth Theatre in the city.'

'Viv wants to be an actress?' I had no idea. It seemed so unlikely.

'Yeh, she's a deep one, lots going on you wouldn't notice.' I'd never thought of Vivienne Cooper concealing hidden mysteries but what did I know? Not much it seemed. The more I found out about Vivienne the more surprising she was. Not only did she have a boyfriend but she totally got that Sadie was dangerous and had even explained why.

Mum opened the front door.

'Is Dad back?' I asked.

'Listening to his programme.'

I felt a knot inside me loosen with relief and let out a big sigh. With Dad home I could stop worrying about Mum and Thomas.

He was in the front room sitting in his leather chair with head phones on. I went and curled up next to him. He always listened to 'Sizzlin' Jim' on Radio

Hoxton on Thursday nights when he got back from Leicester. He said the show relaxed him.

'I've been chosen for the dance show,' I told him. He frowned and shushed me with a finger to his lips. He hadn't seen me for three days but all I got was a shush. Mr Cooper had given Viv a big hug. Dad took off one side of his head phones.

'Early Louis Armstrong, pre 1925, with Bessie Smith on vocals. I've never heard it before. Extraordinary the recordings Jim gets hold of.'

He had his laptop open and was downloading tracks. He had thousands of old songs.

When Dad was away I longed for him to come home but he didn't really make much difference. He knew about Mum's panic attacks but hadn't bothered to find out how we were coping. He always had something; his music, or local history, or work, anything, to avoid being with us. He didn't seem to care anymore. He'd been promising to take Thomas to the football for weeks now but he never did. I wished I could talk to him like I had to Mr Cooper. My Dad didn't even want to know about the show and yet Viv's Dad was interested in what I was trying to say with my solo.

I retreated to my room. Dad was selfish. He spent his time lost in the past – either listening to his old fashioned jazz or obsessing about World War 2 and finding out where bombs had fallen in Birmingham. What about the things that were going on now? Like Mum being depressed and Thomas skiving off school. Looking after them shouldn't be my responsibility. I'd got enough to do with exams coming up, plus the dance show. I'd always thought of Vivienne as a loser but I'd swap my useless parents for hers any day.

8

On the night of the dance show I was sitting on top of my desk with my feet on the chair in front when Vivienne suddenly shrieked out.

'Oh my God, Pen.'

I kicked out in surprise and the chair fell back and banged into the desk in front. That was typical of Vivienne, wherever she was, noise was close by. She was reading my dance show programme and eating her sandwiches at the same time, getting greasy finger marks over the cover.

'What is it?' I fished the chair back upright and picked up one of my sandwiches. 'Have they spelt your name wrong?'

Mrs Hadley had said I needed someone to do the lighting cues for me. Tamasin acted as if the dance show didn't exist and as Vivienne had done lighting with her youth theatre I asked her. Tamasin wasn't really the back stage type.

'You're the only one doing a solo like out of the whole school,' Viv finished her sandwich and wiped her hands down her trousers. 'There's two sixth formers doing a duet, otherwise it's all groups.'

I put my sandwich back in the tinfoil wrapper. I didn't feel hungry any more. All day snakes had been squirming around my stomach and now they'd started crawling through my intestines heading for my bowels. Vivienne's helpful comments took immediate effect.

'I've got to go to the loo,' I said and sprinted for the toilet.

When I got back Vivienne had her mouth full of chocolate cake.

'Muuumsentissss' she said and handed me a slice. I couldn't eat - not even Mrs Cooper's chocolate cake.

'I'll save it.'

I put the cake into my lunchbox next to the uneaten sandwiches. The wall clock said six thirteen and I wasn't due on stage until seven forty five. Vivienne saw me looking at the clock.

'We've got ages yet. Do you wanna play a game? I've brought some cards.'

What I wanted was to disappear, to become a tiny speck of dust floating about at the fringes of the cosmos. If Vivienne hadn't been there I would have gone and sat underneath Daisy's desk in the far corner of the classroom. Instead we played *Racing Demons*. Vivienne slapped down the cards squealing 'Out!' as if she'd won a million pounds. Generally I'd be determined to win but tonight I didn't care. Mrs Hadley appeared at the classroom door just as Vivienne was screaming 'Out!' for the third time.

'Keep the noise down,' she said, 'the audience is arriving.'

Vivienne and I stared at her. Usually her hair was tied back in a bun but tonight it was flowing over her shoulders. She was wearing a long silky green dress. The neckline was so low you could almost see her nipples. I didn't dare look at Vivienne.

'You should get changed now Penny and remember to do your warm ups.' She walked over and put her hand on my shoulder. 'You'll be fine. Just concentrate on the music. Good Luck.'

She slinked out of the room. Our classroom was right by the front entrance with the door open we could hear the burble of voices out in the corridor.

'My Dad's going to get a right eyeful,' Vivienne said making me laugh. Mrs Hadley was quite tall and Mr Cooper wasn't. Vivienne was standing at the classroom door watching the people arriving through the foyer.

'I'm going to see if Mum and Dad are here yet. They promised they'd come early to get a good seat like. Do you wanna come look for your folks?' I shook my head.

'I'm going to get changed.'

Vivienne went out banging the door behind her.

I'd got the family tickets for the show but I didn't think they'd be there. This morning Mum had been shaking so badly she'd broken two of the breakfast bowls. Even if Dad got back in time I didn't know if he'd manage to get her out.

I was dressed in the tracksuit and t-shirt I'd worn for rehearsals. I wished I could do the dance in them. Wearing a leotard and tights made me feel as if it was my body and not the dance that was on show. Mum had ordered the leotard online and it was a tight fit but there wasn't time to order a bigger size. I kept remembering what Tamasin had said about not being seen dead in a leotard. My hands trembled as I took off my tracksuit bottoms and pulled on the black footless tights. I got into the leotard underneath my jumper. The classroom was bright with electric strip lights and the wall of windows projected an identical classroom onto the school lawn. I climbed up on a chair in the middle of the room and stepped barefoot onto the desk. I pulled my jumper over my head and stared at myself in the glass. Something terrible had happened to my body. My skinny legs and bony elbows should have made hard sharp lines but dressed in skin tight lycra I curved. I looked like Mrs Hadley, for God's sake. Things stuck out, breasts jutted from my chest and my stomach, hips and bottom were all circles. This tight black sheath had stolen my body and replaced it with someone else's. I wanted to run away. I couldn't go through with the dance, not looking like this.

I was getting down from the desktop when Vivienne came back.

'Mum and Dad are at the front in the middle. I couldn't see your parents but the hall's like completely packed. I think every seat is taken.' Then she noticed the leotard, 'Wow Pen.'

Trust Vivienne Cooper to make me feel a hundred times worse. I hurried to pull my jumper on and Vivienne managed to stop herself from saying what she was going to say and instead said, 'you've changed,' as if she was trying not to comment on the fact that I'd grown another head.

I sat down on the chair.

'I'm going to be sick.'

Vivienne went all Florence Nightingale, fluttering around me.

'Ok, put your head between your knees, breathe deeply, it's just nerves. I get them before a show. Take deep breaths.' She put a hand on my shoulder.

'Don't touch me,' I shook her off. 'Just leave me alone ok. I don't need you fussing around me.'

Vivienne had her sad puppy face on. 'Alright, I was just being kind. Please yourself.' The music for the first performance had started. 'If you don't want me here I'm going to watch the dancing.'

She went out leaving the door to bang again. I knew I'd been mean to Viv, that she was only trying to help, but I was too wound up to stop myself. I walked to the window and pressed my hot cheeks against the cold glass. I could run now, just go, disappear.

The square of garden in front of the school entrance was dimly lit by the outside light and looked like an empty stage. I imagined the cool damp grass under my feet and the night air on my skin. The black leotard would be camouflaged by the night sky. The dance was raging around my body like a trapped animal. I wanted to dance but out there on the dark lawn not on a stage. I started to pull my trainers on. I couldn't go through with this.

Then I saw Mum, Dad and Thomas making their way along the drive towards the entrance. I couldn't believe it; Dad must have come home early especially and brought Mum. She was clutching his arm while Thomas held her other hand but there she was walking up the steps into school. No way could I chicken out now. If Mum could leave the house then I could dance. And maybe if Dad was proud of me he'd spend more time with us.

9

Somehow I got myself to the wings of the stage five minutes before I was due to start. A group of year eights were finishing their comical routine. They were dressed up like robots in outfits made out of cardboard and silver foil. One moment the audience were clapping and then it was my turn.

I walked out into the centre of the dark stage and knelt in my starting position. My heart beat was crashing in my ears. I couldn't remember anything, not a single move. With my eyes closed I began to hear the sounds of people in the hall, voices murmuring, chairs scuffing and squeaking across the floor. I wanted to be beamed up to another planet. Inside I was trembling as if a trillion tiny feelers had been set to vibrate. My nostrils flared as I drank in the dark earthiness of the wooden floorboards. I looked down at my hands spread out underneath me and was surprised at how steady they were.

The music started and a spot light caught me in a bright circle. The music was my life raft and with every part of my body I listened. My brain had jammed stuck but my muscles began to move by themselves. Like a dog trained to respond, at the first trill of notes I swayed my head and then in the silent pause that followed I began to arch my back. Rolling forward on the next musical phrase I came up slowly to stand facing the audience. With the spotlight beam directed straight into my face I couldn't see anything just total blackness. Out there hundreds of eyes were fixed on me but I couldn't see them.

My mind turned inwards and settled. In the centre of my belly was the ball of fire. I let out a long slow breath and as the fierce music kicked in I erupted. Lava flowed through my veins from the soles of my feet to the roof of my scalp. I had never felt so much energy. This was my dance; and I would dance it just for me.

Every move that Mrs Hadley and I had invented was waiting to be expressed. I kept to the pattern and punched out the story. The stabbing motif that we'd woven through the dance marked the discords in the music; arms, knees, feet, elbows, even chin, every part of me played a version of the theme. I was fighting for my life. I was trapped. I was dying. I was the chosen one, the sacrifice. Anger poured out of me into the dance. I was doing the moves as I'd never done them before, higher, sharper, deeper, right out of the centre of me.

When the frenzied section of the music ended and the orchestra played the final strong, slow phrases I came to the front of the stage, and stood in a single spotlight reaching up and out. I felt mighty and humble at the same time, as if I'd cracked open and the sun had risen inside me, a glowing ball of scarlet, gold and palest pink. My body throbbed with life but my brain had rocketed out into the sky.

The spotlight went off and the applause was immediate and louder than even the loudest parts of the music. There was stamping and whistling. Someone I think it could have been Mr Cooper shouted 'Bravo'.

I ran to the side of the stage. Mrs Hadley was there and she grabbed hold of me. 'Curtain call,' she said and pushed me back onto the stage.

That was the absolute worst moment. All the stage lights were on full. Giggling year seven and eights were watching from the wings and I could see the audience looking at me. I had to walk to the front in my leotard and bow. I assumed my family were somewhere at the back of the hall. I could see Mr and Mrs Cooper down at the front. Mr Cooper was clapping like a loony, cheering as well. I thought he was going to stand up. I would have died.

10

I couldn't wait to find out what Mum and Dad thought. My body was buzzing in every cell, purring with delight. I ran back to the classroom, pulled on my tracksuit and grabbed my stuff. I'd put my real self out there on stage and amazingly people had loved it. I hadn't failed like Mum. It had gone better than I could've dreamed. The happiness inside me felt bigger than Jupiter.

Mum and Dad had said they'd wait for me in the school foyer. I was running down the corridor when someone called my name.

'Pen,' it was Tamasin's Mum. She wore high heels that clicked on the tiles as she trotted towards me. Tamasin was with her, wearing jeans and new boots that I hadn't seen before.

'Darling, you were amazing,' Tamsin's Mum gave me a giant hug, 'so exciting and dangerous. What a star you are; I'd no idea you could dance like that.' Tamasin's Mum was a lawyer who wore super stylish clothes. She could be a bit over the top but I really liked her.

'Thanks Mrs Fox,' I answered.

'Yeh, and you rocked that leotard,' Tamasin grinned at me. I wasn't sure if she was being sarcastic.

'We haven't seen you for ages,' Mrs Fox carried on, 'you must come over next week.' She looked at Tamasin who just said, 'text you later.'

'I need to find Mum and Dad,' I said, escaping.

My family were standing near the front doors and Miss McBride was with them. Mum was holding onto Dad's arm with her left hand but otherwise looked like a normal Mum. She'd washed her hair and was wearing a new blue dress that she must have ordered online. She squeezed my arm when I came up.

'Well done sweetheart, you were wonderful. I'm pleased you've inherited something good from me,' she laughed and looked happier than I'd seen her in ages.

Dad was talking to Miss McBride.

'Can we go now?' Thomas said pulling at his sleeve. Around us crowds of parents and kids were leaving. A cold wind blew in through the open doors defeating the school's central heating system. I felt shivery despite my jumper.

'I'd better let you go,' Miss McBride said, then focusing on me, 'very good Penny, very brave.'

I could feel water rushing up my throat and I got the sharp pain at the end of my nose I get when I'm going to cry. I gulped the feeling down and Miss McBride moved off to talk to another family. Dad turned and guided Mum towards the front door. I bounced after him.

'Well, what did you think?'

'You were fine. I hadn't realised how busty you'd got.' He walked onto the forecourt. 'All these cars, we'll never get out.'

'Can we have fish and chips on the way home?' Thomas asked.

How dare Dad say that? I wasn't busty - it was just that stupid leotard! What about the dance? I wanted to hit him. He'd spoiled everything.

'Stop pestering,' he said to Thomas.

'I'm hungry,' he insisted but Dad ignored him.

The car park was packed and Dad couldn't remember where he'd put our car. He pulled away from Mum walking ahead of us with his hand in his coat pocket jiggling the car keys. Without Dad to hold onto Mum's left hand began jerking. She tried to catch up but he marched off in front of her scanning the rows of cars for our Volvo. I could tell Mum was starting to panic so I caught up with her and held her hand. Her skin felt rough because of the eczema which broke out whenever her nerves got bad. Spasms of tension shot up my arm every time her hand jerked. My body stopped purring and locked into defensive tightness.

Dad found the car and he had the hand break off and the engine revving while we were still climbing in. With everyone leaving at once the school drive snarled up. People were reversing. Dad pulled forward into the line of cars waiting to get onto the main road.

'This is bloody ridiculous,' he said. 'We could be here all night.'

Mum said, 'there's no need to swear, calm

down.'

'I am calm,' Dad shouted.

The cars shunted forward and we started to move down the drive. Dad was revving the accelerator and driving close to the vehicle in front.

'You've been in a mood all evening,' Mum said. 'You'd think you could miss your precious history society for one night?'

'Don't start that again.'

'Please, Mum, Dad, don't argue,' I asked.

'When did we last go out as a family?' Mum ignored me. 'You never take us out anymore?'

'Stop this Jenny, you know the work pressure I'm under.'

I got my phone out and plugged my headphones in, turning the volume up as loud as it would go. Vivienne had sent me a message saying my dance was brilliant. Nothing from Tamasin.

When we got home Mum leapt from the car as we pulled onto the drive. She slammed the passenger door shut and ran into the house. Thomas found a football on the lawn and was kicking it against the front wall.

'Are we going to see City this weekend?' he asked Dad.

'Get in,' Dad pushed him through the front door. Mum was already in the living room with the door shut.

'You two had better go to bed. Take your brother up, Penelope, it's late.' Dad went into the living room and closed the door behind him. Thomas looked at me, and his round blue eyes were filling up.

'Are you still hungry?' I said. As if I needed to ask. I hadn't eaten anything all day and realised I was starving. In the kitchen I made jam sandwiches and poured us each a glass of milk. We could hear them next door.

'You've got to get a grip on yourself Jenny? You're not doing the exercises the doctor gave you.'

'You're supposed to help me with them.'

'You can't depend on me for everything.'

I remembered Mrs Cooper's chocolate cake and got it out of my school bag. There was easily enough for two. I cut it in half and Thomas pounced on his slice. Next door Mum was screaming.

'Just leave then, you obviously don't want to be

here?'

'If you're trying to get rid of me you're going about it the right way!'

'Gooooood cake,' Thomas had a chocolate ring around his mouth.

'I'm taking mine upstairs,' I said. 'You'd better come to bed too.'

'You don't understand how unhappy I am.' Mum was crying now.

'And that's my fault I suppose.' Dad voice sounded like he was giving up.

As we climbed the stairs to the landing I asked Thomas, 'What did you think of my dance?'

'It was good but I liked the robot one best.'

'Yeah,' I said, 'that was funny.'

I heard Mum rush upstairs and slam the bedroom door. Dad went into the front room and the distant sound of jazz music drifted into my room. He always played Bessie Smith after they'd argued. She had the saddest voice I'd ever heard, as if the sound was coming out of the darkest, bloodiest, part of her insides, like she'd spent her whole life chained up on a slave ship.

There was no way I could get to sleep. Lying still my muscles started twitching. I closed my eyes but the bad colours went wild behind my lids. I'd been so happy that Mum and Dad had come to the show but now that was ruined. They seemed to hate each other. Was Mum right? Did Dad want to leave or was she just being paranoid? I didn't know whether to cry or scream.

The music downstairs stopped and Dad came upstairs and stood at my bedroom door, a dark silhouette with a crack of landing light behind him.

'Penny?' he whispered. 'Are you awake?'

'I can't sleep.'

He came into my room and sat down at the end of my bed. I waited for him to say something about my show. Surely he must be proud of me. People were cheering. He patted my leg.

'Miss McBride says you're doing very well in your history GCSE, she wants you to do History A' level.' Why was he going on about exams? Why didn't he mention my solo?

'What about my dance?' I snapped at him.

'That was fine,' he said getting up.

'Fine!' I shouted. 'You didn't like it?' I couldn't believe he was being so horrible.

He turned back.

'Look your Mother wanted to be a professional dancer and failed. Every teenage girl in the world dreams of being a dancer but you're clever Pen, you've got this opportunity at Kings, you can do anything you want with your life.'

'Except dance,' I shouted.

'Dancing is fine as a hobby,' he got up again. 'Now get to sleep.'

I wanted to hurt him like he'd hurt me.

'How come you're never here? You know Mum's been really bad but you don't care about us.'

'Not you too! It's because I care that I'm away, working to earn money to keep this family afloat.'

'You don't know what it's like being left to look after her. What about me?' I was kneeling up in bed shouting into his face. I watched something flick over in his eyes.

'Don't I? Don't I?' Dad was shouting back at me. 'She's on the phone every day. I get it from the moment I walk in to the moment I leave. There's no escaping her needs. What kind of marriage is this? She's choking the life out of me.' And then abruptly he turned away and walked quickly out of my room switching off the landing light even though we always left the light on because of me and the dark.

I couldn't go to sleep, not after that. I was boiling with rage. I got out of bed and stalked around my room. The silence in the house banged against my ears. I had the worst, most awful parents in the universe and I hated them. Through the gap in the curtains came a pale blue light that made diagonal shadows on the opposite wall. I pulled back the curtains and saw the full moon. I tiptoed onto the landing and listened. Everyone else was snoring away. I put on my clothes and climbed out through my window.

11

The moon was a ball, hanging fat and white overhead. Cold night bathed my skin but inside I was boiling over. I ran up the road faster than a forest fire. I wished I could destroy everything in sight. Punching out my dance moves, I hit out at Dad, imagining him in front of me, pummelling him with my knees and elbows, then head butting him in a running charge.

How dare Dad say that 'every teenage girl' stuff? So patronising! I hadn't said anything about wanting to be a dancer. I just wanted him to be proud of me. Just to say I'd been good. I'd worked hard for weeks on my routine and poured all my thoughts and feelings into it. Why didn't he understand how important that was for me? Mum and Dad were both so wrapped up in their own stuff they didn't care about me and Thomas.

I remembered how I'd felt at the end of my dance, blazing with light. Now I wanted the darkness to fill me up, I wanted to drink in the cool night until I froze inside and couldn't feel anything.

He'd spoilt it for Mum too. She'd been so brave going out, even looking pretty and normal and happy for once, poor Mum. Dad was supposed to look after us but instead he'd ruined everything for everyone.

I raged my way to the end of our road with kick boxer style dance moves until I reached the junction with Lordswood Road and the main route into town. Last time I'd stopped here daunted by the wider emptiness. The houses were ginormous with a hockey pitch of grass separating their drives from the edge of the road. If I went any further I was leaving the safety of our estate.

I was deciding what to do when I heard male voices. I crouched down pressing myself against a hedge. In the silence of the empty streets I could make out everything they were saying.

'Man that would be freakin' cool?' said one voice.

'If Chas borrowed his Mum's car we could drive down,' the second voice was deeper.

There was a twig digging into my shoulder just beneath my armpit. I wriggled to get more comfortable and leaning forward slightly I saw two boys storming along the pavement from the direction of Harborne towards the Kings Head pub. One of them was huge, a walking wardrobe, in a long coat. I recognised the smaller one striding to keep up with the big guy, Mick Taylor. He'd been at my primary school but was two years older. His brother Wilf had been in my class.

'Are they only playing in London?' Mick asked.

'Or Glasgow,' the wardrobe answered.

They passed the pub, turning the corner onto the dual carriageway into town, and I couldn't hear them anymore. They were wandering about as if it was ordinary. If Mick Taylor could walk brazenly along the main roads at night then why shouldn't I?

I crossed over the grass, avoiding the brightly lit pavement and stayed in the shadow of the hedges. I couldn't hear any traffic, not even far off, just my own breath, panting in my ears. I practised moving silently like a Cherokee tracking. I was pretty good on the grass but when I had to cross a driveway every step crunched. Cherokee hunters didn't have to negotiate gravel when they were slipping unnoticed through the forest.

The pub on the corner loomed like a castle against the moonlit sky. There was a gap of about a hundred yards between the King's Head and the nearest house, and the back wall of the pub cast a great black shape across the space. Faint music drifted out from somewhere inside but I couldn't see any lights on in the building.

This was a major junction and usually there would be queues of traffic waiting for the lights but it was past midnight so there was only the occasional car and a few lorries zooming past. I dashed across the pavement and into the shadow of the pub wall. Then I slunk my way along the bricks and round the corner onto the side facing the dual carriage way. I could hear the music clearly now, coming from somewhere underneath the pub. A wall lamp lit up a flight of steps leading down to a basement room and the boys were heading towards them. There must be some kind of club beneath the pub.

Just as the boys got to the top of the steps

another figure appeared out of the dark.

'Hiya,' she said. It was the red haired girl from the bus stop who'd I'd seen the first time I'd gone out night dancing.

'Oh hi Mel,' Mick answered, 'you coming in?' She followed them down the steps and out of sight. The basement door must have opened because loud rock music belched out. I heard a booming man's voice speak loudly.

'She's not cummin' in. I've told 'er – I'm not riskin' me licence. Do yurself a favour duck and gu home. You've 'ad a skin full. Off yow trot - there's a gud girl.'

The door must have closed because the music went quiet again.

I wanted to meet this girl who was out on the streets at night just like me? I inched my way out of hiding and waited for her to come back up the steps. Minutes went by but there was no sign of her. Maybe she'd gone inside after all. I tiptoed towards the basement stairs.

The girl was sitting on the steps leading down to the club, her head leaning against the pub wall, eyes closed. In the pool of light from the lamp I could see her pale skin and hair the same colour red as the bricks. She had a deer's soft face, a little wild creature, hunched inside a thick black coat. There was something delicate and magical about the way she looked, like she was from an older fairy world. Eyeliner had smudged onto one of her cheeks. She seemed to be sleeping, her mouth slightly open and her body completely relaxed.

I looked up and down the road and couldn't see anyone coming. I dashed out of the shadows down the steps and crouched beside her.

'Are you ok?' She was breathing heavily. I touched her arm gently not wanting to frighten her. The boy had called her Mel. 'Can I help you, Mel?'

Her head swung away from the wall towards me and one of her eyes half opened.

'Get us a drink?' she said and I couldn't stop myself from laughing. It was so ridiculous. Both of her eyes opened then. They were large and brown with specks of orange round the pupils.

'Who're you?' she asked.

'Pen,' I took hold of her arm and putting it over my shoulder, lifted her to her feet, 'd'you live near here?'

'By the old ice rink,'

'Silver Blades?'

'Ah huh'. *Silver Blades* was at the bottom end of Bearwood High Street. When I was a kid we used to go as a family. Dad would sit with Mum and they'd watch while Thomas and I went round and round. Thomas was so young he wore these tiny little boots.

It was hard work getting Mel up the steps, like dealing with someone who couldn't stand up on the ice, her knees kept going and she seemed determined to sink back to the ground. She stank of alcohol and cigarettes. At the top of the steps she lurched away from me, jack knifed and was sick over the pavement. It was disgusting. She straightened up wiping her mouth on her coat sleeve. Now we were under the street lights I could see her properly. Even after being sick she looked pretty, with her elfin face and copper hair. Under a black donkey jacket she wore a denim mini skirt, with striped tights and big army style boots. I'd never seen anyone who looked as cool as she did.

'God I hate spewing,' she said.

Sick was splattered over the pavement between us. The girl didn't look at me but turned and stepped into the road. She couldn't walk straight, and her body lurched from side to side as she staggered forward, zigzagging across the four lane road. She was going to fall over in the middle unless I did something.

12

I ran after her and put my arm round her waist keeping her upright against my body. I could feel the point of her hip bone even through the thick jacket. She smelt of vomit now. I got her to the other side of the junction. She was leaning against me with her head flopped onto my shoulder. I tried to untangle myself but she clung on. I wasn't sure what to do. She seemed to have gone to sleep.

'Come on Mel, wake up.' I shook her gently but she didn't open her eyes. I couldn't just leave her on the pavement so I started to walk down the High Street in the direction of the old ice rink, supporting her weight against my hip and shoulder. Her bones felt thinner than the finest branches of the lilac tree and

I worried that if I dropped her she'd snap. Her legs moved but she kept her head on my shoulder. I seemed to be carrying most of her weight. For a skinny girl she took a lot of shifting. I appeared to be the only one of us battling gravity.

Who knew Bearwood High Street was so long? I'd never been here at night before. It was seriously spooky with the shop windows lit up and the mannequins staring out at us with their mad round eyes. Between the shops black alleyways threatened unknown dangers. The hairs on the back of my hands were prickling with fear.

I was about to tell Mel I couldn't go any further when I realised we'd reached the old ice rink. The double doors still curved around the corner but they were boarded up now. Must have been three years since the place closed. I remembered the cold air, woody smell, and walking on skates down the rubber path to the ice, clumsy and wobbly, then zooming off in clean sharp swoops once you were on the rink. The older kids had seemed so cool in their skinny jeans and leather jackets. How exciting it'd been. But now it looked pathetic.

I shook Mel awake.

'There's the ice rink, is your house somewhere near?' I asked.

She pulled away from me and I felt as if I'd been released from a Vulcan death grip. I rubbed my sore shoulder. Mel shifted her whole body towards the ice rink as if she couldn't manage to turn her head at the neck.

'Oh yeh,' she said, 'nearly there,' and staggered back against me, 'this way.'

Still clutching hold of my arm to stay upright, Mel led the way. It was like taking Mum out. As we walked down the side of the ice rink I peered in through the dark window at the old coffee bar.

'Did you ever go there,' I asked Mel, 'when it was open?'

'All time,' she slurred her words.

'Did you have lessons?'

'Get lost, I was a Blader!'

A hundred yards along the road, Mel turned right into the back entrance of a council estate. I didn't know what a 'Blader' was but I remembered these kids in bomber jackets that used to turn the rink into a speed track. When they came on everyone else got out of the way quickly. We'd sit and watch them bending forward so low that their hands could touch the ice, moving fast enough to blur going past. Mainly they were boys but there were a few girls. I imagined Mel as one of them.

We walked through a double row of garages and turned into the main estate. The flats were in three storey blocks built out of concrete. I'd never been here before. The place had a bad reputation for drugs. That was why the ice rink had closed because of the drug dealing. Four blocks along we turned into a stair well that was grim and scary. The wall light on the ground floor was smashed. Getting up the stairs in the dark was tough. I had to feel my way along the wall and I didn't know where the steps were or what was lurking in the corners. At the first floor junction there was a lamp that worked and it lit up the graffiti scrawled in red and black on the wall. I gulped when I read the words and hurried past. Mel led me along the first floor walkway, moving faster. She knew which door was hers and had a key in her pocket. There were no lights on inside and I guessed her parents must be asleep.

'You ok now? Will you be alright?' I asked.

'No probs,' she was leaning against the door

frame rather than me. After a few misses she managed to get the key in the lock and opened the door then turned and looked at me struggling to bring my face into focus.

'You're an angel,' she said nodding her head to emphasize the words, 'Melody Jones never forgets a kindness, never.' There was a pause, 'Angel,' Mel added, this time shaking her head. Then she closed her front door in my face, leaving me standing on the concrete walkway in the dark.

I was completely alone on a drug-fuelled council estate. I ran back along the walkway, leapt down the two flights of stairs, and sprinted back to the High Street. There might be people in the doorways, addicts or pushers, or drunks. I was sure there were eyes watching me. I wondered if Mel would be in trouble with her parents for coming home late and being drunk. *Melody Jones* - she sounded like a pop star. I reckoned she was older than me, maybe seventeen or even eighteen.

I ran back to the traffic lights Cherokee style, low to the ground, silent and fast. There were no cars at the junction and I noticed the bird song for the first time. I couldn't see the birds but their voices were weaving a skein of notes across the road.

When I got onto our road I slowed down and walked the rest of the way. A wind had blown up and the daffodils in our front garden were bobbing about like demented choir boys singing for their lives. What a strange, wild night this was; my solo, Mum and Dad's argument, me and Dad rowing, then meeting Melody. Ok she was drunk but I could tell there was something unique about her. She was way more stylish than Tamasin. I'd never met anyone like her and I hoped that somehow I'd see her again.

13

I was crouched down low, hands behind my back, the sides of the rink blurring as I sped past. Melody Jones was skating next to me. We both wore black satin bomber jackets. Melody accelerated ahead and I pushed with my thighs to keep up. We were going faster and faster.

'Pen,' Thomas was screaming from the side of the rink, 'Pen help me.'

I wanted to go to him but I didn't know how to stop.

'Pen,' Thomas was yelling and I crashed into the barrier and out of my dream. Jolted suddenly awake I realised Thomas was calling from downstairs.

'Pen,' he screamed again, real fear in his voice.

I leapt down the stairs three at a time. The front door was open and Thomas was on the pavement outside the house trying to lift Mum up. He had her arm round his neck but she was too heavy for him. Mum was slumped on the concrete clutching her chest with her hand, shaking violently. She made small whimpering noises.

'Can't breathe,' she managed to gasp as I knelt down beside her and took hold of her hand. It was slippery with sweat, water was dripping off her face and I wiped her forehead gently.

'Ok Mum, lean against me, hold onto me,' I braced against the contact, steadying myself. She pressed into me and I felt her frightened, fluttering, energy and tried to absorb it.

'I'm having a heart attack, call the ambulance,' she gasped.

'You're ok, you're not having a heart attack. I'm here, feel my breathing,' I took long, slow, exaggerated breaths down into my belly, 'breathe with me. There's nothing to be frightened of. You're not going to die. You're going to be ok.'

Thomas had started crying.

'She's going to be fine Thomas, she's just scared. You come and hold me as well and breathe with us. I'm going to count now, breathe in one, two, three, now we wait, breathe out one, two, three.' Thomas started counting with me, and gradually Mum joined in and her body began to unwind to a manageable trembling.

We must have looked right idiots, the three of us bundled together, me in my pyjamas with bare feet, sitting on the pavement facing the road, cars roaring past us as we counted out loud. At least it wasn't raining, though the ground was damp, and I seemed to be breathing in nothing but exhaust fumes.

'Not really sunbathing weather,' I said, not much of a joke but Mum managed a weak laugh. I took hold of her left hand. The skin on her index finger had split open and inside was as pink as a sausage with red bits of clotted blood in patches.

'Your poor hand. Is your heart still racing?' I asked her.

'Better,' she said.

'Come on then, let's go inside, my feet are soaking.'

Mum stood up no problem, but she held

onto my arm so fiercely I thought she'd dislocate my shoulder. Last night Melody and now Mum I was going to be permanently disabled at this rate.

The moment we got inside and closed the front door she started to sob.

'We ran out of cereal so I wanted to buy some more. Your Dad says I've got to go out, but I can't, I just can't. It's hopeless.' Tears were running down her cheeks and my heart lurched.

'Don't cry Mum,' Thomas said.

I took her through to the living room and got her to sit on the sofa. Thomas snuggled up next to her.

'Where is Dad anyway?' Why was I having to deal with the results of his unkindness? I was so angry with him.

'He went to work,' Mum said.

'What time is it?' The wall clock said ten past nine. I was mega late for school. 'Why didn't you wake me?' I shouted.

'You were dead to the world, must have been tired after the dance show, so I let you sleep in.' Mum explained.

'I've got history this morning. I need to get

going. And why isn't Thomas at school?' I was panicking now.

'I don't want to go to school,' Thomas said.

'You've got to. Mum, he needs to go. You can't keep letting him stay home.'

'Off you go Pen and get ready,' Mum was recovering, 'don't miss your next bus. I'll phone Kings and tell them you're on your way. I'll see if Mrs Bell next door will walk Thomas to school.'

I rushed off to get dressed. But the sight of Mum and Thomas still huddled together in the corner of the sofa cut through me like a razor.

Getting the bus at nine-thirty was weird. I had the top deck to myself, downstairs was all mums with pushchairs. I sat on my favourite seat at the front half asleep. The white sky was too bright to stare at for long but a line of rooks flew over the rooftops heading out of the city to the fields. Helping Mum was like a weird blood transfusion, only it wasn't blood I was donating. I gave her my calmness and in return her panic spilled into me. I felt like a pinball machine with jumpy sensations ricocheting around inside.

From the top of the bus I looked over the horse chestnut trees along the edge of the park, lime bright with new leaves. The dew was still on the grass and the playing fields spread out in sheets of sparkling emerald, so much beauty and Mum never got to see any of it. A great globule of sadness started to push up through my throat but I gulped it down, and forced myself to stop thinking about Mum.

14

It was break time when I finally got to school and most girls were outside in the playground. I went straight to our classroom. There was a piece of A4 paper on my desk, probably a handout from the Math's class I'd missed. But when I picked up the print out I saw a photocopied image of a pole dancer dressed in a black leather corset. Someone had photo-shopped my face onto her body and there was a speech bubble coming out of my mouth saying, 'I just love to twerk.'

I recognised Tamasin's handwriting. Why had she done this? Why would she do something so awful when I was her friend?

Vivienne came crashing in through the classroom door. She was breathing heavily as if she'd run to get there.

'Pen, you're here,' she could never resist the obvious, 'I missed you last night. Did you get my text? Your dance was awesome.' She moved across the room until she was standing too close and kept on talking, 'We were looking for you. Mum and Dad wanted to say well done.'

'Have you seen this?' I waved the photocopy at her.

'Oh take no notice of that. Throw it in the bin.' She stepped forward to take the paper from me but I stared at her and she backed off. Shame poured through me as I looked down at the stupid image. Why had Tamasin done this? Surely she'd realise how exposed I'd feel after the dance show.

'Forget it Pen, you know what Tamasin's like, it's just like a silly joke. She's jealous because everyone's talking about your dance.' Vivienne was trying to help but she made me feel worse.

Girls were piling in through the classroom door for the end of break, and I was still holding the paper. Was everyone laughing at my solo? Had I made a total fool of myself? I remembered Mum's scabby finger this morning and I felt like that, flayed and raw, as if the skin on my whole body had split open.

Tamasin was amongst the last back to the classroom, coming in with Sadie and her gang. I probably should have thrown the paper away, like Vivienne said, but I couldn't let it go. With everything last night and Mum this morning my emotions were churning like a river running through rapids. I walked over to Tamasin's side of the room.

'Your work?' I said lightly, pushing the paper towards her.

Tamasin laughed. 'You should get one of those corsets for your next dance – looks good on you.'

'Why have you done this? I don't understand.'

'It's a joke, no big deal, don't be so uptight,' she mumbled. There were two pink spots on her cheeks and she was avoiding looking at me directly. The bell rang for lessons and I could hear desks opening and some girls started chatting. Vivienne came over.

'Come on Pen,' she touched my arm, 'history in a minute,' but I shook her off.

'I don't think this,' I flicked the paper at Tamasin, 'is funny. I think it's mean.'

Tamasin let the paper fall to the floor and glared at me.

'You take yourself soooo seriously these days Pen. You used to be fun.' She turned her head away from me, twisting her body until she found Sadie's face then raised her eyes back in my direction, in a 'can you believe this' way. Sadie stepped forward and picked the paper off the floor.

'We couldn't find a picture of a fat pole dancer,' she said, laughing. Her nose fanned out as her nostrils expanded. I should have guessed Sadie would be behind this. There was something of the lion about her, with that great mass of frizzy light brown hair, flat freckled nose and wide spaced eyes. She was excited at the smell of blood. I didn't care if her Mum was dead. There was no way I was backing down now. If Sadie wanted a fight she was getting one.

'I'm not talking to you. I'm talking to Tamasin.' I tried to get eye contact with Tamasin but she'd moved away, whereas Sadie had planted herself right in front of me. We were eye to eye.

'Yeh? Well she's not talking to you.' Sadie was enjoying this. 'You think your dance was cool? Nah ah

– you looked like a total dork.' She moved away and threw over her shoulder, 'ask anyone.' '

Miss McBride came in at that moment carrying a heavy pile of books which she dumped on the table at the front. Everyone else was sitting down. There was only me left in the middle of the room.

'Ah Penny,' she said, 'while I remember, Mrs Hadley wants to see you. She's got some exciting news for you.'

Sadie made a vomiting noise and then changed it into a cough and the girls around her tittered. I walked back to my desk over by the window. As I was getting out my history books I dropped my pencil case on the floor and the stuff inside went flying. I had to crouch down and pick up the pens, pencils, and rubbers that'd spilled everywhere.

'When you're quite ready, Penny, we'll start,' Miss McBride said, and lots of people laughed then, as if they'd been given permission to hate me. I could feel my cheeks boiling. Did everyone think my dance was stupid? I clamped down fiercely on the end of my biro and the plastic splintered. When I spat out the bits there was ink in my mouth.

Vivienne was watching me with her big sad potato face. I didn't want her to pity me. I tried to take notes, forcing myself to listen to what Miss McBride was saying but my broken biro kept smudging leaving blobs of ink on the page. Why was I taking notice of anything Sadie Thompson said? I started scratching into the ink blots with the jagged plastic end of my broken biro, making webs and arrows, a whirling flock of black marks. I imagined the rooks I'd seen on the bus turning vicious and bombing down out of the sky, attacking Sadie and pecking her eyes out.

15

Mrs Hadley was wearing the pleated navy mini skirt she wore for netball practise. Her thighs loomed giant and white when I sat down in the tiny room that was her office. I had to look away as she pulled on some tracksuit bottoms.

'Lots of people have been saying how much they enjoyed your solo Penny. You should be pleased. I know how hard you worked.'

'Thanks for helping me,' I said. Surely if Mrs Hadley thought the dance was good then it must have been. What did Sadie know about dance anyway? Mrs Hadley was searching through reams of paper on her desk. It was a real mess.

'Here we are,' she had a blue paper file in her

hand. Her eyes locked on my face and I felt as if I were a notice being stapled to the wall.

'I think you should take your dancing seriously. In here there's a leaflet for a dance show by an exciting new company called Tartan Fling. They're holding a workshop and I think you'd enjoy it so I've booked you a place. I've also put in some details of ballet classes. You haven't done any?' I shook my head and she went on. 'If you're going to go any further as a dancer, you'll need to get to grips with a basic vocabulary, build up your strength and flexibility, so that means ballet. You're starting late but you can catch up if you're prepared to put the work in. I've also given you a Prospectus for the London School of Contemporary Dance just for you to look at and get a sense of possibilities.'

She handed me the file and the silence in the room was as round and fat as one of the pumped up netballs in the corner. I needed to grab the ball, say something, but my brain wasn't coming up with anything. My speech bubble was totally empty. Mrs Hadley started to laugh.

'Don't look so worried Penny. It's a lot to take in I know. Just look over the information and think about it in your own time. There's no hurry.'

'My Dad wants me to go to University. He doesn't think dancing's a good career,' I blurted out. I didn't know why I'd said anything and immediately, wished I hadn't.

'Well you're not going anywhere for a few years yet. But why don't you think about what *you* want to do?'

I walked back along the corridor towards the cloakrooms, put my coat on and went outside. I skirted the hockey pitches and made for the boundary furthest from the school buildings, where you could look over into the park next door. I leant against the top bar of the fence and stared across the flower beds.

Yellow crocuses popped out of the dark soil. Banks of daffodils were shouting away. Yellow was such a loud colour and always cheered me up. What did I want? Apart from Sadie Thompson to choke on her own vomit and die.

I remembered how I'd felt on stage at the end of my dance. Could I really be a dancer? Surely I wasn't good enough. You had to start when you were like three years old. But Mrs Hadley'd given me the file so she must believe in me? Dad would hate the idea but maybe Mum'd support me. A pulse started in my belly, raced through my thighs, down my calves and into my feet, not stopping there but moving further, pushing into the brown, sludgy, earth. Somewhere deep inside a new green force was sending out secret roots. Could I, Pen Flowers, really grow into a dancer?

16

I didn't dare look at Mrs Hadley's blue file until I was safely home and in the privacy of my bedroom. The leaflet was for a show by Tartan Fling at the studio theatre of the Birmingham Rep. The publicity photograph showed a man with caramel coloured skin and short dreadlocks, with a bare chest but wearing a kilt and leaping impossibly high off the ground. I stuck the picture on the wall next to my bed. If I trained day and night I wondered if I could learn to jump like the man in the photo.

The London School of Contemporary Dance Prospectus was the most exciting book I'd ever read. The pictures were stunning, with loads of fit looking guys. If I went there the other students wouldn't laugh at me for loving dance. You could do a degree in Dance so maybe Dad wouldn't mind because it'd be the same as going to University.

I went online and found Tartan Fling's website. The leaping man in the picture was the choreographer, Jock Briggs. His Dad was a Scottish communist and his Mum, a Cuban ballet dancer – how romantic was that? He didn't start dancing until he was fifteen – like me. He'd been a footballer first. But then he'd trained with the Royal Ballet for two years before going on to the London School of Contemporary Dance. He was only twenty three and already a worldwide super star. There was a video clip of him dancing. I watched it again and again.

While I was online I saw that Tamasin had posted a load of photos of her and Sadie messing about with a group of boys in Kings Heath. In one photo Grant Barker had his arm round her. Tamasin looked well pleased. In the war between Sadie and me it was becoming pretty obvious whose side Tamasin was on.

Was that it then - the end of our friendship? Surely it couldn't happen like that? Not in one day!

I needed to talk to her when Sadie wasn't around. Explain why she'd upset me, make her understand. School would be awful without Tamasin. I'd be really lonely, especially now I wasn't rehearsing for the dance show.

I went up to bed but when I closed my eyes the bad colours were waiting. My head was going bonkers with too many things to sort out. As soon as the house was quiet I climbed onto the roof.

The moment the night touched my skin I relaxed. The rich, smooth, chocolate blackness poured over me. The moon still looked full, pumped up to a ball of brilliant white. Lots of girls go mad for sunbathing but I preferred moon bathing. I wanted to rip off my clothes so that my skin could soak up the silvery magical glow. Obviously I didn't because it was freezing. But maybe I could dance out my problems.

My life, it seemed, was demonstrating the first law of emotional dynamics – if one area starts going up then the others take diving lessons. I tacked across the road between the lampposts. On the up was dancing. I copied Jock Briggs' amazing jumps, flinging myself up into the air. On the down, I crossed back over the road, was Tamasin, Sadie, School, Mum and Dad; a long list. I dragged my feet, hung my head low, and kicked out at the garden walls. But then on the up, I twirled back to the dancing side of the street, was me and the night with an ocean of space to dance in. When I was dancing I didn't care if Tamasin had betrayed me, if I had to look after Mum, if Thomas didn't go to school, if Dad abandoned us. The answer to my problems was simple – all I had to do was keep dancing.

Part 2:
Trial by Water

17

Dancing was the answer to all my problems. After Dad left for work on Sunday evening I went through his CD's looking for unusual music for a new routine. I found a track by John Coltrane called '*A Love Supreme*' that was really wild and built to a frenzy of saxophones. The music writhed and snaked making me want to ripple and flicker like a flame. I imagined myself auditioning for the London School of Contemporary Dance. They were blown away by my brilliance. It was easy being stupendous in our front room. Going to my first ballet class was harder.

I didn't know what I ought to wear. Plus that morning I'd grown a giant green tipped spot that exploded when I squeezed it so that my whole left cheek was like a volcano crater. What a fabulous first impression I'd make. I got the bus straight from school, along Kings Heath High Street, through Moseley and into the city.

School hadn't been as bad as I'd feared, Sadie and her gang were pretending I didn't exist and Tamasin was avoiding me, but the dance show was forgotten history. At lunch time I hung out with Vivienne in the library. Turned out she wanted to go to drama school in London. We discussed how we could live together if I went to dance school and googled maps to find out where the colleges were. As the bus rumbled along I imagined my new exciting dancing life in London.

At the traffic lights in the centre of Moseley most of the passengers got off and I moved to my favourite seat upstairs at the front of the bus. We zoomed past the end of Tamasin's road. I hadn't been to her house once this term whereas last term I'd been almost every week. I still wanted to talk to her and sort things out but I couldn't ever get her by herself. Sadie was determined to keep us apart.

Mrs Hadley had given me directions to the ballet class. I had to get off in Digbeth where I'd never been before. My Mum should be taking me. It was tough always having to sort everything out for myself. But in the end it was easy. There was a huge white sign saying *Digbeth School of Dance* that I spotted from the bus. Mrs Hadley had said I couldn't miss it. I thought it was a sign, well obviously it was a sign, but you know what I mean, the thing was, I got there.

'You must be Penny.' A woman was smiling at me but not in a way that seemed friendly. More as if a smile was an expression she didn't like to use. There was something dangerous about her pinched little face and red rimmed eyes; she looked like a white mouse but I sensed something more vicious on the inside. Even under her tracksuit I could tell she was incredibly thin. I was easily the fattest person in the room and I was normal size.

There were about ten people in the dance studio, all older than me, sadly only one man, (I'd been hoping for a room of fit guys like in the London Dance School prospectus). They seemed to know exactly what to do. They were mainly dressed in leotards like me, but with little wrap-over skirts on top of them. The coolest girls, and the man, were wearing baggy track suits. The teacher was called Wendy but I'd already decided to call her Rat woman.

I had a funny effect on teachers, some of them liked me but others really didn't. Rat woman, I sensed immediately, wouldn't be joining my fan club.

'I don't generally allow students to start half way through a term.' Rat woman looked at me suspiciously. 'Mrs Hadley said you'd be able to keep up. I certainly hope so - it isn't fair to slow the others down. How much ballet have you done?'

'None,' I kept my voice low.

'None at all,' she shrieked so that everyone could hear. 'Good grief – well do what you can. Stand here at the front where I can keep an eye on you.' She pointed to a freestanding bar in the middle of the room where two older girls, probably over twenty, were already warming up. The one on the right side moved back to leave a space for me. I started copying what they were doing.

There were mirrors, floor to ceiling, on three sides of the room. I could see why ballet dancers were anorexic. By the time Rat woman put the music on and I'd worked out what was first position – I'd decided never to eat again. Watching myself dance in the darkened glass of our front room window, I was a smoky mysterious siren. Looking at my lumpy body in these brightly lit mirrors, as I struggled to point and flex my feet, was just horrible. All around me willowy young women slid their feet out and snapped them back with iron limbed strength and diamond cutting precision.

'Pull up,' Rat woman ordered me, 'suck your stomach in until you feel it coming out of your mouth.'

She took hold of the middle of my body with a fierce grip and tipped my top half forward. 'Now, shoulders down, relax them!' She made no effort to speak quietly - in fact she was shouting even though she was so close I could smell her mint flavoured breath.

'Keep breathing,' she told me without relaxing her hold on my rib cage,
'don't tighten up. Pull up here,' she pushed her fingernails into my tummy, 'now!' I had nothing left to pull without bursting.

'Better,' she said, finally releasing me. I'd have liked to squeeze her until she popped out of her own skin like my spot this morning. Roughing me up like that, humiliating me in front of the class. This was my first and last ballet class.

We started on the next limb-twisting torture and I looked in the mirror trying to copy the girl next to me. Amazingly something had changed - I'd grown taller. I'm not talking miracles, but somehow, I'd definitely become less lumpy. Rat woman was evil but effective. Maybe I'd give her a second chance.

My legs were wobbly by the time I'd finished the class. I'd never worked my body so hard, not at night, not even doing the show. Getting to dance like Jock Briggs was going to hurt, I realised. Every muscle I had seemed to be throbbing. I didn't know how I was going to manage the long walk down Lordswood Road to get home.

I fell asleep on the bus and nearly missed my stop. Luckily I half opened my eyes and saw The Kings Head pub looming towards me so I had time to leap down the stairs just as the bus lurched to a halt. I lost my balance and staggered forward knocking into two girls getting on the bus.

'Oi watch out,' a short skinny girl with greasy

hair pushed past me roughly. The other girl was Melody Jones.

'Melody?' I couldn't believe it. I was so pleased to see her again that I beamed.

In daylight, dressed up to go out, she was absolutely stunning. Her bobbed auburn hair was washed and gleaming and she had sparkling turquoise arches painted over her eyes. She was wearing the same big boots and mini skirt but this time under a man's jacket belted at the waist. Somehow wearing men's clothes made her look more delicate than if she were wearing a frilly dress. She smiled back at me blankly as if she didn't have a clue who I was.

'You're Melody Jones, right?' I repeated.

'Who the hell are you?' But she said it quizzically not aggressively. She had a shining open face with peachy skin.

'I'm Pen. I took you home the other night, from The Kings Head, to your flat.'

The blonde girl was half way up the stairs.

'You coming Mel?'

Melody laughed then.

'Of course – I was shit-faced – I remember -

you're my mystery angel.'

The driver shouted.

'You girls getting off or staying on?'

'You live near?' Melody asked as I stepped off the bus.

'Bottom of Knightlow Road.'

'Give us your number?' Melody got out her mobile and tapped in the number I gave her.

'What's your name again?' she asked but the bus driver closed the doors.

'Pen,' I shouted as the traffic lights changed, 'Pen Flowers,' I called after the moving bus.

I watched Melody climb up the stairs as the bus accelerated up the hill and I wondered where she was going. Maybe that new Club in Quinton where I'd seen loads of young people queuing to get in. Her life was obviously way more exciting than mine.

18

Two days later, when my phone started ringing, I assumed it was Vivienne - calling with details of her upcoming birthday extravaganza in which I was a key participant. But it was a number I didn't know

'Hello, who's this?'

'Angel?' I recognised the voice at once

'Melody, you called,' hanging out with Vivienne was rubbing off on me, now I was stating the obvious.

'I'm in the park with some mates – come and join us.'

'It's a bit late, I don't know...'

'By the swings – see you,' she shouted and called off.

I told Mum I was lending some revision notes to a new

girl who lived nearby and legged it out of the house and up the road. I assumed Melody meant Bearwood Park. The main gates were on the corner diagonally opposite The Kings Head but the park stretched for miles, right past The New Inn and up towards Quinton. The playground area with the swings was behind the stone boat house. After that it was just grass and trees until the golf course.

I was sure Melody would have left by the time I got there. But when I came round the side of the boathouse, catching my breath because I'd run all the way, she was sitting on one of the swings. She had the chains twisted to the top ready to spiral out. Sitting next to her, were the two boys from Friday night, Mick Taylor and the big guy. There was another one on the roundabout. I suddenly felt shy.

'Here's my little angel,' Melody stretched out her long legs. She wore fish nets over laddered sheer black tights – I'd never seen that before. She let go of the chain so that the swing sprang out of its spiral and clanged to a halt. Rising out of the seat, she skipped towards me, and put her arm around my shoulders. I felt like her baby sister. I'd always wanted a sister;

brothers like Thomas were pretty useless. She smelt of tobacco and cider. The boy on the roundabout was drinking from a big plastic bottle.

'This is Angel,' she introduced me. 'She appeared from nowhere, out of the night. I thought I'd dreamt her.' As if to prove I was real she dug her fingernails into my arm. The next minute she ran at the roundabout, grabbed hold of a handle, and pushed hard, jumping on as it spun.

'My turn,' she grabbed for the cider bottle but the boy holding it was too quick for her.

'Y' just had it.' The boy I hadn't seen before was tall and very thin with short brown hair that stuck up straight from his head in jagged clumps. 'Mel is a thief and a drunk and a tart,' he told me, as if he was saying – she's five feet six and wears size five shoes. He took a big swig at the bottle and then passed it to Melody who was laughing.

'This is Dog and he's a liar and a sheep shagger because no woman'll touch him. You wouldn't, would you Angel?'

The thought of going anywhere near Dog was terrifying but I didn't say anything. I turned away not wanting to be caught in his hungry eyes.

The boys on the swings were much less alarming. Mick was smiling at me with screwed up twinkly eyes. He had a mess of black curly hair and thick black eyelashes. His teeth were a bit crooked but not in a way that would put you off. I'd always thought he was pretty fit. The bigger one had a fleshy face and a fringe that covered half his face. There was something bear like about him.

'Come and sit here.' The bear indicated the swing seat between them that Mel had just left.

'I'm Yogi,' said the bear, clearly I wasn't the first to note his spirit animal, 'this is Mick. Ignore those two they're disturbed.'

'I'm Pen.'

'What's a good girl like you doing with a bad girl like Mel?' Yogi grinned at Mel and she pouted back at him. Mick laughed. You could tell they adored her. Mel came over and took my hand.

'Be nice, or me 'n Pen'll go.'

'Hey, don't finish that, you dirt bag,' Yogi shouted at Dog who took no notice. He drained the cider bottle and threw it into the bushes. Dog looked older than the other boys.

'You're for it now, Man.' Yogi shouted and he and Mick leapt off the swings and ran at Dog. He was too quick for them and sprinted off like a starved greyhound. They hared after him and the three of them disappeared into the grassy bit of the park. That left me sitting on the swing with Melody standing in front of me.

'Crazy dudes, whatever,' she sighed then sat down next to me and started to swing slowly backwards and forwards. I kept pace with her.

'So Angel, tell me your secrets.' I didn't know what to say. How could I possibly interest someone like Melody? But I wanted her to like me.

'I don't have any.'

She slowed down her swing and caught hold of my chain, squinting her eyes at me, 'So how come you're out alone in the dark of the night?'

Melody was looking at me with a funny one sided smile, like she already knew the answer. I struggled to explain.

'I don't know why but I feel more alive at night.'

She gave a yelp of laughter.

'Me too, sister.'

'The empty streets are mysterious and I feel so free.'

Melody focused on me with her big brown eyes like she totally got what I said. Then she jumped off her swing, grabbed hold of my legs and pulled so that the swing came up really high. I screamed and she laughed then walked off abruptly like she'd suddenly got bored. I jumped off as soon as my swing slowed down and followed her.

'You're like me,' Melody said putting her arm around me again, 'not scared to do your own thing. Come on – let's find the guys.' She started off towards the golf course, in the direction the boys has gone. Running, her long slim legs were awkward and gangling. I followed after her. A bright light had been switched on above me. At last someone had seen who I really was.

Along the Hagley Road the street lights had come on. Bushes were turning into boulders and trees into frozen giants. I should have gone home but I didn't want to. The boys were on the Pitch and Put course. There was no one playing in the twilight but they'd found a golf ball and were kicking it about on one of the greens, trying to get it into the hole.

Mick kept staring at me. Melody didn't stop at the green but kept going. I followed her and Mick came over and walked beside me.

'I think I know you,' he said.

'Station Road Primary, I was in Wilf's class.'

'Gotcha. Ever play golf here?' he asked. Melody disappeared down the far slope on the other side of the green and I sped up to stay with her. Mick kept close to me.

'Sometimes,' I lied.

'We should have a game,' he said.

'I'm not very good, I mean I haven't played much.'

'That's ok, I'm ace,' he grinned at me with his crooked teeth smile. 'I'll teach you. It's all about the swing.' He put his arms round me, holding out my hands so that my arms were straight in front of me, and then he moved them so I was making an imaginary golf swing. His cheek was against mine. I couldn't speak or breathe. He nestled his chin on my shoulder.

'You smell nice,' I could feel his breath on my

neck, 'clean.' My cheeks were getting hot. His body was pressed up behind mine. Melody shouted for us to catch up. I broke away and ran towards her. She and Yogi and Dog were at the bottom of the steep bank that led down from the Pitch and Put course to the car park at the back of The New Inn.

'He said he'd be here by nine,' Dog was talking. 'Better not keep him waiting. You got the money?' Yogi nodded. There was something furtive about the way they were talking. As if they were a bit scared or doing something they shouldn't be. I felt uneasy but Melody didn't seem worried. She put her hand in Yogi's jacket pocket, rubbing her cheek against his shoulder.

'Come on beautiful, I'll buy you a drink,' he said and they started walking towards the pub. I ran to catch up with them.

'I've gotta go,' I told Melody.

'Come for a drink.'

'Can't,' I'd never been in a pub without an adult. Suddenly I felt like I wanted to get home.

'I'll text you,' Melody said.

'Bye,' I said to the boys, though part of me wanted to stay and hang out more with Mick.

He smiled at me. I liked his sweet crinkly face.

'We'll play golf sometime.'

'Ok,' I moved away, flustered, and half walked, half ran, back towards the Bearwood traffic lights. I was just turning into our road when my phone bleeped.

'C U soon Angel. Mick says sweet dreams.'

I ran the rest of the way home leaping like a gazelle.

That night I lay for a long time with my eyes open under the duvet thinking about Mel and I being adventurers together and about Mick and the golf swing. Snakes were running all over my body but not in a horrible way – it was like the saxophones in '*A Love Supreme*'. Of course I couldn't sleep. When I heard Mum snoring I climbed out of the window and ran up Knightlow, onto Lordswood, and crossed over the junction to the Bearwood side.

The park gates were locked after dark, but as they were made of wrought iron, with a fancy leaf pattern, there were easy footholds. I pulled myself up to the top, then stepped between the spikes and jumped down inside.

There was something magical about being locked inside the park railings at night. You could almost hear the trees breathing. I danced down the main pathway, bowing to the avenue of silver birches as if they were courtiers making an arch for me to pass beneath.

The playground was utterly still. The swings hung straight down in vertical lines, and the seesaw was a balanced horizontal. I skipped around the playground, sprinkling fairy dust as I went, bringing back the evening that had just gone. Mick appeared on the swings, smiling at me, I sat down next to him. *I'd like to play golf, here's my number, give us a call.* Melody arrived spinning on the roundabout and I flew towards her. *I'm going to be a dancer, Mel, travelling the world. Let's go together, you and me, global adventurers, roaming wild and free.*

Pushing the roundabout, I ran and ran, until I'd got it going as fast as it would ever go. I leapt on and lay there with my arms and legs stretched out in a star shape and looked up. Inside my head I could hear the crazy saxophones in *A Love Supreme* building to a crescendo. Zillions of stars circled above me and I was spiralling up and up to join them.

19

The next morning I overslept and was late for school. I hadn't finished my biology homework and had to do the last questions on the bus. I knew when I handed my book over that I was going to get a low mark. Our mocks started soon and I was behind with loads of work. In Maths I fell asleep at my desk and Mr Whitehead gave me a detention so I was late home.

Mum was in the hall when I came in and she passed me the phone, 'Dad,' she said.

'You're back late,' typical that he'd actually notice today. Usually he hadn't got a clue what was going on.

'Practising a new dance routine after school,' I lied.

'I hope this dancing malarky isn't interfering with your school work. Your exams start next week.'

'I know!' Dancing malarkey! How dare he? 'Anyway when are you coming home?'

'I'll be back on Thursday as usual. Mum says you're away for the weekend.'

'Yeh, I'm staying at Viv's, it's her birthday. We're going to see Dominic Sawyer at the Hippodrome.'

'Well make sure you get your homework done before you go. Have you started revising?'

'Oh Dad, stop going on. Of course I'm revising. Do you want to speak to Mum? I'll get her.'

'Mum,' I yelled and stomped upstairs. Dad made me so angry always going on about exams and putting me down for dancing. But I did feel guilty because I'd hardly done any revision

At break time the next morning Vivienne was doing her usual business with the Creme eggs and I was trying to learn my French vocabulary for the exam we had coming up. Without looking up from my book, I heard a loud squawking as if a gaggle of geese had landed at the back of classroom. The noise centred on

Tamasin's desk. Stacked in front of her were a pile of envelops, clearly party invites. Maybe she'd changed her mind about the trip to London and was having a party instead.

My stomach started to churn – Tamasin and I still hadn't made up since the fight over the pole dancer photo. She seemed to be sewn to Sadie's side. It was Sadie who gave out the invites. The envelopes were pink with the names written in gold pen and everyone in Sadie's gang got one. I put my head down trying to concentrate but I seemed to be reading the same sentence again and again.

Sadie stopped by my desk and I looked up. She smiled at me and held out an envelope. I smiled back at her and went to take the envelope but she snatched it away.

'Oh sorry, my mistake, this one's mine,' she said grinning.

I took my hand back quickly. Why had I let Sadie play me like that? I was such an idiot. She moved away laughing.

The sentences in my book were beginning to blur. I looked over at Tamasin but she was surrounded by admirers clutching their envelopes. I'd been to all her parties. I was her best friend, or I used to be. Well if she was going to behave in this nasty way, I didn't care. A party dominated by Sadie and her gang would be awful anyway.

I squeezed down so hard inside myself that I nearly stopped breathing but there was a limit to how much emotion I could contain without exploding and tears seeped into my eyes. I had to get away where no one could see me.

I walked quickly to the door, looking straight ahead and biting into my cheek. Once I was outside the classroom I ran down the corridor to the toilets and locked myself in a cubicle and let the tears spurt out.

Looking down at the floor where the grey tiles were marked with streaks I felt so lonely and defeated that I wanted to lie amongst the dribble. Not being invited to Tamasin's party, being left out, was unbearable. Rejection stank. I slunk down onto the lino and curled up with my head on my arm. The stench of urine was overwhelming and I wanted to be sick, but it matched how I felt.

The door to the toilets opened and someone

came in. I stopped sobbing and lay completely still and silent on the floor. Feet walked over to the cubicle and tapped on the door.

'Is that you Pen?' Vivienne called out.

I didn't say anything. I felt stupid lying on the floor. I didn't want her to see me like this. But a big gulping sigh burst out of me.

'Pen,' Vivienne rattled the bolt on the door, 'let me in, Pen.'

I didn't move. There was a sound of shuffling and then Vivienne's face appeared on the floor underneath the door. If she was surprised to see me looking back at her she didn't show it.

'Oh Pen, come on, open the door. Sadie's like such a bully. Who wants to go on a minibus to London with her lot? It'd be hideous.'

So they *were* going to London. I'd never ever been to London and I wanted to so much. Tears gushed out of me. I was as bad as Mum.

'Pen,' Vivienne banged and rattled the door making enough noise to alert the whole school. 'Open or I'll climb over the wall and knowing me I'll like fall on you and break something.'

I pushed myself up still lying on the floor and pulled back the bolt. Vivienne came in and crouched next to me, patting my arm as if I were a dog.

'Don't cry Pen, you mustn't let them get to you. You're strong, remember. Here have some loo paper.'

She rolled me out a wedge of paper that was soon reduced to a soggy lump. I remained sprawled on the floor, my arm on the loo seat.

'You like it down here or something?' Vivienne squatted next to me. 'Eau de urine and fabulous art work.' Someone had drawn a hairy penis on the wall with arms and legs and labelled it Mr Richards. Vivienne went on, 'would you say that was like an accurate portrait?'

I managed a weak giggle.

The bell went for lessons to start.

'Come on,' Vivienne hauled me up to my feet. 'You can't stay down here. It's like totally repulsive.' She looked me over. 'You'd better wash ya face girl.'

Looking in the mirror I was puffy from crying and blotchy red.

'Shall I tell Miss McBride you're ill? I could take you to the sick room.'

I plunged my face into cold water until my skin tingled. I didn't want to miss history but I didn't want anyone to know I'd been crying.

'Do I look ok?' I asked Viv.

'Like totally normal,' she said. I knew she was lying but I was grateful.

20

We were late and Miss McBride was already sitting at her desk. The room was abnormally quiet with none of the usual chattering and shuffling. One glance at her desk and I knew why. She had a great pile of essays in front of her, ready to give back. We'd written them ages ago but she'd taken forever to mark them. No one was supposed to know anyone else's grade but Miss McBride always gave the papers back starting with the person who got the highest mark and going down to the lowest. Waiting for your name to be called was agony and everyone knew exactly where they ranked. I really could have done without this today.

Julia Worth was almost always the first name called. So when Miss McBride said,

'Excellent work Julia,' no one was surprised.

Sometimes I came second. It was usually either me or Tamasin.

'Tamasin,' Miss McBride held up her essay. 'Very good Tamasin, you could have put in more details, but otherwise - well done.'

Miss McBride kept giving back essays and mine was nowhere. I remembered I'd written the essay as if I were a slave – so stupid, I'd really messed this up. Miss McBride gave all the essays back apart from one. How embarrassing that mine was the worst in the whole class?

'I've kept this essay back for a reason,' she announced. 'It was difficult to know how to mark, and I have no idea what an examiner would make of it, but it was both original and powerful. Penny, I'd like you to read out your opening page.'

The class room dropped into the silent expectancy of an execution chamber. Sadie glared at me suspiciously. I tried to say no but Miss McBride was adamant. My hands trembled as I took the essay off her. I kept my eyes on the paper and started in a whisper.

'My name is Upepo, meaning runs like the wind, I am a hunter.'

'Don't mumble Penny, speak up, we know you've got a loud voice, so use it.'

She was determined to destroy me. This day was turning into one of the worst in my life. When I'd written the essay I'd never thought I'd have to read it out loud. My face was so hot that I started to sweat. I carried on reading.

"I would run for many days to catch antelope to feed my village. Now I am chained inside this dark, stinking ship and I cannot move a step. I try to remember the feel of sunlight on my skin, the smell of the grass on the plains."

Every line made me cringe; it was so over the top. Tamasin was looking over her glasses with an incredulous expression and Sadie actually laughed out loud at the bit about people dying that was meant to be heart breaking.

When I finished no one said anything; there was total, echoing, silence. Why had I written something so childish and ridiculous? It was worse than standing in front of a room of boys with no clothes on. I rushed back to my desk with my head bowed.

'So why was that so effective?' Miss McBride asked. Why couldn't she leave me alone? 'Vivienne?'

'Pen made the experiences of the slaves come alive, she made it into a dramatic story rather than boring history.' I suppose Vivienne was trying to help.

'I don't think anyone should describe the shameful treatment of slaves as 'boring' but you're right – the strength of Penny's essay is that it imagines vividly what it would feel like to have lived through the events we're studying. Now bearing that in mind, you've got,' Miss McBride looked at her watch, 'twenty minutes to answer this question.' She wrote an essay title on the board. 'Try and write something I might enjoy reading. Give me vivid details, like Penny did, don't just regurgitate the facts.'

I tried to concentrate on the exam question but I couldn't get my mind to focus. I kept going over the words I'd read out loud, reliving the shame. Most girls had started writing except for Tamasin. She'd got her phone out and was busy texting. She grinned at Sadie who immediately sneaked her phone out of her pocket and grinned as she read a message.

I willed myself to concentrate but Sadie was texting Tamasin back. Tamasin read the reply and snorted with laughter which she tried to change into a cough when Miss McBride glared at her.

'Was that your phone I saw Tamasin?' Miss McBride had her suspicious stare on full beam.

'No,' Tamasin responded with her best innocent face, but Miss McBride was no fool.

'As we only have ten minutes left I suggest you start writing your *essay*.'

'Yes Miss McBride,' Tamasin put her head down. A text was obviously moving round the class. Razi and Sonia were sneaking out their phones. They were up to something and my stomach did a loop the loop. I'd only written three lines. This was going to be my worst mark for history ever.

Vivienne and I were on the way to the library at lunch time when Mrs Hadley stopped us. She'd had her hair dip-dyed in rainbow colours that matched her floral leggings. She looked like a multi coloured sausage.

'Pen, I wanted to catch you. I've got something for you. How's the ballet going?' I pulled a face.

'That bad,' Mrs Hadley looked sympathetic. 'I'm afraid Wendy can be a little brusque.' Talk about understatement.

'It's tough but I enjoy it,' I admitted.

'Oh well that's good – I've got two complimentary tickets for that new dance group I told you about at the Rep next week – Tartan Fling.' She meant Jock Briggs, the leaping man, whose dance I'd tried to copy. 'I thought you might like them.' She seemed to be including Vivienne, who jumped in,

'Wow thanks - that's like so cool, you'll love that Pen, what night is it?'

'Monday,' Mrs Hadley said. I didn't think that Dad would be very happy with me going out to a dance show just before exams started. But Vivienne was already answering for me.

'Great I don't have rehearsals.' Maybe she thought I was too broken to answer for myself.

'And the workshop is next Tuesday, Penny. Luckily your exams don't start until Wednesday, so the Head has said you can go, but you must promise to make up the school work you'll miss. Come and get the tickets.' Dad would really not like me missing school for a dance workshop. Maybe I wouldn't tell him.

We followed Mrs Hadley down the corridor, trying to avoid staring at the orange and magenta bouquet stretched across her backside. The office was as untidy as ever, but she managed to find the envelope with the tickets in.

'Thanks, this is brill,' I said and Mrs Hadley smiled at me.

'Tell me what you think of the show and how you get on at the workshop.'

I pushed the tickets into my satchel. I felt a surge of love for Mrs Hadley, and had to stop myself hugging her. It didn't matter that she wore stupid clothes, this was a horrible day and she'd made it better. So what if I wasn't going to London with Tamasin, I'd much rather be going to see Tartan Fling with Vivienne.

21

Every Friday afternoon, before we finished for the week, we had School Songs in the hall. It was totally awful and embarrassing and everyone hated it and mucked about. Basically, the whole school, even sixth formers, had to come and sit in the hall to sing together. I guess it was supposed to be some sort of bonding exercise. The songs were either old fashioned ballads like *Skye Boat Song*, or show tunes from musicals, or hymns, seriously uncool. If Melody or Mick ever saw me in School Songs, I would honestly have to kill myself.

Luckily, the ordeal only lasted half an hour. We were nearing the end, with a boisterous version of *Land of Hope and Glory*, when, as we got to the chorus, the row behind me, where Tamasin and Sadie were sitting, started singing, *'Wider still and wider Flowers' Big Head swells, God who made her shite-y, bring her down a peg, God who made her shite-y, bring her down a peg.'* At first you could hardly make out the altered words but each time the chorus was repeated they became clearer. It wasn't just Sadie's gang either, others in our class were joining in.

This must have been what Tamasin's text was about. Younger girls in the rows in front were starting to turn round and laugh. One of them pointed me out to her friend. I didn't know what to do. I felt as if my skin was being torn off in strips. I couldn't bear sitting there while everyone was laughing at me. The teachers knew something was going on. Mrs McBride had left her seat at the front of the hall and was walking along the rows listening. Of course, nobody sang the Flowers version when she was near. But once she'd passed by us, on the last chorus, they went for it, really loud and clear, so it sounded as if the whole school was joining in. Tamasin and Sadie looked so pleased with themselves that I wanted to push my fingers into their eyes and rip their faces off.

'Come on Pen,' Vivienne had stood up, 'let's just go.' She didn't even wait for the song to finish she pushed past the girls on the end of our row. You were meant to file out in class order but none of the teachers stopped us. We went straight to the cloakroom and grabbed our coats and bags while the others were still filing out. Vivienne was really angry.

'That was horrible– you'd think they were like six years old. I know Tamasin's supposed to be your friend but I think she's a vain, immature, stuck up bitch.

22

When we turned into Vivienne's road there was a clump of purple balloons tied to her gate, like a giant blackberry floating in the air. A homemade sign 'Happy 16th Birthday Vivienne' hung on the front door. I didn't think I could handle being with Vivienne's family.

'Look Viv maybe I shouldn't stay. I don't want to spoil your birthday but I'm not feeling much like a party.'

Vivienne grabbed hold of my wrist with a grip that Wendy, my ballet teacher, would have been proud of. She thrust her face up against mine.

'You're staying with me. You're going to forget about those stupid idiots, I want to kill them. We're going to have a good time and I'm like going to look after you, ok?'

'Ok,' I agreed, rubbing my arm, and not daring to say anything else, 'but please don't say anything to your Mum or Dad.'

'Alright, if you don't want me to, I won't, but I like really think you should tell yours.' The door opened and Vivienne's mother was there in a bright orange dress.

'The birthday girl's here,' she shouted and pulled Vivienne into the house and her bosom. I was next. Orange enveloped me and my eyes blurred in a tangerine haze as I breathed in the scent of cake mixture and flowery perfume. Large squishy breasts pressed against my chest. There was nothing jumpy about Mrs Cooper, rather something so comforting in her warm, soft, body that I nearly let go of the tears that bubbled inside me. But I pulled away and escaped into the house.

The party wasn't too awful. It stopped me thinking about the hideousness of school songs. Vivienne's Nan and Pop were there and her Auntie and cousins and as they were all as loud as Vivienne, I could be quiet and no one minded. Everyone was sweet to me and there was tons of food. I didn't eat much at first because I was so churned up but when I'd relaxed I couldn't resist the birthday cake and ate two slices.

Mrs Cooper had laid out a mattress for me on the floor of Vivienne's purple grotto. After what had happened at school I knew I'd never be able to sleep.

'Are you ok down there Pen?' Vivienne asked. We'd changed into our pyjamas and were lying down with the bedside lamp still on.

'Sure.'

'Did you have fun? You weren't like thinking about school too much?'

'Not much,' the sheets over the mattress seemed to cling to my legs, making me feel sweaty.

'I know you don't like talking about it Pen, but don't you think you should tell your Mum and Dad about today, and the other stuff, like Sadie picking on you, the porno photoshop?'

I tried to think what I'd say, to imagine Mum and Dad listening to me, but I just couldn't.

'When Sadie was bullying me,' Vivienne carried on talking, 'my parents went to see the Head and Sadie got a warning. She hasn't been so bad to me since.' I thought: no, because now she's picking on me. Thanks Viv.

'Why do you think she needs to pick on someone?' I asked.

'Mum says she's probably hurting inside so she like wants to make others hurt too.'

That made sense but what about Tamasin why did she want to hurt me?

'I still think you should tell your Mum and Dad,' Vivienne continued.

'Look Viv, I get what you're saying, but my parents aren't like yours. I'm alright, I can manage this myself. Can we stop talking about it now?' I rolled over and turned my back to her.

'I think they'll just get worse unless you do something to stop them.' I was trying to stop Vivienne and not doing very well. I had a brain wave. I rolled back over and leant up on my elbow so I could see her stretched out on the bed above me.

'So what's the play you're rehearsing tomorrow?'

My strategy worked, she was off.

'It's called *Mother Courage* by Bertolt Brecht and

it's incredible – Louis's directing. He's the one I've told you about who used to be part of our theatre group but who's at college now doing drama. His grandparents come from Jamaica. You'll meet him and Samia and Sasha - Samia's my closest friend, after you.'

It was hard taking on board that Vivienne Cooper was part of this whole other world. I had to keep adjusting my idea of her.

'I can't wait for tomorrow,' she said. 'Shall I switch the light out now?'

'Sure,' I said and my heart lurched as the room plunged into darkness. Lying on the floor, shadows crept towards me from every direction. Right next to me was the space under Vivienne's bed. I faced into it to so as to be ready for anything that might come out of there.

'If you could have any boyfriend in the world who would it be?' Vivienne was whispering. Mick Taylor's crooked teeth smile and crinkly black eyes flashed into my mind.

'Not telling,' I said thinking about the feel of his arms around me when he did the golf swing.

'Me neither,' Vivienne laughed, 'but I'm going

to dream about mine.'

Did Vivienne really have a proper boyfriend? Maybe she was only imagining Dominic Sawyer, hard not to with his face glaring out at you from every wall. Within seconds I could hear Vivienne breathing noisily up above. I risked closing my eyes and waited for the bad colours to start.

Weird lavender light bore down on my eyelids. I opened my eyes and realised I was in Vivienne's bedroom with daylight streaming in through her purple curtains. My mobile said 10.00 and Vivienne's bed was empty. I must have fallen asleep and slept through the whole night without waking. That never happened to me. I lay there in the soft lavender haze with Dominic Sawyer grinning above me. His relentless twinkle was really menacing.

'Hey Pen, you awake yet? Breakfast's ready, we've got to get going,' Vivienne was yelling up the stairs.

23

Mrs Cooper, Vivienne and I headed for the city centre and I have to admit, I was excited. I hardly ever went clothes shopping to real shops because Mum couldn't. We got everything online. I'd never even been to the Bull Ring before. As we walked through the entrance, past the restaurants into the body of the Mall, I couldn't believe how many shops there were. We went into one big store and there was rail after rail of clothes. How could you even begin to know what to pick with so much choice? Vivienne and her Mum zoomed around taking a quick glance at each stand, going 'no' or 'yes', and grabbing something. I couldn't keep up with them. One minute I wanted to buy everything, the next moment I hated it all.

'I'm going to try this lot on, are you ready?' Vivienne asked. I hadn't chosen anything but she had a great pile of stuff. I felt totally overwhelmed.

'I'm not bothered.'

'Well, bring some of mine in for me, will you? I've got like too many to take in one go.'

We had to queue to get into the changing rooms. Mrs Cooper sat down on the cubicle chair while Vivienne tried her dresses on. Waiting outside by the mirrors, I watched other young women emerging from behind their curtains and parading about. My own reflection was hideous in the brash yellow lights. I hated everything about the way I looked. Even my shiny chestnut hair which I was quite proud of looked dull and straggly. Where did these tall super skinny girls come from? Maybe the shop hired them in specially to make you feel bad about yourself.

Vivienne came out wearing a dress that Mrs Cooper had chosen for her. On the hanger it looked dreadful, sack shaped, black with a flower pattern, but on Vivienne the dress worked. She had big breasts and hips but a small waist, so the stretchy material made her body into an hour glass shape and the dark colours suited her black hair and olive skin. She looked really grown up and I could see that in a strange way she was attractive– not pretty but striking.

Mrs Cooper went into ecstasies over her. They found a black tailored jacket and when Vivienne put it on over the dress she could easily pass for eighteen.

'But Mum,' Vivienne was holding the price tag on the jacket, 'that's too much money and you've already got me the tickets for the show.'

'You only get to be sixteen once. All you need now is a pair of boots and you'll look smashing.'

'Mum,' Vivienne squealed and threw herself at her mother, hugging and kissing her in the changing room. I walked away and handed back some of the clothes Vivienne didn't want. Seeing the way Viv's Mum looked after her, made me feel jealous. I had to work everything out for myself. If I had a Mum who could show me around maybe I wouldn't feel so lost.

Mrs Cooper went to pay while Vivienne, who wanted to wear her new clothes straight away, got changed. I stood by the shop door until they'd finished. Just once, when I'd had to get my school uniform and you couldn't buy it online, we'd gone shopping as a family. Mum found shopping really frightening. She'd been shaking and twitching, holding onto Dad. She shouted at the assistant because she was so wound up. Thomas was bored and whining and Dad stood there wishing he was somewhere else. Vivienne didn't know how lucky she was.

We carried on through the mall until we found a shoe shop. While Mrs Cooper and Vivienne hunted for a pair of boots, I wandered off on my own. Loads of the shoes had stupid pointy heels. They looked flimsy and would be useless for dancing. But I found a pair of black lace up leather boots just like the ones Mel wore. I asked the assistant if I could try them on. The lacing took ages but when I'd got them on I wanted to go jumping around the shop. It was one of those moments when you didn't know what you wanted and then you saw something and you knew immediately that was what you'd been looking for your whole life.

Mrs Cooper came over.

'Have you found some'at you like?'

'I love these - they're really comfortable.'

'They're DM's, Doc Martens, John wears 'em for work. Are you sure you don't want some'at more feminine?'

'I like these, I'm going to buy them.' I was bobbing up and down on my toes, doing a ballet exercise that strengthens your legs for jumps. Mrs Cooper smiled at me and put her hand on my head, smoothing back my hair.

'Good for you, Pen. Bring the box over to the till. They'll let you wear 'em if you want. Let's see if Viv's decided yet. She's got two pairs she likes.'

When Vivienne was dressed in new clothes from top to toe, Mrs Cooper went home. I was trying hard not to be envious because Vivienne looked great. We sat on a bench in the park by the Cathedral and ate the sandwiches Mrs Cooper had made us. Pigeons kept up a constant attack and I threw most of my bread to them. Hanging out with the Coopers involved almost continuous eating and I wasn't up to it.

'Can you like keep a secret Pen?' Vivienne spoke in a whisper even though there was no one near us.

'Of course I can,' but I wasn't sure I wanted to. I had a feeling she was going to tell me about her mystery boyfriend.

'I don't really like Dominic Sawyer anymore.'

'What,' I burst out laughing because Vivienne looked so guilty, 'I can't bear him,' I said, 'but I thought you were crazy about him?'

Her face was so tragic I couldn't stop laughing.

'I used to be and Mum and Dad ordered the tickets like ages ago and they cost loads. They think it's a massive treat and I can't bear disappointing them.'

'How mad is that,' I was relieved that Vivienne had trouble with her parents too.

'That's the problem with being an only child. They wanna keep me as a baby. It's like unbearable how much they love me.'

I looked at Vivienne. How could being adored be bad?

'You'll have to tell them sometime or they'll keep buying you tickets. Imagine being eighty and still having to see Dominic Sawyer.' I said making Vivienne laugh.

Vivienne lying about Dominic Sawyer made me feel less jealous. I was pleased that she didn't have the worst music taste in the world, and that I wasn't the only one with problems. It was a sunny day and the line of trees around the park were in blossom. Sitting with the sun pouring over my face, wearing my new boots, I felt like a tree drinking in the light. Having a good night's sleep had made me feel stronger. Maybe life wasn't so awful. I closed my eyes and enjoyed the feeling of the heat on my skin. Hanging out with Viv was relaxing.

'I've got an idea,' she announced.

'Oh yeh?'

'Why don't we go down to London together – we could get the coach, it's like really cheap. We could go for the day.'

I sat up.

'Could we do that?'

'I don't like see why not, once our mocks are over. I've done it with Mum and Dad and Dad would pick us up from the bus station if we like got back late.'

'Oh my God, Viv that would be soooo brilliant.' I leapt up and grabbed hold of a tree branch shaking it so that blossom floated down over my head.

'Let's do it.' Viv got up too. I ran around the trunk of the tree kicking up the fallen blossom with my new boots. She copied me and we ran around the park kicking up splashes of white and pink petals.

'Hey Pen!' Someone was shouting my name, 'Pen, over here.'

24

Melody was waving to me. She was standing by the burger stall at the side of the park. I ran over to her. She was with Dog, who was gobbling up a hot dog, getting tomato sauce over his hands. Melody's hair was bright red, not her natural auburn, but fire engine red. With her hair sticking out like a star burst from her head and thick black eyeliner round her eyes she looked like a cartoon drawing of someone who'd been electrified. On anyone else it would be harsh but on Melody the red hair just emphasised her sweetness, like a kid pretending to be bad.

'Who's the babe in the floral outfit?' She asked nodding towards Vivienne.

'Viv, my school friend, I'm staying with her for

the weekend.' I wished Melody hadn't seen me running about like a total twat. 'I like your hair. What are you doing in the city?'

'We're off to *Records Rock* – they've got a load of cool vinyl, David Bowie, Sex Pistols, original albums, seventies and eighties stuff. You should come.'

Melody was looking over my shoulder with raised eyebrows like she was watching something funny. I turned and Vivienne was walking towards us.

'Hiya,' Vivienne was all gummy smiles.

'Viv, this is my friend Mel and oh, this is Dog.'

Melody and Dog didn't say anything they just stared at Vivienne. Then Melody said to me.

'Why don't you come with us?'

Records Rock sounded like a cool shop and part of me wanted to go with them but I couldn't desert Vivienne, not after Melody had been so rude to her.

'Sorry Mel, I can't, but I'll see you next week.' Melody was already turning away and walking after Dog towards New Street.

'Ok, and nice boots Angel.'

'Who are those two? They're a bit weird aren't they?' Vivienne said as she led me at a fast pace in the opposite direction across the park towards a large redbrick church hall.

'Mel's shy with people she doesn't know,' I improvised. 'Dog's ok when you get to know him.' Mel could've been friendlier but at least now Vivienne knew that I had cool friends outside of school just like she did.

The entrance to the church hall was down a little side road. We pushed through a large wooden door painted red. Inside was a square reception area with theatre posters stuck over the brick walls. There were two big wooden doors facing us and Vivienne pushed through them.

'Ta daa!' she sang throwing wide her arms and leaping into the room. I followed behind her into a hall with wooden floorboards, a stage at one end, and maroon velvet curtains drawn over the windows down the opposite side. It was gloomy after the bright sunlight and my eyes took a while to adjust. A group of young people were sitting on chairs in front of the stage and there was an older woman with glasses and long dark hair. As Vivienne walked over they burst out singing *Happy Birthday to you* and Vivienne did a twirl holding her new dress out and finished with a curtsey. Everyone was getting up and hugging her. She even had presents from two of the girls.

'Hey everybody, this is Pen, my friend from school,' Vivienne waved me over. 'This is Samia-Aimer-Sasha-Stacey-Cos-Dickster-Bob and Louis.' She said without drawing breath. The lady with the glasses stood up and walked over smiling.

'Hold on Viv, calm down, Pen will never remember all those names. I'm Maggie – Viv told us you were coming, have a seat by me.' I felt shy in front of so many new people, lots of them boys.

They all climbed onto the stage to rehearse the opening song. I couldn't believe she hadn't told me, but Vivienne was playing Mother Courage. She had the main part! She stood on a flat luggage trolley and two of the boys pulled her round the stage while they sang. I knew that Vivienne had a loud voice but not that she could fill the whole hall with sound and stay in tune. She was singing about soldiers needing food and boots in order to march into hell, strutting around the stage like she was the most confident person in the universe.

I'd never seen Vivienne like this at school. Here, with her theatre friends, she was like she was at home with her parents, a really extrovert and lively person.

Maggie and I sat in the hall watching while an older boy called Louis directed from the stage. I thought Vivienne was brilliant. She put so much emotion into her voice but Louis kept getting her to repeat the song. He made her crouch on the trolley like she was on a surf board while the boys pulled her faster. They finished the opening song but then Louis wanted Viv to practise her solo. The other kids jumped off the stage and went out through the big doors.

'There's coffee and squash in the green room,' Maggie said, 'if you want some.'

Sasha and Samia, the sisters Vivienne had told me about, came over to talk to me as I reached the door. They were smiling and friendly.

'Viv says you're a great dancer,' Sasha said. She was wearing a beautiful emerald green sari and had amazing eyes. Samia wore glasses and looked younger.

'Not really, Viv's just being kind,' I said, not wanting to boast.

'Y' right there, Viv is super kind. When I was in

hospital having my appendix out, she came every day to see me,' Samia said. 'I had to tell her to stop making me laugh because I thought my stitches would burst.' I'd never really thought of Vivienne as funny but maybe she was. At school Tamasin was the person who made everyone laugh.

When I got back to the hall Vivienne, Louis and Maggie were sitting on the chairs in front of the stage chatting. Maggie said she had to clear up and we helped her push the chairs to the side of the room. As we left, Louis came to the door with us. He seemed kind, handsome too, in a cool, laid back, grown up sort of way. He and Vivienne were obviously good friends. He knew about the Dominic Sawyer concert and, I suspected, knew Viv's true feelings because he was teasing us when he said,

'You kids have a great evening and don't scream too much.'

Outside there was a brilliant orange and pink sunset. I was going to say something about how attractive I thought Louis was but then I didn't. The park looked so beautiful with the blossom on the trees, the golden glowing light and the fiery sky over the buildings' rooftops.

Vivienne linked her arm around mine, 'I'm so glad we're friends now.' My face flushed as I remembered how rude Tamasin and I used to be about her. I couldn't believe I'd been so horrible.

'Me too,' I said and Vivienne started to run, pulling me with her as we skipped across the park. I wasn't even pretending. Samia and Sasha were right about Vivienne, hanging out with her was surprisingly good fun.

25

Mr and Mrs Cooper were waiting for us at Captain America's Burger Bar. I was used to Vivienne and Mrs Cooper wearing mad clothes but up until now Mr Cooper had dressed like every other Dad, in jeans and a blue or grey t-shirt, so when he took off his coat I nearly screamed. His shirt had broad emerald and white stripes with a ruffle down the front. My eyes couldn't leave it alone. I must have been staring because Vivienne said.

'What do you think of Dad's shirt?' I gulped and she carried on. 'I gave it to him for Christmas. I like paid for it with my babysitting money.' That was the moment I realised Mr Cooper was the kindest man in the world. There was no way my Dad would ever wear that shirt.

We ate burgers, of course, with four different sorts of relish, and sesame seed buns, and fries. They did these ice cream Sundays that were so gigantic, an Inuit family could be living inside one of them. Thomas would have been in heaven and I thought I'd ask Dad to bring us here for my birthday.

Life size cut-outs of Dominic Sawyer guarded the entrance to the Hippodrome. At the doors there was a crush as everyone compacted together to get through and I was glad I had my DM's on because girls kept treading on my feet in their pointy heels. The air smelt of hairspray and vinegary perfume that caught at the back of my throat. Mr Cooper was looking around grinning. He squeezed my arm and whispered in my ear.

'Don't let anyone hear me say this, but I'm not a great Dominic Sawyer fan. I just love watching Viv's face, seeing her so happy.'

How ridiculous it was that we were all pretending to love Dominic Sawyer when none of us did! Our seats were in the middle about half way back in the stalls. When Dominic Sawyer finally came on stage the place went wild. The noise was horrendous, high pitched squealing, and shrieking, the sounds you imagined when you looked at old paintings of people being thrown into the fires of hell. You couldn't hear anything he was singing. I put my hands over my ears. Next to me Vivienne was 'being' excited and her Dad was looking at her with fatherly love. Good job she was a convincing actress.

The opening chords of Dominic's latest hit caused a surge of even louder screeching and around us girls leapt to their feet. I don't know why but I suddenly felt like I wanted to join in. I opened my mouth and a silly noise like a parrot squawking came out. I took a deeper breath and stood up and screamed. The sound was amazing, loud, harsh, angry and coming out of me. I didn't care about Sawyer but I enjoyed screaming. I breathed in again and screamed even louder. Vivienne looked surprised but then stood up beside me and she started to scream too. Vivienne was loud. But I was louder. It turned out I could roar like a lion. Mr Cooper had his hands over his ears but he looked really happy watching us and laughing to himself.

26

On Sunday mornings the Coopers went to church in Bourneville. We bundled into Mr Cooper's window cleaning van. Mrs Cooper sat in the front and Vivienne and I were in the back, bouncing around with the ladders and cleaning stuff. They were dropping me back home afterwards.

When we got to Bourneville, there wasn't a real church just a wood panelled room with some chairs in a circle. It turned out they were Quakers and Quakers didn't have churches or vicars or crosses with Jesus dying in agony. Mrs Cooper explained that everyone sat in silence for an hour but you could get up and say something if you felt moved to. I didn't think I'd feel the spirit calling.

There were only about twenty people sitting on the chairs including me and the Coopers. An old lady read out notices, then at ten o'clock it went quiet, no bells or gongs, not even anyone saying 'begin'. I didn't realise we'd actually started. I was sitting between Vivienne and Mr Cooper. At first the silence was a bit odd and I felt like giggling but then it was quite relaxing. Vivienne was wriggling about in her chair, only she could be so noisily silent, but after a while she stopped. You could hear the birds outside.

Sunlight came in through the windows and made rectangles of light along the floor. The wooden tiles were laid out in a circular pattern and gleamed as if they'd been recently polished. There was some terrible footwear on show, squishy potato shaped lumps of shoes, worn with patterned socks. Not a Doc Martin in sight, apart from mine, I admired my new boots and danced my feet along the floor, fitting them into the shapes of the wooden tiles around my chair. I was starting to feel a bit bored and looked at the clock. We'd only been going for ten minutes. I had to sit there for another fifty.

I ran through my exam revision; history,

biology, French vocabulary, English Lit, I had so much to catch up with. I looked at the clock again, only two minutes more. This was going to drive me crazy. What a waste of time. Everyone was looking down at their hands. Even Vivienne seemed to be peaceful now. Was I the only one going bananas?

From out of nowhere my mind started to fill with the sound of the whole school singing *'wider still and wider Flowers' big head swells'*. Everyone, not just our class, would be laughing at me, in assembly, in the corridors and the playground, on the bus home, girls sniggering behind their hands. Anger rushed through me, making my face boil. I could see them, Sadie and Tamasin, exploding with laughter, and I wanted to lash out and kill them, to make them stop. But then everyone would hate me even more for being a maniac.

The fierce anger drained away and I wanted to howl, great baby yells of unhappiness into the silence of this sunlit space. Stupid silence, I hated this stupid room, sitting here was horrible, I should just go, get up and walk out - no one could make me sit here.

I was about to run out when an old man started to speak. He had a big oval head, white hair and thick glasses. He leant on a stick and used it to heave himself up to standing. Everything in his face was big, big nose, big chin, big spectacles, but it was a nice face, because all the bigness came together in a soft way.

'For the last few years I have felt comforted by the presence of God.' He spoke slowly in that quavering way old people talk. 'When I was a boy I would stand outside my Grandmother's room and know without doubt that inside that room was love for me. That's how I feel now in this room, certain of the presence of love.' Then he sat down again. I didn't know what to make of his speech. My Mum and Dad didn't believe in God. Dad said he was for the weak minded. The old man didn't seem weak, just gentle.

Next to me Vivienne shifted in her chair and then she started to speak. I should have guessed that Viv couldn't possibly go for a whole hour without talking.

'I've been finding it hard at school so I prayed for a friend I could trust and now I've got Pen.' I kept my head down staring at the floor, Vivienne was so embarrassing.

'But I like feel bad because now Pen's having

a tough time. So I wanted to pray for Pen, that things get sorted out, and to thank her for being such a good friend.' She squeezed my hand but I couldn't look at her. I didn't deserve to be thanked. I wasn't a good friend. I'd spent ages despising Vivienne, and laughing at her. I'd been almost as bad as Sadie. Now that I knew how awful it felt to be picked on I realised that I should have stood up for Vivienne, not joined in mocking her.

A huge sigh escaped out of me into the silence of the room, Vivienne was right, I should do something about Sadie and Tamasin. They had to be stopped. If it wasn't me then they'd only start bullying someone else. I decided to tell Mum and Dad about everything.

27

Our house was full of delicious cooking smells when I got back, almost as if I was still at Vivienne's. Dad must have done a proper food shop and Mum must be feeling better. Roast dinner had to be a good omen. Mum was in the kitchen and I sat down at the table to talk to her.

'Did you have a nice time darling?' she was stirring the gravy and her left hand looked pretty relaxed holding the handle of the pan.

'Yeh, it was good.'

'Thomas has been asking when you're getting back.' Mum turned round wiping her hands on her apron. Seeing my face she said, 'are you ok Penny, you look upset?'

I searched Mum's face, she did look concerned. I took a deep breath, I wasn't sure how to explain everything.

'You know we have school songs on Friday,' I started, 'well Tamasin, no really it's Sadie, but Tamasin is joining in, so I suppose it is her as well,' I stopped because Mum wasn't listening she was watching next door's dog Pepe in the garden through the window. She was obsessed with that dog.

I was just wasting my time. I picked up my bags and went upstairs, dumping them on the floor of my bedroom and throwing myself onto the bed. Bright sunlight came in through the window and shadows of the lilac branches danced on the wall opposite. The lilac tree was bursting with greenness so new and bright it glittered. The blossoms were tiny green balls waiting to explode. I saw that Mum had gone into the garden and was on her hands and knees feeding Pepe through a gap in the fence. She loved that ridiculous dog much more than she did me.

Maybe Dad would help me.

He was in the front room with the dining table covered in old maps and photographs. I sat opposite him trying to work out what to say while he squinted at an old black and white photograph. He was writing a pamphlet about the districts of Birmingham that were destroyed by bombs in the Second World War for the local history society.

'Dad can I talk to you about something, about school.'

Dad didn't answer, he had his glasses pushed up on his forehead. He passed me the photograph.

'Can you read that shop sign,' he said.

'I think it says 'Blackstones',' the photo was blurry. I used to go out with Dad exploring strange parts of Birmingham looking for any pre-war remains. But now he mainly went with Suzanne, from the society, who was another history nut.

'About school Dad,' I tried again.

'I'm right in the middle of this Penny, can't you wait until lunch time? I want to get this done before I leave.'

Dad didn't care about me either, all he cared about was his pamphlet or jazz music, or work, anything apart from me. Mr Cooper loved Vivienne so much, and Mrs Cooper, they both did. They hadn't let her get bullied. My parents wouldn't notice if I was being stabbed to death.

'There's no need to slam the door, Penny,' Dad shouted after me.

We sat at the kitchen table for lunch and Thomas was going on about how Birmingham City had won yesterday, trying to get Dad to take him to a match. He was describing every goal in huge detail. It was really, really, boring.

'You're quiet Penny,' Dad said, 'didn't you want to talk about school?'

'No,' I said. What was the point of asking him? He didn't care about me or Thomas.

'How's your revision going? When do your exams start?' he asked.

'Wednesday.'

'Well I hope you'll get down to some serious work this week, no more partying until exams are over.'

I scowled at him and didn't say anything about the tickets Mrs Hadley had given me for the Tartan Fling show, nor the workshop. There was no way I was risking the only good thing left in my life. He wouldn't even know I'd gone until it was too late.

Dad left soon after lunch. He used to drive to Leicester on Monday mornings then he started going on Sunday evenings. He seemed to leave earlier every week.

I'd just opened my history text book when my mobile bleeped.

'Meet u top of Fitzroy Ave in 15 mins. Mel.'

28

Fitzroy was one of the most exclusive streets in our area with huge detached mansions that had their own drives. Dad would cut off his right leg for the chance to live there.

'Where are we going?' I asked Mel lengthening my stride to keep up as she galloped along. She was wearing her man's jacket over a white t-shirt, with a bear riding a bicycle on the front, plus her usual silver chains and bangles. I'd give anything to look like her.

'Chas's house,'

'Who's Chas, does he live on Fitzroy?'

'My boyfriend.' She turned into the drive of a red brick house with turrets on the corners and ivy growing up the walls. We crunched up the gravel to the front door. There were carriage lamps on either side of the porch and the door had stained glass panels and a big brass knocker. It was even grander than Tamasin's house. Chas's Dad must be loaded to live here.

'What does Chas's Dad do?' I asked.

'Some kind of banker – they've got a place in London as well.'

'I thought Yogi was your boyfriend.'

'Ugh no, he's just a mate.' Melody rang the bell and you could hear it go off all over the house. She put her face to the glass and looked inside. There was music coming from somewhere. No one answered and she rang again, keeping her finger on the button so that it made a long continuous drone.

'They're in the basement and can't hear us,' she started on the knocker, banging so hard that I worried the glass would break. I felt anxious about meeting a boy who lived in a house like this and I thought that even Melody was a bit nervous. She was chewing her index finger so that her bangles rattled.

Mick answered the door. I'd sort of hoped that he'd be there.

'We're still rehearsing,' he said and turned away,

walking back along the hall. Melody followed him. I shut the front door behind me and shuffled after them. Music was coming from below and there were steps leading downwards.

The basement room must have run underneath the whole house because it was the size of a hockey pitch. There was a table tennis table at one end and opposite the table tennis table, in one of the dark corners, was a sofa and two armchairs, with a giant flat screen TV mounted to the wall. In the furthest, darkest, corner there was some kind of stage where the boys were playing music. Chas appeared to have his own private youth club.

Yogi and Dog were playing electric guitars. Mick clambered over a tangled mess of wires, to sit behind the drum kit, and started bashing away. Around the stage area, pale green egg boxes were stuck to the walls and ceiling, so it looked like an underwater cave. Yogi stood at the front of the stage next to a tall blonde boy with a microphone. The singer had to be Chas.

They were making an awful noise, far too loud with lots of electric distortion. Chas was shouting rather than singing into the microphone. They didn't stop when we came in and Melody switched the telly on and flopped down on the sofa. I sat near her on the armchair but half turned so I could watch the boys.

Chas was incredibly good looking with a tangle of mousy blonde hair and cheek bones that stuck out like triangles. I couldn't help staring at him. He wore very tight jeans and a white t-shirt. You could see his hip bones above the jeans and a little line of dark hair on his tummy. Just staring at him was making me blush. Trust Melody Jones to have an absolute stunner of a boyfriend. She had her back to him. It was impossible to hear the TV because of the noise they were making so Mel used the remote to turn up the sound.

'Turn that off,' Chas shouted at us. Melody took no notice. 'I said stop that,' Chas put the microphone down carefully and came over. The others kept on playing.

'Look, I told you we were rehearsing,' he spoke to Melody and didn't even seem to notice I was there. She ignored him and carried on watching TV – it was on a music video channel.

'So rehearse. I'm not stopping you,' she'd stretched out along the sofa and looked at Chas with big innocent eyes. He knelt over her and they kissed - a long slow kiss that made me look away and stare hard at the TV.

'Switch it off, babe,' Chas stood up again, 'who's your friend?' He turned to smile at me and I fell in love immediately.

'This is Pen, my guardian angel.'

'Hi Pen, feel free to chill. We'll be finished soon,' he spoke with a sort of cockney accent but you could tell he was putting it on. Underneath, he was as posh as his eyes were blue, and his eyes were as blue as the sky on a sunny day in May.

Mel and I watched the boys for a bit then Mel got up and did a duet with Chas. They looked incredible together. Mel had a sweet voice not as powerful as Vivienne's but sexy and husky. She was better than Chas.

When they finished Chas and Mel disappeared upstairs. Left on my own with the other boys I felt like a spare part. I should go home – I ought to be revising. I'd told Mum that's what I was doing with Mel. She hadn't even asked where Mel lived.

'Fancy a go?' Mick asked me nodding to the

table tennis.

'Ok,' I said. Mick switched on the overhead light and we started to knock the ball about.

'Do you know how to play a game?' he was patronising me but I just smiled and nodded. 'You can serve first,' he threw me the ball.

Tamasin had a table at her house and we used to play on it for hours plus most lunch times at school. Mick wasn't bad. The first time I did a forehand smash, catching the table corner, he looked surprised but when I did it again he got worried. He started slamming the ball as hard as he could which meant he kept missing the end of the table, so my points mounted up. I'd never played against a boy before. It was fun – really fast. I had to leap all over the place.

'She's whooping his ass,' Yogi noticed, sounding pleased, 'go for it Titch!'

I'd got a nickname already, like I was part of their gang. Yogi and Dog started watching us play. Jeering at Mick when he missed and cheering my points. I won easily but Mick took it well. He grinned at me and gave me a little kiss – not like Chas and Melody - just a peck on the cheek.

'Return match? I'll teach you to play golf. You'll be good at it.'

'That'd be great,' I said, thinking maybe Mick would be my boyfriend. I couldn't wait to see Sadie and Tamasin's faces if Chas and Mick came and met me from school.

Mick started putting a back spin on his forehand. I had to really concentrate. Yogi bet Dog a quid that I'd win. I was really enjoying myself, when the shouting started upstairs.

'You're not coming to London– stop banging on about it,' Chas yelled, 'guys only road trip, you're not invited.'

'You're a shit – you know that,' Melody screamed back.

The atmosphere in the room changed. Chas came downstairs and sat next to Yogi and Dog. Melody called down the stairs

'You coming, Pen?' She sounded upset.

'Sorry, I'd better go.'

'My game then?' Mick caught the ball and put down his bat.

'Ok,' I heard the front door opening, 'got to

go.'

I ran up the stairs but Mick followed me and in the hall he held onto my shoulder and kissed me again. It was my first ever proper kiss and our teeth clashed. Trust me to mess up.

'I've got to go,' I pulled away.

'See you again?' he asked and I nodded but made for the door.

'Got to go, sorry,' I headed out across the drive.

'Don't let Mel run you around,' Mick called after me, 'she's a crazy maker; you know that?'

29

Melody was already a long way down the road and I had to sprint to catch up with her.

'You ok?' I gasped. My heart was pounding from running. Melody should have been in the Olympics as a walker. I'd never known anyone who could move so fast without actually jogging.

'I've got work this evening,' she explained.

'Oh I didn't realised you worked,' I'd assumed she'd still be at school.

'At The Beehive, I'm on early shift tonight.'

'Oh,' I was impressed. The Beehive was the new club in Quinton. It was so cool that people came from all over Birmingham and queued to get in.

We walked in silence. Melody seemed to have retreated inside her big jacket and I felt I'd lost her.

Half way back along Fitzroy Avenue we were passing my all-time favourite house, a big square Victorian red brick, with gate posts that had concrete lions on them. I tugged on Melody's arm.

'When I was little, I'd walk down this road imagining where I'd live if I could choose any house, and this was the one,' I pulled her gently towards the entrance of the drive. 'I liked the lions, of course, but it was messier than the others. They had bikes and toys thrown down on the front lawn and an old camper van. I thought there must be a great big exciting family living here.'

I was looking at the house like I used to - as if I had x-ray eyes to see through the brick. Melody stared past me towards the front door of the building.

'No cars here now,' she said.

'That was ages ago,' I felt like I'd given away something precious and could never get it back. 'Don't know why I said that.'

I started to move away but Melody held me back.

'Maybe they're away – let's look,' she started down the drive.

'Mel,' I whispered to the back of her head, 'Mel, we can't.' But she kept moving towards the house. As I ran after her the outside lamp over the porch clicked on automatically and flooded the driveway with yellow light. There was a dim glow from somewhere inside the house at the back of the hall.

'I don't think there's anyone in,' Melody said, 'let's try and get round the back.'

'We shouldn't, what if someone comes out?'

'Chicken,' Melody grinned at me and then pushed her way through the bushes at the side of the house. I followed her, my heart on a trampoline. We scrambled through the undergrowth into the back garden. My hair caught on a thorny branch and I had to rip a chunk off to get through.

I stood in the shade of the hedge warily surveying the back garden. Melody was already crouched beneath the back window where there was a bright light on. My heart was doing double and triple bounces.

'Come on,' Melody beckoned me over. We poked our heads up above the window sill. The kitchen was empty.

'They're away, I'm sure,' Melody said, 'the lights

are just to put off burglars.'

'Let's go,' I said. Melody ignored me and ran over to the other side of the house. By the back gate where the bins were lined up was a milk crate with four empty bottles. Melody fished out a note stuffed into one of them.

'No milk this week,' she handed me the paper, 'told you, here, help me with this.' Melody was lifting one of the huge bins. I put back the note and took the other handle. Between us the bin was easy to carry.

'What are we doing?' I asked her.

'Shhhh,' she signalled to me. We carried the bin round to the back of the house. Melody stood it underneath the kitchen window and climbed on top.

'Mel, don't be crazy,' I hissed.

She had one foot on the bin and one on the kitchen window sill. The kitchen window was made up of a large square pane of glass with a second narrow horizontal window pane across the top. The little window had been left on the latch. Melody reached inside and opened the narrow window as wide as possible. Holding onto the top ledge, she got both feet onto the window sill, and swung one leg up behind her through the window. Her body lay horizontally along the lip of the window while she balanced on tiptoes with one leg inside and one outside.

'Mel, you idiot, stop it —what if they've got a burglar alarm - we'll be arrested.' I tugged on the outside leg. She grinned at me with a big Cheshire cat smile.

'I used to get in and out of Oaklands like this all the time, same sort of window,' and she slipped her other leg inside and jumped down. No alarms went off and we were facing each other on different sides of the glass. Melody was waving at me.

'Come on,' she mouthed, gesturing at me to follow her.

'I can't.'

Melody climbed up on the sink again and whispered through the window.

'It's easy, just put one leg on the bin and the other on the sill.'

'We shouldn't be doing this. It's breaking and entering.'

'No one will know – it's just for fun, don't be all wet.'

I absolutely knew that I shouldn't but I did it anyway. The thrill was incredible. Like Melody had said, it was easy. Using her method I just seemed to roll through the window. In seconds I was standing next to her on the kitchen floor with my heart hammering and wild feelings surging through my body. We hugged each other and did a little cat burglar dance, capering around the kitchen.

The house was exactly the way I expected it to be, much nicer than Chas's. They had a big pine dresser where lots of brightly coloured vintage plates were displayed. Kids' drawings were pinned to the walls which were painted a soft eggshell blue. Melody opened the fridge door but there wasn't much inside apart from jars and a half packet of Edam cheese.

'See - empty fridge – definitely away.' That'd be no guarantee in our house. Melody found a bottle of vodka in the freezer compartment and opened it. She took a swig and passed it to me. I shook my head. She didn't put it back in the freezer but carried it with her as she led the way to the staircase. Whenever a floorboard creaked, I expected someone to come rushing out of an upstairs room with a gun, and shoot us. For the first time I understood the phrase 'heart in your mouth'– if I hadn't kept my mouth closed, for sure, my heart would have been skidding across the floor on one of the rugs. I got this overwhelming urge to giggle. There was an explosion of laughter inside me. We made it to the landing and Melody stepped inside the first door that opened onto the back of the house.

A night light dimly glowing on a chest of drawers revealed a child's bedroom. The curtains were open and you could see the sky had faded to pale grey, not yet dark but bled of all colour. There were two single beds, fluffy toys piled at the bottom of one and dolls lined up against the wall on the other. I couldn't hold the laughter in any longer. I threw myself down on the nearest bed and buried my head in the pillow to smother the sound.

'I'm sorry,' I said but I kept laughing. I thought my stomach would split open. Melody flung herself onto the other bed, and started laughing too, without even trying to be quiet.

'I can't stop,' I said gasping for a mouthful of air.

'Me neither,' Mel said. And then we both did.

As suddenly as it arrived, the laughter went away, and we were lying on our backs on the single beds looking up at the ceiling. Mel took a swig from the vodka bottle. I was clutching a pillow to my chest. We lay for a while in silence listening to the house tick.

'I always wanted a sister to share a room with, so I wouldn't be on my own in the dark,' I whispered.

'I'd have killed for a room of my own.'

'Was Oaklands your school? Were you a boarder? You said you used to get in and out through the window?'

'It's the kid's home in Bearwood.'

'Oh God, I'm sorry Mel.'

She didn't say anything but she made a little noise – half huff half sigh. My very worst fear was that if Mum went totally nuts Thomas and I would end up in a children's home; poor Melody.

'Apart from having to share a room and never feeling your stuff was safe, it was alright. And now I've got my own place.' I realised how grown up Melody was. She was in a different league to me.

'Did your parents die?' I asked thinking of Sadie.

'Nah, they're smack heads. Friggin' Losers.'

I didn't know what to say. I wanted to comfort her somehow.

'You've got an amazing voice,' I said.

'Yeh, I'm going to be famous,' she laughed, 'and rich, super freaking rich.'

I didn't know if she was being serious.

'I'm going to be a dancer and choreographer and travel the world,' I said in the same semi joking semi real tone.

Melody rolled on her side to look at me,

'Get you my little Angel! You got wings to fly so high?'

'We can be adventurers together,' I suggested.

'Why not,' Melody could have been laughing at me as she swigged back more vodka.

The sound of a police siren in the distance made us both jump up.

'We'd better get out of here,' Mel said and I hurried after her.

Now I was a dancer and a cat burglar. Hanging out with Melody was electrifying - you never knew what was going to happen next.

30

Rain made the morning pretty; grey and misty, with the air softened by water vapour. Everywhere smelt fresh. On my way to the bus stop I put my face into a branch of cherry blossom and sucked in the sweetness. The bus windows were steamed up, and the city shrouded in fog. I felt cosy and cocooned, falling asleep as soon as the bus started moving. I was always tired these days. In my dream world I was dancing a duet with a sensitive but fit boy who looked like Mick. He was holding me in his arms and spinning me round.

If only I could have stayed on the bus forever, but if I didn't go to school then I couldn't go to the Tartan Fling show. Somehow I had to get through the day. I was so far behind with my revision that I knew I'd do badly in the mocks which would send Dad ballistic. But I was too tired to care.

Exams started that morning and fear had rolled into Kings, settling on the grounds like the carpet of mist that covered the hockey pitches. Everyone took exams seriously – our first written paper wasn't until Wednesday but we had French orals today and the classroom was subdued when I walked in, with lots of girls revising instead of the usual chatter. Vivienne wasn't there and I remembered that she had a doctor's appointment. Without her I felt totally isolated. I got out my French vocab book and tried to drill the words into my brain. I was rubbish at French even when I worked hard.

Sadie and Tamasin came into the classroom together and immediately rushed over to Razi's desk, not far from mine, and went on about their weekend. How they'd been ice skating at Top Rank with Grant Barker. Everything that I used to do with Tamasin, she was now doing with Sadie and I couldn't help but feel hurt. Tamasin seemed so full of herself, going on about how she'd snogged Grant, and speaking so loudly that I was sure she wanted me to hear. They were making plans for her birthday trip to London.

I stared out of the window, blocking my ears, and drifting off into a dreamy trance. The sky was bright white as the sun attempted to blaze a hole through the clouds. The mist had gone and the blossom was out on the trees around the hockey pitches. Nature was having a wedding, with the wind sending handfuls of petals floating across the grass to settle like polka dots on the green fields. I longed to drift away like a petal on a breeze.

Mr Richards took a laid back approach to the morning giving us a pile of practise exam papers to work through while we waited for our French oral. People were being called out in pairs to go to the language lab. I hadn't thought about it but as the register was alphabetical Tamasin and I were called out together. She looked as alarmed as I felt and walked quickly to get ahead of me through the door and along the corridor. When we got to the lab Mrs Enby, our French teacher, told us to sit outside until she called our names. There were two chairs placed next to each other. We sat down in silence, staring straight ahead at the wood panels opposite.

I decided to be brave.

'This is silly Tamasin, us not talking,' she didn't answer or look at me so I went on, 'I don't understand why you're picking on me. What did I do?'

'I'm not,' she said refusing to look at me.

'Come off it, what about school songs? You've been ganging up on me with Sadie.'

'Well you went off with Vivienne first,'

'No I didn't.'

'You chose her to do the lights for your dance show. How do you think that made me feel? I thought I was your best friend.'

'I didn't think you'd want to.'

'You could have asked me.'

'But I…'

'All you care about is dancing and you know I'm a rubbish dancer.'

'That's not true, I like table tennis and history - lots of stuff,'

Mrs Enby came out of the lab.

'We're ready for you now Penny,' she held the door open waiting for me so I had no choice.

'Bonjour, comme s'appel?' asked the French

assistant.

'Err, Je m'appel Tamasin' I was so flustered I even got my name wrong. Had I really abandoned Tamasin? Was everything my own fault for being a rubbish friend?

31

I'd sent Mum a text warning her I'd be late home because I was seeing a show after ballet class. Then I'd switched off my mobile in case she or Dad called and made a fuss. Vivienne's phone bleeped as we climbed on the bus. She was coming to watch my lesson and then we were going straight on to the theatre for the Tartan Fling show.

We got off the bus in Digbeth and walked down the hill towards the ballet school. A tall black man was walking towards us from the city, he looked familiar.

'Isn't that Louis – from your theatre group?' I asked but I didn't need an answer because he was waving and smiling at us and Vivienne was going red, more like beetroot, as if she was embarrassed.

'We're going over one of my songs while you're at your ballet class,' she explained. I stopped walking.

'I thought you were watching me. Why didn't you say?'

'Louis only just sent me a text. Hi there,' Louis had caught up with us. I'd watched Vivienne rehearse on Saturday, she could at least have watched one ballet lesson.

'Are you ready then?' Louis had his hand on Vivienne's arm. He seemed in a hurry to be off. Vivienne hesitated as Louis started walking towards the city centre.

'You're ok about me going?'

'Sure – I'll see you at the theatre.'

Climbing the stairs to the studio I was confused, wondering why Vivienne had abandoned me with no warning. From the first floor landing I looked out of the window and watched her catch up with Louis. He put his arm round her shoulder and they walked off together. Surely Louis wasn't her mystery boyfriend? No way, he couldn't be, he was gorgeous and loads older than us.

When I got to the theatre Vivienne was already waiting for me and there was no sign of Louis.

'How was your class? I got us ice creams.' She handed me a tub.

'Thanks.' After ballet I was always ravenous. 'It was good. Wendy, my teacher, knows all about Tartan Fling. She was dead impressed I was doing the workshop tomorrow.' Several of the older girls in the class had given me looks of pure envy. I always felt brilliant after ballet. My body hummed with power, like I was a warrior, like I could deal with anything. I was so excited about seeing the show. So what if Tamasin and her new friends were going to see Westside Story. Tartan Fling were much cooler.

I bought a programme and we went and sat down in our seats in the auditorium. Vivienne didn't say anything just slowly ate her ice cream. I read her bits from the programme.

'Jock Briggs, the choreographer, started this group when he was still at dance school.' This was so amazing that I expected some response. She knew all about me wanting to go to Dance School. Something was up with her.

'How was your rehearsal?' I asked and Vivienne looked as if she was going to cry. She reached out and grasped my hand. My ice cream spoon went flying.

'I suppose you've like guessed,' she blurted out in her full on drama mode.

'Guessed what?'

'About Louis and me - cross your heart and swear to God that you'll never tell anyone.'

'What about you and Louis?'

'Swear.'

'Alright I swear.' The house lights went off for the show to start. People around us stopped talking. Vivienne carried on in a whisper.

'We've been seeing each other for a year now.'

I was glad it was dark so she couldn't see the shock on my face. That Vivienne had a boyfriend as good looking as Louis was surprising, but how could they have been going out for a year? I'd only had my first proper kiss last week. Louis must be nineteen or even twenty if he was at college and Vivienne had only just turned sixteen.

'Why didn't you tell me before?' I whispered.

'I haven't told anyone except you.'

The music was starting and lights were coming up on the stage. The man in front of us turned round, glaring.

I didn't know what to think, Vivienne and Louis? Incredible. My mind was turning somersaults trying to make sense of this latest bombshell.

Dim lights flickered on the stage revealing four dancers, with two hangings of transparent white cloth, lit by a twist of blue light. The dancers began by swaying gently against each other, hardly moving, then two of them wrapped the drapes around their bodies and rolled slowly into the air, inch by inch. They lifted off the ground and stretched into impossible shapes while the dancers on the ground worked with the hangings so that the air borne dancers circled and swayed above them.

I was transfixed. I'd seen loads of dance numbers on the telly, ballroom dance shows like *Strictly* that Mum loved to watch, but I'd never in my whole life seen anything like this. The dancers were strong and flexible but it wasn't like gymnastics, or circus. I don't know how to find the words because it wasn't about words - no words - the way they moved their bodies was like poetry. They were telling stories about human relationships.

There were six dancers in the group and they did three separate dances; the first slow air borne dance, then a duet, and a final piece with the dancers wearing kilts and strange antlered headdresses. From the start I was trying to work out which one of the dancers was Jock Briggs. I was pretty certain he was the smaller of the male dancers in the first piece.

When he did the duet I knew I was right. I swear I had never seen anything as beautiful, as sorrowful, or thrilling. I don't know how he managed to create such powerful emotions. Watching the two dancers I expanded on the inside like a great breath had blown into me and I'd grown an interior cavern of giant proportions. The dancers were saying things I knew but could never express. They did this one spin where the female dancer was balancing on the man's chest with her legs stretched out behind her. It didn't seem humanly possible. They danced a love story that descended into violence and heartbreak and terrible sadness.

The dance with the kilts came last and was wicked. The men had bare chests rippling with muscles and they made these incredible high leaps. I was going to learn to jump like that if it killed me.

When they finished I was near to exploding. I knew with absolute certainty what I wanted to do with my life. I clapped and cheered until my hands were sore. Vivienne was clapping enthusiastically next to me.

'Wow,' she said, 'that was really good.'

Vivienne was struggling into her coat and fussing around and the rest of the audience were getting up from their seats and rushing out. I carried on staring at the stage, soaking up every last bit of the after vibration. I didn't want it to be over.

We walked out of the theatre through the gardens and past the Central Library in silence. I was quiet, reliving the duet in my head.

'Pen, can I ask your advice?' Vivienne interrupted.

'Sure,'

'Do you think I should like tell Mum and Dad about Louis?'

I thought for a bit.

'Probably best to,'

'That's what Louis says as well, but I'm like scared,' I'd never seen her look so worried.

'Why? Louis's lovely and so are your parents.'

'You don't know my Dad. He won't be happy.'

'Is he a racist?'

'No of course not, but he won't like me having an older boyfriend, I know he won't. What if he like stops me seeing Louis?'

'Stop being such a drama queen. You're imagining problems before you've got any.'

'You really think so?'

'Yup,'

We'd arrived at Vivienne's bus stop. I had to cross over to the other side of the road and get the number ten.

'Maybe you're right, I should like be brave and tell them,' Vivienne gave me a hug. 'Thanks Pen, I need to be a fighter like you.' I hugged her back.

'I'm sure it'll all be fine. True love will prevail. There's my bus.' I ran across the road dodging the traffic and leapt on before the doors closed.

I climbed up to the top deck and waved to Vivienne through the window but she wasn't looking. She was busy on her mobile. Probably speaking to Louis. A flood of loneliness rushed through me. I wished I had a boyfriend I could talk to about important things.

I leant against the window and as the bus pulled off I closed my eyes and pushed the sadness away. Dancing was all that mattered I told myself and conjured up the duet, feeling the patterns moving inside me, weaving around my muscles, winding in and out of my ribs, changing me into a different shaped being.

32

'You should've told us you'd been given tickets to a dance show,' Mum said. 'Your father is worried you'll fail these exams.'

I carried on eating my cereal, ignoring her.

'He wants to speak to you this evening,' she continued.

'They're only mocks! Dad doesn't really care he just likes saying – "Penelope's a straight 'A' student." I got up from the table and crashed my empty bowl into the sink, heading for the kitchen door.

'That's not true,' Mum was siding with him. I hadn't told them about the dance workshop either and wasn't about to. They'd only make me go to school instead.

'I don't like you keeping things secret from us Penny,' Mum called after me.

I left the house early pretending to go to school as usual, but when I got to the bus stop I carried on walking. It wasn't as if Mum would catch me. She'd have to go outside to do that. Vivienne's Mum would have taken her to the theatre telling her how brilliant she was and not to worry. I had to do everything by myself.

At the theatre there were about fifteen other people waiting, mainly women but I counted five men, loads more than in my ballet class. Everyone looked older than me and I guessed that they were either dance students or professional dancers. The organiser lady walked us through to the studio. We were going to be dancing on the actual stage where Tartan Fling had performed. Beneath my baggy tracksuit I was trembling; part nerves, part excitement.

The stage was in the middle of the room with raked seating rising up on three sides. We sat on the red velvet theatre seats while the organiser ticked off our names on a list. When Jock Briggs walked into the room everyone stopped talking. The organiser lady introduced him, and said he'd be leading the workshop himself. I couldn't believe I was in the same room as this famous dancer. He wasn't much taller than me, and standing next to the stately, elegantly dressed woman introducing him, he seemed ordinary; a slight young man in scruffy tracksuit bottoms with short dreadlocks, wearing white tennis pumps. He wasn't even as good looking as Louis though he did have a lovely smile.

'Come and sit down,' he said, waving us over. He sank down cross legged in the middle of the stage and we gathered around him on the floor. I stayed near the back.

'So tell us, why you're here?' he spoke with a soft Scottish accent.

At first no one said anything and then one of the men said how much he admired Tartan Fling's work and he wanted to know more about their methods. A girl said she was a dancer and she wanted to learn new techniques. Jock listened and smiled at the answers and soon everyone apart from me had given a reason for being there. The room went quiet and Jock looked over at me.

'What about you?' I felt as if his eyes were

drilling right through me. I had to say something so I blurted out,

'I want to know how you make a dance that changes everything – like yours did last night.'

'So our dance changed you?'

'Inside, yes.'

'Good,' he leapt to his feet. 'Most people, most dancers even, think that dance is about movement. Wrong, it's about ideas. We dance to find out who we are and why we're here. Not just in this room but in this world. By the time you leave the theatre this afternoon, I want you to have learnt something new about yourselves, not just a sequence of dance steps. Let's warm up.'

And so began the most physically gruelling three hours of my life. Jock Briggs was far more demanding than Mrs Hadley or even Wendy but his energy was magnetic so all I wanted to do was please him. I was trying so hard I thought I would erupt out of my own skin. At one point he was watching what I was doing and I'm sure he was laughing at me. Not in a horrible way but because he could see that I was almost bursting with determination.

I didn't care if everyone else was older and better than me. I didn't even think about the others. All I thought about was trying to do the moves and how they made me feel and who I thought I was.

Jock taught us a sequence from the dance with the kilts. Once we'd learnt the moves, we had to keep repeating them, and he walked amongst us making corrections. I was doing this bit where you came up on your toes with your legs wide apart and made a sort of running motion on the spot. At the same time you had to do fast, complicated, arm movements above your head. Jock stood in front of me so I could copy him as he did the move.

'Higher on your toes, faster legs, pull up through your trunk, no keep the knees bent so that you're grounded. The energy comes from the floor, now relax the shoulders, what's your name?'

'Pen,' I managed. I could hardly breathe let alone speak. We were still running and doing the arms superfast.

'Breathe Pen, remember to breathe, the move must come from your centre. Find your centre.' Then he moved off to the next dancer.

'Everything is in motion. We live in a vibratory creation. Everything that exists is humming together at different rates of vibration.' Jock started the next session. 'This afternoon I want you to connect with your own unique vibration and develop a series of moves that express your essence.' That was the challenge he set us when I got back to the studio after lunch.

I thought my sequence would be huge and violent and angry like my dance solo had been. That was how I started off dancing but as I did the exercises Jock gave us, and tried to listen to my own vibrations, my moves got smaller. I came up with this tiny, fluttering, softness of a move that totally surprised me. We had to show each other our sequences and then Jock combined them into a dance.

He put me in the centre of the stage and every time I started my little move, the other dancers had to stop theirs, look at me and make a movement in response. By the time we finished I felt really close to the whole group even though I'd hardly spoken to any of them. It was like being part of a new family. Lots of them came up and hugged me when we said good bye.

There was such an atmosphere of love in the room that I wished I could do this every day of my life.

I was putting my boots on when Jock came over to talk to me.

'I liked your work today Pen, you have good energy. I could feel the joy.'

'Thanks,' was all I could manage, my heart had turned into a butterfly.

'How old are you?'

'Fifteen, nearly sixteen,'

Jock handed me a card.

'That's got our contact details, website, email, phone. Stay in touch, we might be able to sort you out some work experience, if you'd like that?'

I could only nod and try to remember to breathe. He laughed at me again.

'Nice, little fledgling move you came up with.'

Even though I was more knackered than I'd ever been in my life before, and my thighs felt as if they'd been razored open, I ran to the bus stop. When the number ten bus dropped me at The Kings Head, I skipped and leapt and twirled all the way down Lordswood and Knightlow and it wasn't even dark.

The sun was going down in lakes of damson, magenta and tangerine, a Vivienne Cooper colour combination if ever there was one. What a day, what an amazing, wonderful day.

Dancing my way down our road I made loads of decisions. I was going to phone Dad and apologise for not telling him about the show and promise to work hard for these exams. I was going to be nice to, and look after, Mum and Thomas. I needed them onside. My whole life was falling into line behind one purpose. I was going to be a dancer and I'd do whatever that took.

33

In line with my new strategy of buttering up Dad, I spoke to him on the phone and apologised and promised I'd concentrate extra hard on my school work. I didn't mention the workshop, no need to complicate matters.

I got down to some serious revision for my history exam. I was working through my notes when the doorbell rang. I felt a flush of guilt – Mel had been texting me, asking to meet up but I'd ignored her messages. I still had loads to do before tomorrow and I knew she wouldn't understand. For a cowardly moment I thought about pretending I wasn't in, only Thomas had already opened the door.

'Friend for you,' he shouted up the stairs. I looked at my notebook – I had another three decades still to learn.

'Coming,' I shouted and shuffled my books into a pile. I'd have to be strong and say no to going out, even if that meant missing Mick.

But it was Vivienne, not Mel, standing in the hall, her face bloated up so you could hardly see her eyes.

'Pen, I'm so sorry,' she said and then threw herself at me. She was heavy and wet. Either it was raining outside or she'd been doing some serious crying. Her damp hair stuck to my cheek. Thomas was staring at her.

'Go away Thomas, go and play a video game or something. Shhhh now, shhhh,' I held Vivienne tight and stroked her back like I did with Mum when she was in a state, 'come on now, calm down, breathe deeply, let's go upstairs.'

Vivienne hadn't been in my room before and looking at it with a stranger's eye, I was ashamed. I'd dropped my school skirt and shirt on the floor and my pyjamas were still there from this morning. I hadn't bothered to make my bed and there were more clothes piled on the chair. My walls were blank with holes in the paintwork where the paint had chipped off. Tamasin had come round and laughed at my Dominic Sawyer posters so I'd ripped them down but hadn't bothered to put up any more pictures apart from the flyer of Jock Briggs dancing by my bed.

Vivienne didn't notice anything. She sat on the edge of the bed sobbing. She had mucus running down her face from her nose. I nipped into the bathroom to get her some toilet roll and tried not to think about her hair being full of snot.

She blew her nose with an elephant's fury. The whole house shook but she managed to stop crying for a moment.

'I've run away from home. Oh Pen, can I like stay with you? I've got nowhere else to go.' She clutched at me holding onto my jumper.

I wanted to be kind and sympathetic but when she went into full on Shakespearean tragedy mode it put me off.

'You told them?'

'You said I should,' she started sobbing again.

'Hold on,' I wasn't taking the blame for this.

'But I didn't,' she wailed. 'Louis said I should

too, you both told me, but I didn't.' The pitch of the words rose violently at the end of the sentence and turned into a wobbly, throbbing squeal. I'd read '*she wailed*' in books, but until now I hadn't understood how it would sound. You had to give it to Vivienne: she had a powerful voice. The neighbours were probably calling the fire brigade.

'Viv, calm down, take some deep breaths, I'm sure it's not that bad.'

'It is,' but she stopped and took a few slurping gulps of air. I waited.

'They found out. My Dad's like so angry.' She started crying again. 'He says it's the feet.'

'What's the matter with Louis's feet?'

'Nothing!'

'So what's the problem?' I was mystified.

'What are you on about?' Vivienne glared at me.

'What are *you* on about?' I glared back.

'Deceit - Dad says it's the deceit – you madwoman,' Vivienne shouted at me. That did it, I couldn't help myself.

'I thought you said "the feet",' I tried to swallow the great guffaw of laughter building inside me. 'I was trying to think what could be so bad about Louis's feet.' The laugh burst out of me and Vivienne stopped crying and punched me on the arm.

'You're like a total idiot, Pen.'

'I'm sorry, I know I am,' another spasm of laughter shook me, 'big feet.'

'What?'

'You know what they say about men with big feet? Big, you know,'

'Pen,' Vivienne screamed.

I collapsed back onto the bed and couldn't stop roaring and Vivienne started laughing too. I had tears running down my face and my stomach hurt. When the attack was over I reached out for Vivienne's hand but stayed on my back looking at the ceiling.

'I'm so sorry Viv, I am taking you seriously, honestly, but don't look at me or you'll start me off again. How did they find out?'

Vivienne sat up on the edge of the bed. She was breathing normally again though she picked up the ruler from my desk and whacked it against her palm in a threatening way.

'You know I had a Doctor's appointment on

Monday? I'm like sixteen now so I went on the pill and my Mum found them in my room. They were waiting for me when I got home from school. So I told them about Louis and how we'd been seeing each other for a year and that it was like a serious relationship. Honestly Pen, I know you think he's wonderful, but Dad went bonkers. He said the most horrible things about Louis and that he'll keep me in my room until I promise not to see him again, which I won't, ever.'

Vivienne was on the pill when I hadn't even had a proper kiss yet? How was that possible?

'Louis has college on Wednesday nights so he's out. When I saw the Number eleven bus, I thought I'd come to you.' Vivienne looked like she might start crying again. I squeezed her hand which was hot, damp and sticky.

'I'm sure your Dad'll come round.'

'He said Louis was a paedo and that he'd have him put in jail.'

'That's a bit harsh.'

'We haven't even had sex, Louis wouldn't - said he'd get into trouble because I was like under age. Going on the pill is my idea not his. But Mum and Dad don't believe that and Dad's gone barmy, which is just what Louis didn't want to happen, so he'll be cross with me too. Oh Pen I've made such a mess of my life.'

I was impressed with Vivienne for having such grown up problems.

'I'm sure it'll work out.' I couldn't see Vivienne's Mum and Dad holding out against their darling. 'When they meet Louis and know he's serious about you, they'll calm down.'

'I've like left Louis a message but his phone's switched off. He'll call me when he gets out of class. I'll skive off school tomorrow and meet him.'

'But you can't. We've got the history exam tomorrow.'

'A good reason for skiving,' Vivienne had calmed down now and was looking around. 'Your room's like a bit of a mess isn't it? How do you find anything? Do you have a biscuit or something, I'm starving. I didn't get any tea.' Trust Vivienne to need food. If she expected our fridge to be full of delicious goodies she'd be disappointed.

I made up some excuse about Vivienne's parents

having to go away and Mum said it was fine for her to stay the night. I made us hot chocolate and jam sandwiches. Thomas nosed in so I made him some too and Vivienne did animal impressions to make him laugh. Her orangutan was fantastic.

We were sitting in the kitchen when my phone rang. It was Mel.

'Why don't you answer your phone?' Vivienne asked.

'Hi Mel, how you doing?' my voice went over jolly because I felt guilty.

'Meet me at The New Inn in half an hour.'

'I don't think I can, sorry, not tonight.'

'You've got to, I'm desperate. Don't let me down, Angel,' she rang off.

34

I told Mum we were popping out to Melody's to pick up some history notes. Vivienne started interrogating me the moment we got outside. .

'Why'd you lie to your Mum about like Mel being at our school? I thought you wanted to do some history revision?' I set off at a pace and she dawdled after me.

'We won't be long,' I said.

Melody was waiting outside the pub. After I introduced Vivienne they eyed each other suspiciously. I was going to have a great time keeping both of them happy. Luckily, Vivienne's mobile started to ring.

'It's Louis,' she said.

I'd never been inside a pub without adults.

There was no way I looked eighteen so I was bound to be thrown out. But as Melody was already through the door I followed. The lounge bar was almost empty, with just one couple sitting at a table by a real fire. The place was old fashioned with dark swirling carpets and red patterned walls.

'You got any money?' Mel asked, 'I ain't been paid yet this week.'

I gave Mel a ten pound note out of my allowance so she could get drinks.

'What do you want?'

'Coke and one for Viv too,' I sat down at a corner table where the man serving behind the bar couldn't see me. With Melody I was always doing stuff I'd never done before. She came back with the cokes and a clear liquid in a tall glass with ice and lemon.

'What's that?' I asked.

'Vodka and tonic – try it.'

I sniffed. It smelt of lemon trees and sunshine. I took a tiny sip – it didn't taste of much but there was a lingering after affect in my mouth that reminded me of petrol.

'Nice,' I lied. Close up Melody looked pale

and she had dark rings round her eyes. 'What's up?' I reached for her hand which was freezing cold.

'Chas won't speak to me. He's stopped answering my calls.' Melody shook my hand off hers.

'But he's crazy about you.'

'Talk to him – I'll give you his number. He'll listen to you.'

'Why won't he talk to you?'

'Cos of London, they're going to see this band to try and get a gig with them. Chas won't take me.'

'Why not?'

'They're staying at his folks' flat and he don't want me to meet 'the Mater and Pater'. What is this *Mater and Pater* shit?'

'I think it's Latin for mother and father.'

'Friggin' arsehole,'

'Why can't you meet them?'

'I'm his bit of 'white trash', good enough for his street cred but not posh enough for home.'

'If that's true you should dump him.'

'I wanna to go to London. This is my chance to make it. I can get them the gig I know I can. Chas knows I'm better 'n he is,' Melody was angry but in a cold way not boiled up like I get.

'What do Mick and Yogi think?'

'Oh they'll do what Chas wants. He's the one with the dosh.'

'Maybe you could go but stay somewhere else?'

'I don't know anyone in London. Do you?'

'No,' but then I did, sort of, know Jock Briggs, 'well I know one person, but not very well.' He'd given me his card but I didn't think he'd want me turning up on his doorstep with a friend.

Mel didn't say anything. She was chewing on her fingernails, looking thoughtful. I still had my history notes to learn. I swigged back my coke.

'I'm sorry Mel but…'

'You've given us an idea…'

'I've got to go.' I stood up.

'You're my guardian angel Pen,' Mel had brightened up. She knocked back her vodka in one long gulp. 'Knew you wouldn't let me down.' I didn't know what I'd done to help apart from listen. Where had Vivienne got to? We left her coke untouched on the table and went to find her.

She was standing in the door of the pub still speaking on the phone, looking much happier.

'We're going now,' I signalled to her and she joined us.

We walked towards the Lordswood Road junction, me in the middle, with Vivienne on one side and Melody on the other. Viv and Mel were both wrapped up in their complicated love lives. I didn't feel it was right to disclose their secrets to each other, which was a shame because they had so much in common. But then again they didn't have anything in common. They were like dogs who didn't fancy the smell of each other, all bristly fur and growling. Mel was going on about this band called *Forest* and how wild they were. Neither Viv nor me had heard of them. Mel was showing off, maybe because Vivienne was there. When we got to the traffic lights she turned to go home.

'Thanks Pen, I can sort this now.'

I was glad she felt better.

'How do you like know her?' Vivienne asked as we crossed over the road.

'I'm seeing a boy that's friends with her boyfriend.' Well, it was sort of true, I had kissed Mick.

Vivienne went quiet for once. I'd given her something to think about. I smiled to myself as we turned down Knightlow into our estate. This was my night dancing territory, patterned with sequences of gravity defying grace and agility.

'There's something like not quite right about her,' Vivienne said, out of nowhere.

'Who?'

'Mel. I've been trying to work out what.'

'Because she's got dyed red hair?'

'Of course not, it's like she's pretending. Louis says when you're acting you have to 'be' the part not 'pretend' to be it, otherwise it feels fake. That's like what she is - fake.'

Vivienne didn't understand about putting on an act to feel brave, nor about having to manage on your own, like Melody had to. She was fussed over and looked after the whole the time, she couldn't possibly know what life was like for Melody. I changed the subject.

'So was Louis angry with you?'

'He's so lovely,' Vivienne gave a big breathy sigh. 'He's glad it's like finally out in the open and wants to talk to Mum and Dad. I'm sure they'll come round once they meet him. He says if I stay at yours' tonight, he'll meet me from school tomorrow.' Vivienne was virtually skipping down the road.

Great, now Melody and Viv were both happy, but I was going to fail my exams.

There was a white van parked outside our house.

'Isn't that your Dad's van?' I asked. Vivienne's face was pink from jogging beside me but she went totally white.

'Oh my God,' she applied her best iron clamp to my upper arm.

'Come on,' I said, 'he's not going to kill you.'

'Honey bun,' Mr Cooper rushed past me out of our front door and hugged Vivienne to his chest. 'I lost me temper. Sorry honey.'

It was a bit embarrassing, the hugging and stuff, so I went inside, leaving them to talk. Things would work out for Vivienne they always did. My Dad had never ever apologised to me.

Ten minutes later they knocked on the door, both beaming, Mr Cooper was charming to Mum, thanking her, and Vivienne gave me another huge hug, before they drove off home. The Vivienne Cooper love ship was back on course.

I went upstairs and sat down at my desk but I couldn't revise. Both Melody and Vivienne had boyfriends. Maybe Tamasin was going out with Grant Barker now. How come I was the only one who didn't have a boyfriend? Was something wrong with me?

I read a sentence of my notes and then my mind flitted off. I was dancing with Tartan Fling and Mick was sitting in the audience watching me. Next time I looked at my watch it was after ten o'clock. Nothing I read stayed in my head. I was too tired. I got into bed but when I closed my eyes the whirl in my head got worse and the bad colours started. My head filled up with negative thoughts. I was going to fail my exams. I'd never make it as a dancer. No one would ever love me. I had no choice.

The dark world was waiting for me as I tip-toed onto the road. The night was cold and clear, a big starry sky, a tiny slither of moon. Jock Briggs had said that everything had a vibration, I bent my knees, crouched down low and listened to the road. *Let's get moving* was what the tarmac told me, *let's get rolling, no time to waste, we gotta rock and roll our way outta here.* The churning inside my head stilled as I performed the Tartan Fling routine for the empty street. I stretched my arms up towards the arc of the sky, letting the vibrations of the stars fall down and through me.

35

The alarm went off and a great fight broke out inside me - get up you need to go to school versus sleep - you need to sleep. Somehow 'up' won even though I'd only had three hours sleep.

At school Vivienne was all smiles. Louis had been round and her parents had liked him. Now everything was out in the open she felt much better. Louis was picking her up from school this afternoon and going for tea with them.

'Honestly Pen, I can't tell you like how happy I am, that they know about Louis. No more sneaking around pretending and lying.'

I was pleased for Vivienne, of course I was, but I felt weird. Now that she and Louis were a proper couple, maybe she wouldn't have time for me.

Not sleeping had given me a strange hollow feeling, as if my brain and most of my organs had been emptied out and I was filled instead with cloudless sky. The sensation wasn't painful but I couldn't concentrate and was super jumpy. Exams always made me nervous. I felt as if my skin was alarmed and the slightest touch sent sirens blaring. Vivienne was chattering away about Louis. If she told me once more how happy she was, I thought I might drive my compass through her brain. Luckily for her, Mr Richards came in with the Geometry paper.

When the exam was over, Vivienne was preoccupied with Creme egg sales so I sneaked out of the classroom. Last night out on the streets I'd invented some new dance moves. They'd been swooping through my head during the Maths exam and I wanted to practise them. Dancing would wake me up and make me feel better. I made my way to the small gym Mrs Hadley used as a dance studio and as I'd hoped there was no one around. The sun beamed through the wall of windows and the room was already boiling hot even though it was only eleven. I took off my tights so that my feet could grip the floor. My school skirt was catching so I hitched it round my waist and tied my shirt up with a knot.

Starting with the little fledgling move I'd made at Jock's workshop I began to improvise using some of the ideas I'd worked on last night. I wanted to express the conflict I felt, between feeling so isolated and the understanding I'd got from Jock that everything and everyone was connected.

I contorted my body into extreme twisted shapes, trying to show the pain inside, and then slowly untangled myself. I was putting some moves into a sequence when I noticed Mrs Hadley standing by the door watching me. I quickly pulled down my skirt. How long had she been there? She came towards me smiling.

'I wanted to catch you Penny, what did you make of Tartan Fling?'

'I meant to say thank you for the tickets – they were incredible.'

'And the workshop?'

'The best thing I've ever done, thank you so much. Jock Briggs said maybe I could do work experience with them.'

'Did he now?' Mrs Hadley's eyebrows went up. She looked impressed. 'Well, I think we should follow that up. I like the new moves by the way and your technique's improving. Good work Penny, we'll make a dancer of you yet.'

Mrs Hadley always cheered me up.

The second Maths exam was pretty easy but my eyes kept closing. I'd fall asleep then wake up a moment later in this horrible jolting way, like I was tumbling downstairs and hitting the bottom.

It was a lovely, sunny day but I intended to spend my lunch hour revising. I didn't want to mess up this afternoon's history exam.

'I'm going to the library,' I told Vivienne.

'I'll come too.'

'Ok but I want to work.'

'You're turning into a real swot,' she laughed and I walked ahead of her. I was finding Vivienne hard to be near today. On the way out of the classroom Tamasin came towards us and for once Sadie wasn't by her side.

'Pen? ".

'Yes,' I was wary but she was smiling.

'We didn't get a chance to finish talking. I wanted to explain,' she glanced at Vivienne, 'about my birthday trip and everything. Can we meet up by the back of the sixth form extension after lunch?'

I didn't say anything. I wasn't sure.

'Like you said, it's stupid us not talking.'

I was trembling a little bit. I looked down at my hands and then up at Tamasin's face. I thought her eyes behind her glasses were sad. Maybe I had hurt her by becoming friends with Vivienne.

'Ok,' I said.

'On your own,' she held eye contact with me before glancing at Vivienne, 'see you there.' She took off along the corridor towards the dining room. There was no sign of Sadie and the rest of the gang.

Vivienne and I climbed up the main staircase to the library in silence. I knew Vivienne was looking at me, wanting to talk. If Tamasin apologised would I forgive her? We'd been best friends since the first year. I'd never missed one of her birthday parties. We did need to sort things out.

'You're not going are you Pen?' Vivienne couldn't keep quiet.

'I'm sorry,'

'To meet Tamasin? Don't go.'

It was alright for Vivienne, she had Louis now.

'I think that's up to me isn't it?'

'When she found out you'd had the day off to do a dance workshop she was furious. Went around saying how unfair it was. I bet she's up to something.'

I'd had enough of Vivienne telling me what I should do.

'Look Vivienne it's none of your business. Why don't you just leave me alone?'

'I don't want you to get hurt,' Vivienne was pretending to be concerned about me, 'Louis says like…'

'Stop going on about Louis - at least Tamasin won't talk about Louis – which is all you do now. You're totally obsessed. Louis this, Louis that, me and Louis, don't you know how boring it is?' I turned round and ran back down the stairs, leaving her standing with her mouth open and that silly hurt look on her face.

36

The sixth form extension was over the other side of the playground beyond the netball courts. It was on the border with the Boys' School and because of that, lots of girls gathered there. Round the back, on the side away from the main school, was the place where the smokers hung out.

Tamasin had turned into a big smoker so she was often out here. There was no sign of her when I got there. She'd still be in the canteen, sometimes the queues took ages.

The sixth form courtyard was empty so I jumped up onto their wall and sat with my back leaning against the extension. This spot was a sun trap, sheltered from the breeze by the building. I closed my eyes and pushed my face up towards the heat. I was so tired I wanted to go to sleep for ever. My heart was beating fast because I'd lost my temper with Vivienne. I still felt angry. She treated me as if I were some sort of victim, as if I needed looking after. Well, she needn't bother, I was well able to look after myself. She was the one who needed a team of people fussing over her.

'She's here,' it was Tamasin's voice. She walked round the corner of the extension and Sadie and Razi followed her. That hadn't been part of the deal.

'Hi Pen,' Tamasin said.

Immediately I was on the defensive. I jumped down off the wall and faced them. 'Sadie and Razi – wanted to come, they feel bad too.'

They were smiling at me but I'd never trust Sadie Thompson as long as I lived. I had a quick look at my watch. There was half an hour before the start of the history exam.

Tamasin got out her cigarettes and gave one to Sadie and Razi.

'You don't do you?'

I shook my head. They all lit up and took long showy drags. Sadie blew smoke rings - it was one of her tricks, if this was supposed to intimidate me, it wasn't working.

'We've been friends since the first year, right?' Tamasin said and I nodded. 'And I still want to be friends but can I trust you?'

Why shouldn't she trust me? I hadn't been nasty to her. I kept quiet.

'Sadie was really upset about you saying that she was 'rough as shit' and Razi didn't like that you'd said she was 'so stupid you didn't know how she'd got into Kings'. How do I know you don't say things like that about me, behind my back?'

Sadie and Razi were looking straight at me. Why had Tamasin repeated things I'd said to her in private?

'I don't, I haven't. You're my friend,' I stammered a bit.

'Vivienne's your friend but what if she knew you called her 'potato face' and 'gummy' and made fun of how she walks.'

It was true I'd been horrible about Vivienne with Tamasin but that was before. Then I remembered that just now on the stairs I'd shouted at her, a wave of guilt rushed through me.

'I only did that to make you laugh,' I explained.

'Everyone knows you've got the most vicious tongue in the class. That's why they don't like you. I'm telling you this because you're my friend and you ought to know.'

Did everyone really think I was a bitch? It was true that I used to laugh at people with Tamasin - it was what we did. I didn't mean to hurt anyone. I didn't think they'd ever know what I'd said. I could feel the sun on my cheeks and knew they'd be scarlet. I put my hand up to try and cover them.

'And what about your temper,' Tamasin carried on, 'the way you lash out, you're so aggressive that people are frightened of you. You don't realise how scary you are.'

The sun was right in my face beating down on me and I could feel sweat running down my back. I had to squint to look at Tamasin. I wanted to move into the shade but she was standing in front of me with Sadie and Razi either side of her. I did get angry and I said nasty stuff about other girls, it was true. No wonder people didn't like me. I shrunk back against the wall trying to find some shadow to protect myself from the light.

'But that's not the main reason I wanted to see you,' Tamasin took out her phone. She had one of the new large sized versions. 'I don't know whether you've seen this?' She passed me her phone. There was a video clip of me dancing this break time in the small gym.

'It was posted this morning,' Tamasin explained, 'and now it's all over the internet.' Sadie made a funny noise, but Tamasin turned and frowned at her. I watched the clip.

It was hideous. Who had taken it? I hadn't seen anyone filming. They must have been outside the windows with one of those zoom lenses because the shots were really close up. I had my back to the camera and was crouching over with my knees bent and my bottom thrust out. With my school skirt tucked up you could see my knickers and my bum looked gigantic. I was twisting at the waist to look back over my shoulder so there was a roll of fat crunched up in the middle between my shirt and skirt. My face was snarling with flared nostrils. My bottom pulsed towards the camera filling the whole screen. I looked like a fat pink pig in big navy knickers. I hated being photographed but this was the worst thing I'd ever seen. I was revolting.

'It's all over the boy's school. You should read the comments. They're calling it the Giant Arse video.'

My cheeks were hotter and brighter than the sun. Hot water pricked at my eyes. I wanted the extension wall to fall on me and cover me in bricks and earth a thousand feet deep. I wanted to run as fast as I could, somewhere, anywhere.

'I feel bad for you. Maybe there's a way you can get it taken down.' I looked up from the phone as she said this and caught her exchanging glances with Sadie. She had a funny little twisted smile on her face and I realised, one of them had filmed me. They'd posted the video.

'Get lost,' I screamed. 'Just get lost all of you.'

'Now, now, Pen, mustn't loose it,' Tamasin was grinning, 'you must come on my birthday trip on Saturday. You can show us some of your latest dance moves.' She was laughing, actually enjoying my humiliation. Everything went red behind my eyelids. I was so angry I roared - the sound burst out of me. I wanted to grab her stupid bunches and swing her round my head. At least I saw her face go pale as she backed away from me. I threw her phone back at her.

'You bitch, you little bitch,' I shouted. And I lashed out with my hand. I wanted to hit her but I didn't actually think I would. When my palm slapped into her cheek, I was as shocked as she was. She screamed then. I'd left a huge red mark across her face. She turned and ran away from me screaming.

'You're the bitch. You hit me. I'm reporting you. You'll be expelled.'

37

I don't remember clearly what happened next. I know I ran down the school drive and out of the gates and got on a number eleven bus. One was pulling up at the stop and I got on without thinking. I had to get away from school before anyone saw me. The bus was virtually empty. I was the only person on the top deck. Slumping onto the front seat, tears poured down my face and my body was shaking.

I couldn't stop myself - I got my phone out and found the video on Youtube. I looked so lumpy and awkward. Not just fat but clumsy too. How had I ever imagined I could be a dancer? It was an ugly film of an angry looking girl and I'd given them even more evidence of just how nasty I was. I hated myself. I was always having violent thoughts but now I'd actually hit Tamasin. I could remember the sound, a loud smack. The palm of my hand was stinging where I'd made contact with her cheek. Tamasin's father was a school governor, I was certain to be expelled. Dad would never forgive me. And I'd even been horrible to Vivienne, my only friend, who was only trying to warn me. Why had I ever done that stupid dance show? I looked absolutely, hideously, awful dancing. No wonder I didn't have a boyfriend. Tamasin was right about one thing - I could never be a dancer the way I looked. I was never going to dance again.

I stayed on the bus until we reached The Kings Head and then went over to the park and sat on a bench watching the film again and again and reading the posts. There were over fifty comments, most of them from boys, calling me a dog, going on about my piggy face and saying what they would or wouldn't do to me. Lots of messages were crude and sexual, and I felt sick. There were more posts coming in all the time and people kept pressing share so that more people could see the film clip. I knew I'd never be able to stop it. This would be out there now forever. I wanted to stop looking but I didn't seem able to stop myself. In the end I couldn't bear it any longer, I chucked my phone into the boating lake.

38

'Where have you been?' Dad shouted as I opened the door. It was the first time I'd seen him since the weekend. 'Why haven't you answered your phone?' He demanded.

'School,' I pushed past him.

'Don't lie to me,' he grabbed my arm and pulled me along the hall.

'Get off me,' I tried to pull away and Mum rushed out of the kitchen. She looked as if she'd been crying. She was wearing make-up and her new blue dress but her eyes were red and puffy.

'You leave her alone. How dare you hurt her?' she shouted at Dad and reached for me, pulling me close as if to protect me. But her whole body was trembling and her left hand was going crazy clawing at me with sharp nails. She was in one of her dangerous states. 'She's my daughter.' Mum held me so tightly I could barely breathe and I struggled to get away from her. Dad was whiter than I'd ever seen him.

'Get into the kitchen,' he said and somehow we all pushed through into the kitchen.

Dad walked over to the back door and stood staring out over the garden. He was trying to calm himself down. Mum's arm was jerking about.

'Mrs McBride phoned to ask why you weren't there for your history exam. She said you were in school this morning but absent this afternoon.' Dad was trying to keep his voice steady but I could hear how angry he was. 'So I repeat, where were you?'

I kept my head down. I didn't know how to explain.

'Have you been having trouble at school?' Mum asked. Maybe Tamasin hadn't reported me yet. But she would if I blabbed.

'No,' I mumbled.

'I don't understand Penny. You've been working so hard for this exam. Why miss it?' Mum asked.

'Working hard,' Dad exploded, 'away for the weekend, at a Show on Monday evening, and I discover, out last night as well. I told you to put your foot down. I told you she wasn't to go out this week.' Dad was shouting more at Mum than me.

'How would you know how much work she does? You're never here.' Mum screamed back at him.

'Someone has to earn a living.'

'And go to History Society and business dinners and whatever else you do in order to keep away?'

'If she had a Mother who could step outside the front door, then we'd be able to keep an eye on what she's up to.'

'I knew you'd make it my fault. You can't wait to get rid of me.' Mum was flinging her arms about and shouting so loudly that spit was coming out of her mouth.

'Jenny really, not this again,' Dad took off his glasses and put his hand on his forehead like he was trying to wipe us away. Mum was pulling at the sleeve of her dress in her compulsive mad woman way.

'Go on, leave, you don't want to be here, you know you don't,' she started crying.

I picked up my satchel and got up.

'Where are you going?' Dad barked at me. 'Sit down, I haven't finished.'

'Don't shout at her,' Mum yelled at him. 'Do you want to make her hate you too?'

'You hate me now do you?'

I left the room. I could hear them shouting with my bedroom door closed. I lay on my bed and shut my eyes. From time to time I heard my name. Thomas crept into my room and got on the bed next to me. I put my arm round him.

'Did you do something bad?' he asked.

'Yeh.'

'Why?

'Some girls were mean to me.'

'Well I love you Pen,' he gave me a pat on my side and tried to cuddle me but I couldn't comfort him. There was so much writhing going on inside me that I couldn't lay still.

'I love you too Thomas.' But I pushed him away from me, off the bed. 'You need to go to your room because I've got to do some homework.'

Thomas stopped at the door.

'You could work in my room if you wanted.'

'No, that's ok Thomas,' he wanted me to stay with him because of Mum and Dad shouting, but I just couldn't do it. I was struggling myself and I didn't have anything left to help him.

It was the worst fight they'd ever had. Mum completely lost it, she was hysterical, wailing and screaming with Dad shouting back at her. I put the pillow over my head. Sometime later I heard Dad coming up stairs. I was for it now.

'Dad,' I started as he appeared at my bedroom door. 'Don't shout at me, please listen,' I was crying now and he waited for me to speak.

'There's this horrible, horrible video of me dancing that's been posted on the internet, people are saying rude things about me. I can't bear it, I look so ugly.' Saying it out loud made me cry more.

'I knew it,' Dad exploded, 'I knew this bloody dancing would lead to trouble. Right that's it, I've decided, no more ballet classes, no more dance shows. You're like your mother: too emotional. It's not good for you.'

'No Dad don't, you can't, please you don't

understand, it's not the dancing, it's Tamasin and Sadie.'

'Tomorrow morning I'm driving you to school and we're meeting with Miss McBride to see what can be done about your exam.'

I started to shout then,

'All you care about is exams, you don't care about me - you're never here. You have no idea about what my life is like, leaving us with Mum all the time. I hate you. I hate you. I don't know why you even bother coming home.'

'Don't speak to me like that,' Dad went cold and emotionless, cutting me off, 'calm yourself down and get on with some work. I'm disappointed in you Penny, with your Mother the way she is, I hoped I could rely on you to be sensible. But I was wrong.'

He closed the door behind him and I was left staring at my old blue dressing gown swaying on its hook, while he stomped downstairs. I waited for Bessie Smith's lonesome voice to start singing. But there wasn't any music. The front door opened and closed and I heard the car engine start. I dashed to the top of the stairs and heard the car reversing, I ran down into the hall. Mum got to the front door before me.

'Where are you going?' she yelled but the car was already half way down the drive.

'Come back,' Mum was screaming from the door step but Dad drove off down the drive. She turned round. Her mascara and lipstick were smudged across her face and her eyes were huge and bright with red rims. Their glare was at me like arrows. She looked totally insane. I stepped back.

'What did you say to him?' she screamed.

'Nothing, I didn't say anything,' I knew I had to be calm and talk her down, but I didn't have any stillness inside me. I was trembling and crying myself.

'What have you done?' she was right up close to me so that our noses almost touched. I tried to move away but she grabbed hold of my jumper, twisting a clump of wool in her hand.

'I haven't done anything,' I said.

'This is your fault. Get him back, go and find him.' She had both hands on my arms pushing me out of the door.

I couldn't stop myself saying, 'You go and get him.'

'Don't say that,' Mum was jerking me about,

hurting me, 'shut up, shut up.'

'Leave me alone,' I tried to pull away but she held on tightly, her fingers pinching into the flesh on the top of my arms.

'You selfish girl, you don't care what happens to me,' she said and I pushed hard and thrust her away from me.

'It's you that's selfish!' I screamed back, heading for the stairs. 'You're the most selfish, useless, hopeless mother in the world.'

She came for me then before I could get away, flying across the hall.

The first slap was across my mouth, the second got my right ear and her ring hit my cheekbone. I got my arms up to protect my face. Mum had me pressed up against the wall. I thought she was going to strangle me she was so strong. Her eyes had gone dark, almost black, huge black holes in her face.

'Mum, no, please,' I begged.

She pulled back but looked as if she hated me. 'Get out of my sight – you'll stay in your room until you apologise.'

I ran up the stairs.

I watched a fish die once. We were on holiday in Wales and the trawlers were unloading buckets of fish and one fell on the ground and they left it there. First off the fish leapt and leapt, jerking and twisting, trying to get back into the water then the jumps got smaller and smaller until it lay on the ground twitching and finally stopped.

I didn't want to see Mum ever again, nor Dad. I was going out of my bedroom window and this time I wasn't coming back.

I had the shopping money, plus what was left of this month's allowance, plus my money box savings, nearly a hundred pounds altogether. I put everything in my school purse, wrapped the cord tightly around and tucked the purse into the inside pocket of my duffel coat.

The house was silent apart from the sound of Thomas's snuffling breath and Mum's heavy snoring. She always snored loudly when she'd been crying. I put my duffel coat and boots on and climbed through the window onto the roof, then down the lilac tree.

The smell of lilac swooshed into my nose. The tree had just come into blossom. Tonight the darkness was lilac. I breathed the scent deep inside, calming myself down. There wasn't a moon nor any stars. I was alone with the darkest of skies. I climbed down onto the garden wall and into the alley.

Soft fine rain sparkled in the street lights. I turned my face up to receive the water. I wanted to be washed away. I wanted the rain to pour down and flood the street, gather me up and carry me off. Away from Mum and Dad, away from Kings, from Birmingham, away from everything I knew.

I stood beneath the lamp posts watching the droplets falling. The rain grew fiercer, lashing my face. Water raced down the gutters and I ran with it. I was a drop of water obedient to gravity. Water only had one direction - down. I would run and run, until I reached the very bottom, until I had sunk into the darkest, blackest, coldest, wettest place it was possible to be.

My heart was flipping like a dying fish...

Part 3:
Trial by Cheese Grater

39

The junction by the Kings Head was deserted, no cars in any direction. The lights changed from red to amber to green for no reason. The rain was fierce, coming at me hard and horizontal. Water streamed along the gutters. I took a deep breath and crossed. Once onto Bearwood High Street, I ran. I didn't dance. I was never going to dance again.

Only the shop window mannequins witnessed my speed as I blazed down the pavement. I got as far as the old ice rink before my breath collapsed. My hair was soaked and stuck to my face in clumps. I turned off the High Street into the road that led to the council estate where Melody lived.

Melody called me Angel but would she be

mine? She was the only friend I had left to turn to. She was on her own and now I was too. We could look out for each other. Dad had told me this true story about two old women from Yardley who'd been friends their whole lives. During the Second World War when they were only fourteen they'd been evacuated on a boat to America but their ship was bombed so they'd clung together, to a life boat rope, treading water, waiting to be rescued, both of them holding onto the same rope. All the other people on ropes, including some of the ship's crew, had given up and drowned but the two girls had kept each other going for sixteen hours and they'd survived. When they were rescued their hands were frozen to the rope. They'd had to be cut off it. Mel and I would be like them, holding on together, survivors.

Walking through the estate was creepy. The heavy rain made the concrete blocks looked grimmer than ever. Water ran down the walkways and gathered in puddles where the pavement slabs were broken. In the tangerine glow from the wall lamps they looked like pools of poison.

I found Mel's block because graffiti like *the Quinton mob are dead meat* – written in blood red paint was the sort of message you remembered. Her flat was the third one along on the first floor, I recognised the front door, painted a cheery seaside blue, which did nothing to make me feel better. Now I'd stopped running I realised the rain was seeping through my coat.

There was a light on inside, and when I opened the letter box and peered in I could see it came from the room at the end of the hall.

'Mel,' I whispered through the letter box, 'Mel, it's me Pen.'

Nothing stirred. I couldn't hear anything.

'Mel, wake up,' I called louder this time.

'Mel,' I yelled and rattled the letter box. I didn't want to wake the neighbours but there was no response. I didn't know what to do. I'd thrown my phone away so I couldn't call her.

'Mel, Mel, Mel,' I shouted and kicked the door. Then I tried banging on the windows, hammering until my knuckles hurt. Why wasn't she answering? Maybe I'd got the wrong flat. I pressed my face against the window trying to see through the gap in the curtains.

'Mel,' I bent down and shouted through the

letter box again. A hand grabbed me round the back of the neck and I screamed. Jumping round I bashed at the arm holding me. My other arm was ready to punch my way out of danger.

But it was Melody holding an umbrella and laughing at me.

'I swear I could hear you at the Bearwood traffic lights.' She was rubbing her arm where I'd knocked it away. 'After me by any chance?' She had her key in her hand and was opening the door. I followed her in.

'Where've you been?' I was a bit wound up. Mel took off her donkey jacket, shook off the rain and hung it over the bannister. She was more dressed up than I'd ever seen her in an electric blue sequinned mini dress. She'd tied bits of ripped up material into bows in her hair. As usual she looked incredible. She walked away from me down the hall.

'Sorry,' she said sarcastically, 'if I'd know you were coming I'd have gotten home earlier.'

She went through into the end room where a sofa was surrounded by a frill of beer cans, dirty mugs, magazines and saucers full of nub ends. Melody seemed oblivious to the chaos. The place stank. She picked up a couple of mugs from the floor and went into the kitchen which was the other side of a half wall at the back of the room.

'Take your coat off if you're stopping, you're dripping everywhere. You want tea?' I nodded and hung my coat over the radiator to dry. The foul smell came from the kitchen. There must have been something going off in the bin bag that sprawled across the floor. Melody took a milk bottle out of her bag.

'I liberated this on the way home,' she said. 'I've been at work, you plank, I don't finish until two when I'm on lates. What're you doing here?'

'I've run away from home.'

Melody put the kettle on and we waited for it to boil.

'Mum went berserk,' I explained as Melody poured water into the mugs. 'She attacked me.'

'Milk and sugar,' Melody asked and I nodded. She handed me a mug, 'come and sit down me feet are killing me. They make us stand all night. You'd think we could sit down for ten minutes when the bar's not busy.' She kicked away some magazines to make a space on the floor in front of the settee and sat down on one end.

She lifted a pile of papers off the other sofa cushion and threw them on the floor. 'Sit yourself down.'

I slumped down next to Mel. The cushion sloped and I nearly lost my balance as I tilted towards the middle of the settee. I had to brace my legs to keep upright and steady the mug. Mel giggled.

'I should have warned you -that side's messed up. The Sally Army gave it me - must have belonged to a fat bastard, that cushion's sculpted to fit a giant arse.'

My brain went immediately to the video of my bottom. That's what the boys called it – the Giant Arse.

'You look terrible,' Melody was staring at me. Everything I thought of to say sounded stupid and childish so I didn't say anything. Melody took a cigarette out of a packet on the arm of the sofa.

'You don't do you?' she offered me the packet.

'Sometimes,' I said and took one. Melody passed me her lighter and I managed to get a flame and put the cigarette into it. I breathed in but didn't swallow, just let the smoke fill my mouth and then breathed it straight out so that I didn't cough. The smoke tasted horrible and made my eyes water but I managed a second puff. I breathed the smoke out in a straight line so it didn't go up into my eyes.

Melody was pulling the bows out of her hair. 'Tell me,' she said so I told her about Dad leaving and Mum blaming me. I didn't mention the video.

'Friggin' parents – always give you grief,' she finished her cigarette and stubbed it out. I copied. 'I don't have anything to do with mine. Waste of space.' She sounded angry. 'Forget about yours. You don't need 'em. You're better off on your own.'

Never see them again – said out loud – the idea was shocking. How could I manage by myself? What about school, money, food? Where would I live? I couldn't go there. I didn't want to think about that.

'Have you heard from Chas?' I changed the subject.

'Yeh, it's sorted. I'm going to London with them.' Melody grinned.

Was it always like this with boyfriends, one minute over, next back on again?

'That's great Mel, I knew he adored you.'

Melody stretched out her body, arms above her head and yawned,

'I guess he couldn't resist.'

Seeing Melody in this room was funny, in one way she was out of place being so beautiful in such an ugly setting, but in another way she fitted, like this was what made her special.

'We're off tomorrow. Why don't you come?'

'To London?'

'Why not?'

'I don't know,' things were moving so fast. I was supposed to be doing my history exam tomorrow. I couldn't think. 'There'd be room in the car?'

'Be a bit tight but you're only little,' she stood up, 'I know you're a night angel but I'm knackered. You're welcome to crash on the sofa.'

I didn't have much choice, 'thanks Mel.'

I started to undo my DM's and Melody came back with a blanket and a cushion. She threw them onto the sofa and kissed me on the top of my head.

'There you go Angel.'

I heard the loo flush and a door close. Then there was silence and I was alone.

There was no way I could sleep. I got up and wandered around the room. Apart from the sofa there was a plastic topped table and two kitchen chairs over by the half wall. A bottle of ketchup with the top off and some dirty plates were left on the table. What if I ended up living here with Mel? I'd have to get a job.

There was a pile of zines with scrawled drawings and angry writing about getting drunk and taking drugs. On the front of one of them was a photo of Mel and Chas singing. Could I really go to London with them? Dad would freak out if I wasn't home when he came back. Serve him right for leaving us. If I went to London maybe I could see Jock Briggs? Maybe I could get a job with Tartan Fling and a flat in London?

The window in the living room had no curtains and the black square of darkness reflected me back. London was a huge city, I'd be anonymous, no one would recognise me from that horrible video. I didn't know what I should do.

The room stank like a rotting sheep carcass. At least I could clean up a bit. I took the dirty plates into the kitchen and put them in the sink then gathered up the stinking bin bag and went round the living room picking up the empty bottles and cans and emptying the ash trays into it. Then I tied the bag really tightly and left it by the front door. I hoped that would stop the living room smelling so bad. I switched off the lights in the kitchen but kept the lounge one on and lay down on the sofa, pulling the blanket Mel had given me over my head.

40

'Rise and shine,' Melody was standing above me with a cup of tea. 'I'm making breakfast.' She put the tea down by the side of the settee and disappeared. There was a radio on somewhere in the flat and sun blazed in through the window. I sat up struggling to open my eyes. It felt like a long climb to the surface but the smell of bacon beckoned me on.

Melody was in the kitchen, singing along to the radio.

'*This girl is on fire,*' she had a sweet voice, with an unusual poignant quality.

My mouth tasted disgusting, and I felt sick. In the bathroom I splashed cold water over my face. Using Mel's toothbrush I scrubbed at my teeth and tongue trying to get rid of the horrible taste of tobacco.

With bright light streaming through the windows the flat looked a bit better than it had done last night. I took my tea into the kitchen. Melody had a fry up on the go with bacon, mushrooms and eggs spitting together in one pan.

'Grubs up,' Melody said and slid half of the frying pan onto a plate and handed it to me. She put the other half on her plate and carried it through to the table. 'I thought you'd never wake up.'

'What time is it?'

'Not sure, 'bout twelve I think.' The fork full of bacon and mushroom on the way to my mouth swayed in the air before I put it back down on the plate.

'Twelve,' I shrieked, 'oh my god, it can't be.' I stared at Melody and she frowned back at me her mouth full of breakfast. It was the first time I'd ever seen her eat and she was shovelling it down like someone who hadn't seen food for days. They'd know I was gone by now.

'I'm supposed to be at school taking an exam. They'll kill me.'

Melody carried on eating.

'What shall I do?' I got up from the table. I'd said I was never going back but now in daylight I wasn't sure. Dad was going to drive me to school this morning. What would he and Mum think when they found I wasn't there? Would they care I'd gone? What if they phoned school and found out I'd hit Tamasin, that I was going to be expelled? I paced up and down trying to think. Outside the window here were little children playing on the scrubby grass. They had a tricycle and an old plastic car. Thomas would definitely be upset that I'd gone.

'Are you going to eat this or not?' Melody called. I went back to the table and sat down. I put a fork full of food in my mouth but it was hard work swallowing it.

'I'm sorry but I don't think I can,' I pushed the plate away and Melody who'd finished her plate started on mine.

'Do they know where I live?' she asked.

'They don't even know who you are. Mum thinks you're a school friend.'

'So they can't find you here, can they?' To Melody it was simple - don't go back - but I didn't know what to do. Melody was lighting a cigarette.

'Help yourself,' she pushed the packet towards me and I took one. Taking my first draw I thought I was going to throw up. I retched but managed to control it.

'Chas is cool about you coming to London if you want. I'm meeting the guys in town in a couple of hours.'

Mum and Dad would have no idea where I'd gone. That would teach Dad a lesson, and Mum. If she thought I was so selfish, well then, I'd bloody well be selfish, and see how she managed without me. And it would serve Tamasin right too - if everyone thought I'd gone missing she'd be in trouble.

'London will be a ton of fun,' Melody said, 'you should chill out. Have a laugh.'

Did I dare go? In daylight the idea wasn't so scary. London with Melody would be an adventure, better than going with Tamasin and her parents on a mini bus. Or with Viv on a coach. Mick was going. Plus Jock Briggs was in London. That decided it. I took a deep breath.

'Ok you're on,' I said, 'why not.'

'Brill,' Melody stubbed out her cigarette, 'let's get ready. Chas is picking us up at Gary's.' She was off up the stairs, an explosion of legs.

We had such a laugh getting ready. I was worried in case someone I knew recognised me. We decided that I needed to be the *international woman of mystery and disguise*. Melody made me look as cool as she did. I had a pink mohair sweater on as a dress with a wide black belt pulled in at the waist and then my thick black dance tights and my DM's. Over that I wore one of Melody's men's suit jackets plus, to be sure no one recognised me, a black wig and big dark sun glasses. Standing at the No 10 bus stop opposite *The Kings Head* I don't even think my Dad would have recognised me. Even so my heart froze when a green Volvo like ours drove past. But it wasn't Dad.

We leapt off the bus by the Bull Ring and Mel led the way down the hill towards Digbeth near my ballet school. On a side street between *The Carpenters Arms* and a Red Cross Charity shop was *Records Rock* and a hairdressers called *Smile*, as announced by a red neon sign, and a man with a green Mohican was standing in the doorway smoking. He was wearing tight black jeans and a t-shirt that had I F--KING HATE YOU written on the front. Somehow he still looked friendly because his face was round and dimpled.

''ere's trouble,' he said, as we crossed the road, sounding just like Vivienne's Dad. There was a huge photo of a girl with spikey red hair hanging in the shop window and as we got closer I realised the model was Melody.

'Yo Gary, this is Pen,' Melody pushed me in front. 'She's coming to London with us. Can you sort her out?' she pulled off the wig and my hair tumbled over my shoulders. Gary took hold of my hair.

'She looks like Dracula's hippy bride.'

I was quite proud of my hair – it was one of the few things I liked about my appearance, being long and shiny chestnut brown.

'I cut my best to The Cure,' Gary said approaching me with a giant pair of scissors, 'no point dyeing all this.' He brushed my hair flat down my back and then gathered it into a pony tail and sliced it straight off in one cut, just below my jaw line.

'That's better,' he handed me the hank of hair. I looked like my Barbie doll did when I chopped off her hair when I was seven. I'd cried about that and I felt like crying now.

'There's so much, you could knit it into a jumper.' He pointed at the hair in my hand and Melody laughed. 'Or have a wig made.'

'You could sell it,' Melody said.

'How much would I get?' I thought about Jo in *Little Women* selling her hair.

'A hundred quid maybe.' That didn't seem enough for fifteen years of growing. It was weird holding my hair in my hand. Just a second ago it had been attached to me and now it was separate. My hair could have a different life from mine. It could go places without me. I giggled.

'What's funny?' Melody asked. Gary was starting to coat my hair in weird lavender gunk and the smell caught at the back of my throat, making me cough.

'My hair on someone else's head - imagine this being an old man's toupee?' I lifted up my hair.

'Don't move too much or I'll get this in your eye,' Gary said. 'You know they make pubic hair wigs.'

'That's revolting,' Melody said then she started to collapse, 'your hair as someone's snatch.'

'Noooo,' I screamed.

'The Queen's! Your hair's going to be the royal pubes,' suggested Gary.

'No, Elton John!' said Melody.

'Stop it, stop it.' I was squealing.

While my colour was taking, Gary cut and styled a new look for Melody. He had a little fat belly that pushed out over the top of his tight jeans and his square hands moved confidently around her head as he sang along to his records, the scissors moving in rhythm. Her natural hair colour was deep auburn, and he cut it spiky on the top but with the sides shorter and a longer lock plaited and curled over her shoulder. With her cheekbones, pale skin, blue grey eyes and dark eyebrows she looked just like a cat, a wild imperious queen cat.

'Mel, you look just incredible,' I said and she preened in the mirror. I wasn't surprised Gary used her as a model. She was so beautiful.

'The boy's done good,' she grinned at me.

'Make us a cuppa Mel, while I get Pen washed

off.' Gary took me over to the basin and rinsed off the dye. I glanced up to look at Mel in the mirror. She was standing at the back of the shop by the till and I saw her take two twenty pound notes out of the drawer and put them in her pocket. I was shocked and didn't know what to do. Surely she couldn't be stealing from a friend? Maybe Gary paid her for modelling. I hoped so.

When he'd finished cutting he blow dried what was left of my hair super straight and shiny. The new colour made my eyes look green rather than dirty puddle colour and with all the black eyeliner Melody had given me they slanted upwards, so that I was a bit cat like too. I could easily pass for eighteen now. Gary showed me the back of my hair in a mirror.

'You like?' he asked.

I turned my head in different directions checking it out. If Dad ever saw me again he'd go ballistic.

'I feel weird without my hair,' I started pulling faces in the mirror, trying out new expressions, angry, deep, even mysterious. 'I think I like it.'

Gary helped me out of the cape.

'Hot shit,' Melody came in with the tea, 'Where did that other girl go? Gary you're a genius.'

'She looks good doesn't she?' Gary was gloating over me like I was his prize poodle.

I was washing up the mugs and cleaning the plastic trays of hair dye in the little kitchen area, when I heard male voices outside. Chas and Mick must have arrived. Suddenly I felt really shy. Maybe I shouldn't go to London, after all I'd only met them a couple of times.

'Come on Pen,' Melody was calling me, 'we're off.'

I looked at myself in the tiny kitchen mirror. At least I looked cool, even if I wasn't really. I breathed in, holding my stomach muscles tight, and walked into the Salon. The boys were talking to Gary.

Mick saw me first and gave a loud wolf whistle that made the others turn round. They stared at me so I stared back. As I no longer had hair to hide behind I had to bold it out.

'Quelle transformation,' Yogi said in a mock French accent.

Mick didn't say anything but he grinned at me. He had such a sweet smile that I stopped doing my cool glare and smiled back instead. I think he liked the way I looked.

'I want to leave before the traffic builds up.' Chas wore super tight jeans, and a battered leather jacket. Although he looked like a movie star he sounded more like an accountant. There was something pernickety about him. The boys were dressed up. Yogi had gelled his fringe into an amazingly high quiff that bounced on the top of his head. Mick looked better than I'd ever seen him in a tight navy t-shirt that showed off his biceps. He held out his hand to me. My snakes were belly dancing but I took his hand and followed him outside.

The car pulled onto the pavement was a silver VW beetle. Chas got in the driver's seat and the rest of us stood on the pavement peering into the car. Gary, closing up the shop and pulling bars across the windows, laughed.

'Blimey, good luck getting to London in that. Have fun children and don't do anything I wouldn't.' Gary couldn't be that much older than Chas, maybe he was twenty five, but he talked as if he came from another generation. He reached into the back pocket of his jeans and handed Yogi something in a small plastic bag.

'Have a good trip,' he said and everyone laughed apart from me.

'Thanks Gary, you're a Gent,' Yogi gave him an envelope.

'Come on get in,' Chas shouted from inside the car. Yogi stood by the passenger door.

'In *you* go,' he gestured at Melody but she didn't budge.

'I'm in the front,' she said smiling at Yogi.

'I don't think so,' he smiled back.

'For Christ's sake,' Chas started to hammer the horn.

'Come on Pen,' Mick climbed into the car and slid over to the far side behind the driver's seat and I slipped in next to him. I was pressed against him thigh to thigh and that left a tiny space on the back seat.

'Come on Mel, I'll never get in there,' Yogi said.

But she didn't move.

'Yogi - get in,' Chas shouted.

There was a moment of silent stand off and then Yogi shoved his massive shoulders through the passenger door and the rest of his body followed them in. I was pushed so far over I was practically sitting on Mick's knee.

'This is ridiculous,' Yogi said as Melody forced the passenger seat back against his knees and then sat down and closed the door. She leaned over and gave Chas, a long, slow, kiss. Yogi never stood a chance.

'Okay finally,' Chas said when Melody had finished with him. 'Let's go.'

I was on my way to London for the first time in my life.

41

There's something incredibly exciting about leaving Birmingham. Even with Mum and Dad I got a buzz but crammed into that tiny car between Mick and Yogi, well, it was wild. We swooped through the tunnels and up over the first flyover with the car banking like we were in a Grand Prix. We reached Spaghetti Junction and curved our way onto the six lane entrance to the M6. I loved it, the car was so smooth and with no traffic lights or stop junctions, we were just gliding from one road to the next. I felt as if as if I was flying off to a new future. Melody and I squealed as we took the corners. I think everyone in the car had the same sense of possibility.

Not that Chas was a crazy driver, I'd say he was

on the cautious side of sensible because once we were on the motorway he settled down to a steady sixty in the inside lane. Maybe this was all the little car could manage with so many of us crammed inside. Mick was playing music from his phone. I didn't recognise any of the tunes but the others were singing along. Melody had a high pitched breathy style that sounded seriously sexy. It was like we were in a coca cola advert. The problems I had at home and school didn't seem to matter anymore. Every time there was a sign for London we hooted. Watching Melody sing a phrase of music and then stop to light a cigarette for Chas and put it in his mouth I couldn't believe that someone so beautiful and cool and special was my friend.

Mind you the smoke was a bit much. Chas, Melody and Yogi all smoked so the car soon fugged up. I felt a bit sick squashed in the middle.

'Do you think you could open the window a bit?' I asked. Mick rolled it down a couple of inches and as I turned my face into the rush of air, my hair brushed against his face.

'Sorry,' I said and that's when he kissed me, not a peck on the cheek, a proper mouth to mouth job. I looked up at him - we were rammed in so tightly I was only inches from his face. He grinned at me showing off his crooked teeth. I smiled back and he managed to lift the arm that was jammed between us and put it around my shoulder so I was nestled into his body. Wow, things were happening fast. We hadn't even got to the first Motorway Services.

I don't know whether Yogi was jealous but the next thing I felt was a hand on my knee and I realised it was his. The sweater dress Mel had leant me had ridden up my legs so that most of my thighs were exposed. I wriggled so that I could pull the dress down over my legs and managed to push Yogi's hand away without being too obvious. A few minutes later the hand was back with his fingers reaching down between my thighs. I squeezed my legs tightly together and used my elbow to try and lever away his arm. He must have felt me trying to push him off but he didn't stop he just kept working his way up my thigh. In the end I had to peel his hand away from my leg with my fingers. I tried to move closer to Mick but there wasn't much room. Ten minutes later Yogi's hand came back. I didn't want to make a scene but it was as if he was trying to get his hand into my pants.

'Leave it off - you fat bastard. She's not interested,' Mick leant across me and punched Yogi on the arm. Yogi hit him back in the chest.

'Says who?' There wasn't enough room in the back for a fight.

'Says me, actually,' I said.

'Oooh, says me actually,' Yogi repeated in a high pitched voice but at least he stopped. I was grateful to Mick for rescuing me and I let my head rest on his shoulder. He smelt of deodorant and boy.

My eyelids started to feel heavy, being in a car always made me sleepy. When I was little and I couldn't sleep Dad would put me in the car and drive around the ring road until I dropped off. I closed my eyes and found myself thinking about Vivienne and wishing I hadn't been so horrible to her. She'd been right about Tamasin. She probably hated me now. If I hadn't chucked my phone away I'd have sent her a text. I wondered what she'd think of Mick.

The car started to slow down and when I opened my eyes we were turning into a service station.

Chas didn't head into the main car park with the other cars but made for the far corner of the lorry park where several giant trucks were lined up and chose a spot behind them under some trees. He climbed out of the car and stretched his arms above his head so that his t-shirt rode up his torso. It was flat and muscled and I had to look away because watching him made me feel like I was doing something wicked.

'You lot out,' he said and we squeezed onto the tarmac. The sun was shining and the heat on my skin felt lovely. I shrugged off the tin can car and unfurled. I was far too hot in the sweater dress but I couldn't take it off.

'Make yourselves scarce for half an hour. Mel and I want a bit of privacy. Meet back here at six thirty ok?' Chas would make a great dictator he was so good at giving orders. One minute he was in a massive hurry and now he wanted us to hang about. I didn't want to leave Melody but she was still in the car and Chas was blocking the door.

'Come on Titch,' Mick was waiting for me. Yogi had already walked off towards the buildings.

'Bye Mel. See you in a bit,' I called into the

car and then walked over to Mick and he draped an arm round my shoulder. It was like we were already boyfriend and girlfriend. Maybe that was how it happened, you just started doing stuff together.

'Let's get a cup of tea,' he said.

'Ok,' I said and realising I was hungry, 'and cake?'

'I'll buy you a cake, Titch.' And he kissed me again.

Yogi was in the arcade pushing coins into a slot machine. I'd never seen the point of slot machines, they ate up your money and you never won anything. Mick and I played electronic hockey instead then we left Yogi playing the machines and went into the café. Mick paid for the teas. We sat at a circular table by the window looking down over the motorway so that we could watch the cars driving underneath. I felt shy just the two of us.

'So how do you know Mel,' I asked him for something to say.

'She's a friend of Dog's and he's in the band. What about you?'

'Met her out one night,'

'You're not much like her.'

I frowned. Did he mean I wasn't cool or beautiful?

'Don't get me wrong,' Mick carried on, rushing his words, 'I like Mel, she's a real laugh, but she's, you're...' he faded away.

'What? I'm boring?'

'No, I mean, this sounds lame, but you're, well, nice.'

I burst out laughing and Mick laughed too.

'"Nice" wow -you really know how to make a girl feel special.' I was flirting. Flirting was fun. But what did he mean about Mel? Was he saying she wasn't nice? She'd always been good to me.

'Don't I? Let's change the subject.' He picked up the plastic menu and there was an advert for holidays in Florida at Disney World. 'Have you been to America? Chas and I are going to the States next summer when we finish school.' That meant he must be at least seventeen.

'No, but I want to.' I hadn't even been to London, a week in France on a school geography trip was the limit of my international travelling. But Tartan Fling had done a tour of America. Their website listed the cities they'd performed in, New York, Philadelphia, Chicago, Seattle, and I'd imagined myself going with them.

'We're going to drive Route 66 across America like Kerouac,' Mick said.

'Who's Kerouac?'

'You've never read Kerouac, Jack Kerouac '*On the Road*', you must have.'

'No but I will. Do you like reading then? I read all the time.' Mick and I had so much in common like playing sports and reading and wanting to travel. I thought he might kiss me again and I thought that would be alright.

'So you're pretty *and* smart,' he said. I blushed, I'd never had a boy say anything like that to me before, shame he was talking rubbish.

'Do you think they've finished yet?' Yogi appeared by our table. 'It's half past six but I don't want to watch them at it.'

'Knowing Chas it was over twenty minutes ago,' Mick said and Yogi laughed.

'You're right. Come on let's get back, we've got another seventy miles to go.'

We walked through the car park towards the Beetle. I moved slowly so that Yogi got ahead of us.

'You were joking about Chas and Mel weren't you?' I asked.

Mick grinned at me and shrugged his shoulders. I don't know why but I shivered even though I was boiling hot in the sweater dress. Having sex in a car park seemed so sordid.

Chas and Melody were standing outside the car smoking. They were such a glamorous couple. Leaning against the VW in the evening sunshine they could have been on a movie set.

'Are you ok?' I felt concerned for Mel.

'Never been better,' she smiled and offered me a cigarette but I shook my head. 'What about you Angel? Has Mick been kind to you?' Maybe she was laughing at me I wasn't sure.

'Well, he bought me a cake,' that made her laugh out loud.

'Good for him. Hey Yogi,' Melody called. The boys were standing a few feet away talking. 'What did

Gary give you?'

'Smarties,' he patted his pocket and I remembered the plastic bag Gary had passed him before we left the salon.

'Let's have some now,' Melody was at Yogi's side.

'No, we should save them for tomorrow night, for the gig,' Chas was laying down the law again.

Melody's eye's clouded over and her smile disappeared. Chas really annoyed me he was so bossy.

'I can get some sweets for the car if you want Mel, I'll only be a minute. I can easily run back to the shops.' They all laughed at me then and Mick put his arm round me.

'You really are sweet,' he said and kissed me on the cheek.

'Why do you think I call her Angel?' Melody said.

'Get in the car you lot and let's get going,' Chas opened the driver's side door and Yogi climbed inside. Melody got in the front seat again and Mick and I squeezed onto the back seat next to Yogi.

'In the glove compartment,' Chas said to

Melody as he followed the exit signs, 'wait until we're on the Motorway and you can roll one up.'

Chas put the music on again and for a while we drove with no one speaking. Mick was in the middle now and I was by the window. Looking out at the green verges running past stopped me feeling sick. I didn't know much about relationships but if I was ever going to have sex with a boyfriend I wanted romance, candles or moonlight, and at the very least, a bit of privacy.

42

Funny how one minute you could be having the best time in your whole life and then the next minute for no reason you just start to feel sad. We passed a sign that said London forty nine miles and I wondered how far we were from Birmingham? When I drove somewhere with Mum and Dad we played the number plate game where you took three letters and had to make up a phrase with the initials. A silver Corsa over took us with a GFE number plate – so that could be *Gone For Ever*. The thought of never seeing Thomas again made my chest constrict so that I felt as if I couldn't breathe.

A car horn blared aggressively and Chas swerved the car to the left back into the inside lane. He'd been trying to pull out into the middle lane to overtake a van.

'I can't see a thing with you sitting there Mick,' Chas sounded cross. That was probably my fault for changing seats.

Melody lit her handmade cigarette and the car filled with even dirtier smoke than from a regular cigarette. I thought Chas would yell at her because you could hardly see out of the front window for the billowing fumes. I started to cough but Melody was taking huge gulps and Chas didn't shout at her.

'Good girl.'

Melody handed him the cigarette and he took several long deep drags then passed the cigarette back to Yogi. The smoke smelt sweet and musty like burning garden clippings. Next to me Yogi started taking deep breaths too and I realised that there must be drugs in the cigarette. Even Mick who didn't smoke took some drags. I didn't know what would happen to them? But nobody seemed any different to how they'd been before.

'You want some?' Mick passed me the cigarette which had burnt down to half an inch from the end. 'Careful, it's pretty hot.'

I copied what they'd done and took a deep breath in. The smoke was harsh and acrid, like breathing in bonfire smoke. It hit the back of my throat and I couldn't stop myself coughing. Smoke burst out of my mouth and nose as I had a total coughing fit.

'Just take a little toke to start with,' Mick said when I'd recovered. No one was laughing at me, so I had a tiny suck on the end of the cigarette and blew the smoke straight back out. This time I managed not to cough and I quickly passed it on to Melody.

'This is dead,' she said and stubbed it out in the car ash tray.

'Not there, you jerk,' Chas was shouting, ''out the window.'

'Alright, you crazy Control Freak,' Melody wound down her window and a huge blast of air rushed into the car. She threw away the nub end.

'Close the bloody window,' Yogi yelled. But Melody wound it down even further and leant right out.

'Mad bitch, can't you do something Chas?' Yogi was annoyed because his hair, greased back into a perfect quiff was getting messed up. Chas watching him in the mirror started to grin.

'Shut the window,' Yogi yelled. Mick was laughing his head off. Melody put her head back inside the car and turned to look at Yogi and then she cracked up seeing his hair fanned out over his face and dancing in the air. She let the air blow hard for a minute and then wound up the window. The car went quiet for a second. We looked at Yogi. His beautifully constructed quiff had collapsed into a flat clump over his forehead covering his eyes. He looked so silly that we exploded. He was desperately trying to resurrect it with his fingers but it just kept flopping down which was even funnier.

'You look like you're in Abba,' Mick said.

'I don't.'

'Yeh you do. Mick's right,' Melody said and started singing, '*Waterloo, waterloo.*' Yogi leaned over in front of Mick so he could look in the driving mirror.

'Shit I do,' he said.

I thought I might wet my knickers from laughing. I had to grip my thighs together and squeeze to hold it in.

By the time we got to the end of the Motorway and saw the signs for Central London, the light was starting to fade. My stomach contracted with excitement. I squeezed Mick's hand and he grinned at me.

'Did you see which way for the North Circular?' Chas sounded uptight again. Dad always got in a total grump when we went somewhere new. He had to have total silence in the car. I wasn't even allowed to whistle.

'Third exit,' Mick said. He had a map on his phone and was giving directions. Melody was singing along to music from Chas's phone played through the car speakers.

'Shut up and switch that off,' Chas ordered her and I knew there'd be trouble. Melody turned the music up instead and Chas went crazy.

'You stupid cow, stop that and look for the signs,' he grabbed his phone and passed it over to Mick. 'Take this and don't let her get it.'

The whole atmosphere in the car had transformed in seconds. Melody went silent and turned away from Chas to press her face against the side window. Yogi and Mick were peering out of the windows looking for signs. A few times Chas got in the wrong lane or hesitated about which way to go and other cars hooted their horns at him. I was clinging onto the back of the driver's seat to avoid being thrown about. Chas, I noticed, had little rivers of sweat running down his neck.

'Stupid car, Mum needs to get a sat nav.'

'Keep in the left hand lane, for another three miles,' Mick's voice was calm.

To start with I was disappointed in London. We were driving down roads with shops that weren't much different to Harborne High Street, apart from there being even more cars. Then there were streets of big grey terraced houses with iron railings and steps up to the front doors. Most of them were hotels advertising rooms available. They looked so grotty who would want to stay there? As we got closer to the centre, the houses got bigger and grander, changing into beautiful white terraces with pillars and canopies over the steps. There were more people about on the streets, smartly dressed, and I started seeing signs for theatres and giant posters for shows. Despite Chas yelling for directions and putting everyone on edge I felt excited. I couldn't stop myself. I was in London.

'Oh my God,' I shouted making Chas jump.

'For Christ's sake Pen,' he yelled.

'Sorry but this is Trafalgar Square, look there's the column.'

'I know this is Trafalgar Square, we've gone wrong. We're too far south. We need to be east of here, look for signs to the City.'

'Can't we stop, just for a minute, and take a look?' I didn't care if I wasn't being cool. I wanted to sit on one of the lions and put my hand in the fountain.

'Don't be stupid, I'm in five lanes of traffic.'

'You need to get into the middle lane and take the next exit on the left.' I was impressed that Mick knew where to go. He was good at following the directions. We pulled up at a red light three quarters of the way round the square and I strained my neck, contorting myself into stupid shapes, trying to see Nelson on top of the column against the darkening sky. Neon lights blazed out against the inky backdrop. There were people hurrying everywhere and hot dog stalls and street artists. This was exactly how I'd imagined London to be.

'What are you doing, noooo,' Chas shouted but Melody had already opened her door and jumped out, run across the traffic and onto the square. 'Why does

317

she do this? I'm leaving her there,' Chas was really angry. The traffic lights turned to amber and he accelerated forward.

'You can't, 'I said, 'you've got to wait for her.' I'd have got out too if only I could.

'Take this exit,' Mick wasn't panicking, 'and I think you could pull over there on the left.' Chas manoeuvred out of the square and across the inside lane into a wide tree lined road.

'I can't stop here there's double yellows. I'll get a ticket. We don't want the police searching us,' Chas's voice went squeaky and high pitched as if he was going to cry.

'Turn sharp left,' Mick said and Chas pulled on the wheel and we swerved into a narrow street. 'Single white lines we should be ok, look out for a spot.' There were parked cars crammed on both sides of the road but there was a small space.

'I'll never get in there,' Chas wasn't even trying.

'I think you'll fit,' Mick stayed cool and I was really proud of him.

Chas was useless at parking. It took him about twenty goes and in the end there was loads of room.

'I'll get her,' Yogi pushed the passenger seat forward and leapt out of the car.

'I'm going too,' I clambered in front of Mick, and climbed out after Yogi. I was pretty sure Mick would follow us.

Yogi and I ran down the road and back to the square. There were hundreds of young people from all over the world, most of them not much older than me. Loads of tourists were taking selfies and I wished I had my phone. I'd never seen so many pigeons in one place. I kept close to Yogi worried that we'd never find Melody in the crowd but she'd seen us. She was standing on the steps at the top end of the square waving.

'Look at that,' she shouted, pointing at one of the plinth's on the square, 'it's a bloody giant blue cock.' She burst out laughing. There was a bright blue statue of a cockerel, bigger than the lions around the base of the column, and she was right it did look funny, so proud and silly. Melody ran down the steps towards us.

'I want to sit on a lion,' I said to her. We pushed through to the base of the column where loads of people were climbing on the lions. Mel and I scrambled up.

'Take a photo,' Melody shouted down to Yogi.

Mick had followed us, and even Chas had come with him. We waved to them and jumped down. Mick and I walked over to one of the fountains. Illuminated by fluorescent green light, the water was like something from another planet, a source of supernatural energy so that if you bathed in it you'd turn into a super hero. Mick threw a coin into the water.

'Make a wish,' he said. I did and it came true a moment later. He put his arms round my waist and pulled me in towards him and I reached my arms round his neck. He kissed me properly and kept on kissing me. Even when we had to come apart to breathe we went back to kissing again. He had his tongue in my mouth and I put mine in his and felt his teeth. Our tongues were snake dancing. Suddenly water splashed all over us. I screamed and Mick shouted.

Melody was behind us in the fountain, wet up to her knees, running around, splashing everyone with handfuls of water.

'Oh for God's sake, she's going to ruin the upholstery in the car,' Chas had joined us. 'We need to get going Mick, we're already late. My parents have booked a table, they're taking us out to eat.'

Mick took his arms away from me.

'Alright Man, chill out, phone and say we're on our way,' Mick said, taking hold of my hand and turning back towards the car.

Mick and I got in the back and Yogi pushed Melody through into the backseat next to me. She was soaking from the thighs down.

'She's dripping over the seats. Yogi - take your jacket off for her to sit on,' Chas ordered.

'No way, give her yours'

'You'll make the car stink.'

'It stinks already,' Melody flashed me a big grin. 'You know what your problem is Chas – you're a giant blue cock.'

'Shut up,' Chas pulled out into the traffic in front of a taxi cab and the driver hammered his horn in protest. Chas wasn't much of a driver but being fair I realised he must only just have passed his test. Mick was reading out directions from his phone. I was glad he was staying steady because Chas was in a right state.

'We're going to be late. I said I'd be there by nine.'

'Shouldn't take us long now, turn right then get into the left lane.'

'Roll up another spliff,' Melody said to Yogi.

'Don't be stupid,' Chas shouted at her. 'What's your aunt's address Pen? Can I drop you at Hoxton Square and you can get a tube?'

'I don't,' I started to speak but Melody reached behind Mick and pinched my arm tightly.

'Pen's aunt's been rushed to hospital so we can't stay there,' she said. I stared at Melody but she avoided looking at me. She was turned towards the window.

'Why didn't you say before,' Chas's voice had gone quiet, 'before we left Birmingham?'

'Pen only just found out.'

'Pen's lost her phone,' Chas's voice was icy.

'They had my number. We don't mind crashing on the sofa at your parents place. It's no big deal.' Melody's voice was light and breezy but I felt Mick's body tense up.

'Ok take the third exit off this roundabout,' he said as Chas exploded.

'I knew it, you lying manipulative bitch. I've told you and told you, you're not staying at the flat.

You're not invited. My parents are expecting Yogi and Mick and that's it. I've told you a million times.'

'I don't see why it's such a problem,' Melody clutched onto the back of the front seat as Chas took a corner far too fast. I was thrown against Mick and grabbed onto Chas's seat as we all slid together along the back seat squashing Melody against the window.

'I can't just turn up with a couple of tramps.'

'Thanks!' I said.

'You bastard,' Melody screamed.

'I don't want you staying there, you're not my girlfriend. I've been totally clear about that. Don't pretend I haven't.'

I was appalled and looked at Melody but she was still staring out of the window.

'So what am I then, if I'm not your girlfriend?'

'A mate, someone who's part of the scene.'

'Someone you screw,' Melody leant right forward and screamed in Chas's ear.

'This is Hoxton Square,' Mick sounded like a tour guide.

Chas drove off the square and a few yards further down veered into the side of the road and mounted the pavement. He stopped the car and got out, lifting up his seat.

'Out, get out,' he ordered Melody, 'you wanted a lift to London, you've had one. Where you stay is your problem.'

'Sod you,' Melody spat out but she squeezed past Mick and got out of the car. I looked at Mick but he didn't say anything. Surely he wasn't going to let Chas treat us like this. But neither he nor Yogi did anything. I struggled out of the car after Melody who was already walking off down the road. I faced Chas.

'You don't mean that. Go after her.'

Chas ignored me. He put the seat down and climbed back into the car.

'Mick tell him, talk sense, I'll get Mel. You can't just leave us.' I shouted into the car. But Chas was already revving the engine. He did a crazy u- turn across the traffic and headed back to the square.

43

Melody was so stubborn she was already walking away at her superfast pace down the main road. She had her head lowered and her hands in her jacket pockets.

'Hold on Mel, wait a bit,' I shouted after her. I didn't want her to leave me behind.

There was no sign of the VW returning, so Chas really had abandoned us on the streets of London. If I ever saw him again – I'd gouge his eyes out. And Mick, how dare he leave me by the side of the road. If Chas refused to stop then Mick could have got out of the car. Some boyfriend he turned out to be. If he thought he could kiss me ever again, he could go boil his head in oil. How were we going to get home now?

I ran after Melody. Okay so she'd lied to me

but we needed to stick together. She'd been there for me last night and I wasn't going to turn on her now. I didn't know what we were going to do but we'd cope somehow. We were survivors, like the girls on the rope.

There were groups of young people dressed in a super trendy way. I had to dodge between them to catch up with Melody. I thought she might be crying because she kept her head right down and walked in front of me. I jogged after her.

'I can't believe that bastard.'

Melody didn't reply. We were zooming past rows of cool shops and bars but she didn't slow down.

'What are we going to do?' I asked but she just speeded up. I wasn't stupid, I knew exactly why Melody had lied, she'd been determined to get to London and I felt sorry for her that her plan had backfired. I wasn't angry but I was worried about what we were going to do.

We walked in silence past a row of fancy furniture and lighting shops, past several pubs with people spreading out onto the pavement, past a park and an art gallery. I didn't think Melody had a clue where she was going and I certainly didn't. We ended up on a wide main road where they'd obviously had a market in the daytime because there were locked up stalls along the pavement. The kinds of shops we passed started getting rougher, second hand furniture, charity shops, and boarded up windows and doors. The road seemed to go on for ever. Melody was on a marathon. Did the girl think we could walk back to Birmingham?

'Hold on, don't walk so fast,' I called after her. We were speeding past the bright lights of a cafe that looked warm and cosy inside. We should stop and come up with a plan.

'I'm starving let's get something to eat,' I said. 'I've got money.'

Melody turned to face me. Her huge eyes were wet and her eyeliner had smudges. She looked so sad I put my arms around her and pulled her into me. Her body went rigid as if she didn't know how to be hugged. Or maybe she didn't like it. Embarrassed, I let go and went ahead of her into the café. I was relieved when she followed me inside.

I loved this kind of old fashioned egg and chips style cafe. Dad would never take us to them. He said the food was greasy and unhealthy. Well, he wasn't around anymore to say I couldn't, so there, Daddio.

There was an empty booth by the front window and I grabbed it. The red plastic seats, a wipe clean checked table cloth, and tomato shaped ketchup bottles were brilliantly tacky. Others obviously shared my taste because the place was packed. Lots of voices talking at once made the room hum and the sound wrapped around us and made me feel brave. In the next booth were a family with three kids and opposite, were two boys with long hair and ripped jeans. Of course they couldn't take their eyes off Melody but she was concentrating on the menu.

'How much money you got?' she asked.

I got my purse out of the jacket pocket feeling a bit silly unravelling the string and Mel seeing the school crest embroidered on the side. It was a stupid purse to bring with me. I got out a twenty pound note out and put it on the table.

'Let's go mad,' I grinned at Melody.

'We can have the all-day giant breakfast with chips and coke.' She was like a kid who'd been promised a treat and reminded me of Thomas. Melody had odd eating habits.

'I'm like a camel,' she must have read my mind. 'I can go for ages without any food and then eat a mountain.'

'Is that what camels do?'

'Streuth! With water, stupid, to cross the desert,' she shook her head, 'for a girl at posh school you can be pretty thick.' She seemed to have recovered. Her mood changes were faster than electricity. She was looking around the café as if we'd always intended to come here.

'Are you ok? After what Chas said.'

'He'll come crawling back you'll see,' she was smiling.

'But surely you wouldn't take him back? I'm furious with Mick.'

Mel didn't answer but looked up as the waitress arrived at our table.

'You're supposed to wait to be seated,' the waitress was older than Mel, in her twenties with dyed blonde hair pinned in a bun and mascara piled onto her eyelashes so thickly that each lash had a little black castle of gunk balanced on it. It was hard not to stare. She'd obviously decided to hate us. Melody glared at her.

'I'm sorry,' I said, 'we didn't know.' I gave the waitress my biggest smile.

'What do you want?' She showed no indication of softening to my charm.

'Please could we have two all-day big breakfasts with chips and two cokes?'

'And bread and butter,' Melody said to me, 'to make chip butties.'

The waitress looked us up and down.

'We can pay,' I waved the twenty pound note at her. She wrote down our order and stomped off.

'Did you see her mascara, what was that about?' Melody dismissed her. 'You got a pound coin – they've got a juke box?' I gave her two pound coins and she slipped out of our booth and walked across the room to an old fashioned juke box in the corner. The two boys opposite us stopped eating and watched every step she took. I counted the notes in my purse. I wondered how much money Melody had. I was pretty sure I'd got enough to get a train back to Birmingham. Vivienne said the coach was cheaper. I didn't know where the bus station was but I knew the Birmingham trains went from Euston. I put my purse back in my jacket pocket. If Melody didn't have enough for the train maybe I could buy us two coach tickets.

Melody was punching numbers into the juke box, a minute later a loud shouting song came on. As she walked back towards me one of the long haired boys spoke to her.

'Great choice,' I think he said but he had his hand over his mouth and mumbled so I couldn't hear. Melody ignored him.

'Is this *The Ramones*?' I asked and she nodded.

'They haven't got much that's any good. You'd have thought a place round here would have a better selection.'

The waitress banged down our cokes.

'Thanks, that's great,' I smiled at her and Melody frowned at me as the she left.

'Why are you being such an arse licker to that old cow?'

'Trying to cheer her up I suppose.'

'Why bother?'

'I don't know.' And I didn't. Melody was right, it wasn't up to me to make the waitress's life better. I had enough problems of my own. When she arrived with our breakfasts I still said thank you though, I couldn't stop myself.

Melody attacked this breakfast just like the one she'd made earlier. It was hard to imagine we were still in the same day, so much had happened since then. I thought about Thomas and how much he'd like it here. It was totally dark outside and I guessed that by now they'd be seriously worried about me. Maybe I should borrow Melody's phone and call them. But then Mum had attacked me and Dad had abandoned us and I wanted them to feel guilty. I hoped Mum was in a terrible state, Dad too. If they cared at all.

I pushed the food round my plate and ate a few chips and a bit of egg. Melody had nearly finished hers.

'Dwwwn yaw waw yahs?' Melody spoke with a mouth full of chips.

'Sorry?'

She finished her mouthful.

'If you don't want it I'll have it.' I pushed my plate over to her. Mick and I had only started kissing today, so I couldn't really say he was my boyfriend, but I was still upset that he'd left us. Chas had been a total pig to Melody but she didn't seem worried at all.

'How much money have you got?' I asked her.

Melody stared at me. 'Not much, few quid,'

'I've got enough for the train home but if you're short we could find out where the coaches go from,' I said. Melody stopped mid bite and her eyebrows went up. 'They're cheaper,' I explained when she didn't say anything. 'I think they'll still be running.'

'We only just got here,' she said.

'I haven't got enough for a hotel,' I explained.

'You need to relax. Let's get a drink.' She took out a cigarette and put it to her mouth then looked over at the long haired boys at the table nearby.

'Save your money,' she told me, then, 'you got a light?' to one of the boys opposite and the least spotty one jumped up with a lighter. They went outside together. I thought I must have annoyed her. Maybe I was being too bossy because I was used to looking after Mum. I got up and went in search of the loo.

When I opened the door to the toilets a small trendy girl with maroon coloured hair stared at me from the far end of the basins. It took a few seconds to realise I was looking at a mirror and that the anxious looking punk girl was me. I'd taken off the big man's jacket and didn't recognise myself in Mel's tight pink sweater dress. It was a weird experience seeing myself as if I were a stranger. It jolted me. Was I now a completely different person to the Pen Flowers who went to Kings and lived on Knightlow Road? Washing my hands in the basin I let out a huge sigh. I didn't even have a spare pair of knickers with me and yet the Pen in the mirror had rounded shoulders as if she were carrying a giant rucksack on her back.

When I got back to the table the two boys were sitting opposite Melody and she was tossing her head and laughing. I didn't understand why Melody would be interested in such greasy looking wimps.

'Pen,' Melody shuffled up the bench seat so that I could perch next to her, 'Dan and Barty say there's a pub on the next street that has live bands and it's free to get in?'

Dan smiled and nodded wildly. He was the better looking of the two with shiny brown hair that was newly washed but he had bad acne. Whereas Barty's lank mousy hair stuck to his forehead which was covered in giant red lumps, some had green caps. I had to look away. He was positively pustular. (I've always wanted to use that word. It's from Shakespeare and actually sounds like a bursting spot.)

'Yeh, they have neat bands, right, Indie, right.' Dan kept nodding and looking at Barty for reassurance.

'Right,' was the most Barty could manage. He had a much lower voice than you'd expect but they couldn't be much older than me. If Melody paired up with Dan I'd be left with Barty the Pus. I wasn't exactly leaping for joy. But Melody had switched into party mood.

'Let's go then,' she poked at me to get up and let her out.

'Can you pass my jacket, it's on that bench?' I asked Dan and he handed it over. I'd much rather have gone straight to the coach station. It was nearly ten o'clock and I didn't know when the last tube went. But Melody was determined to have fun now we were in London. I wished I could relax like she'd said and stop worrying.

Out on the street it wasn't that cold but I was glad of the jacket and hugged it close around me. Melody and Dan strode off ahead and I ran to catch up. I didn't want to be left with Barty but he stuck to my elbow.

'How far is the pub?' I asked him.

'Corner,' he pointed at the next side street. He only seemed able to manage one word answers. I wondered if he was a bit slow in the head.

'Where's the nearest tube?' I asked.

'Shoreditch,' he pointed further ahead.

'How late do they run?'

'Midnight'

I was relieved. We could go to see the band and still get a tube. As long as the coaches ran all night we'd be ok, even if we had to wait for the first one in the morning that wouldn't be too bad.

The street was much busier than Birmingham's Broad Street on a Friday night, with groups of young people who looked as if they were fashion students. The pub was called The Old Red Lion, a proper traditional red brick, three storeys high with curved bay windows and a big double door. A crowd had gathered outside the pub and two bouncers in black suits were letting people in. Loud rock music poured out of an upstairs window onto the street below. Melody turned and grinned at me and I smiled back even though the squirming in my tummy didn't feel much like excitement.

'Where?' I realised Barty was speaking to me.

'Sorry?'

'Where do you live? What tube you getting?' He stumbled towards a proper sentence with his huge Adams apple wobbling up and down as he gulped between words.

'Birmingham,' I said and that seemed to deprive him of speech entirely.

Melody and Dan pushed their way through the crowd into the pub.

'Mel,' I called after her, 'wait.' There was no way the bouncers were going to let me in. I didn't have an identity card. She didn't hear because the noise inside was overwhelming so I kept my head down and sprinted after her. Passing the bouncers I waited for a meaty hand to drop on my shoulder. But all I felt was Barty bang into me as he was shoved forward by a man pushing his way to the bar.

'Sorry,' Barty shouted.

I couldn't believe I'd made it inside. Once with Tamasin we'd tried to get into a city centre pub with fake ID's. The bouncers had taken one look at us and laughed. With my new haircut I must look older. People were rammed into the pub so tightly that you couldn't see the floor. I had to step and hope I found floorboards and not someone's foot. All I could see were the armpits of the people immediately in front of me. I ducked and squeezed and wove my way through the crowd trying to keep Melody in sight.

There was a long wooden bar that ran down the whole length of the room. To the right of the bar at the back, a staircase led to an upstairs room where the music was coming from. I couldn't see over people's shoulders and a fluttery panic was rising in my body. I had to catch hold of it to stop it from coming any further up. This must be similar to what Mum felt when she went outside. This sensation of having a scared bird trapped inside my body was horrible, poor Mum. If I saw her again I'd be more understanding. I was even glad of Barty being close by. He was taller than me and if I got pushed under he might do something to rescue me. Not that I trusted boys, not after Mick and Chas.

There was a line of people three deep along the bar. Melody and Dan had thrown themselves into it. Melody seemed to be enjoying the pushing and shoving. It was alright for her because everywhere she went people stopped to stare. Even in London she was getting attention from the men around her. I could tell she was spiralling higher on the energy.

'What do you want to drink?' she shouted to me.

'I'll just have a coke?' I said and she pulled a 'don't be an idiot' face, 'Coke's fine.' I insisted. The yeasty smell of beer mixed with stale sweat was making my stomach churn. I stood close to Barty near the bar while Melody and Dan got the drinks. We kept being jostled by people trying to get past us on their way upstairs. I had to shout to get Barty to hear me.

'Do you know where the coach station is?' I asked.

'Victoria,' he shouted back.

'Can we get the tube there?'

'Yeh,'

'Do the coaches go all night do you think?'

Barty got out his phone,

'Birmingham, right?'

I nodded.

Dan and Melody barged their way through to us. Melody had a pint glass and a small glass.

'Cider with a whiskey chaser,' she was laughing and her eyes were wide and bright and moved around the room like a search beam. Dan was balancing three glasses. He gave me a coke and Barty a pint.

'Vodka and coke,' he shouted at me, 'is that ok.'

What could I say? I frowned at Melody but she was staring over my shoulder as a gang of cool looking guys in vintage biker jackets with long hair made an entrance. The crowd parted to let them through and they disappeared up the stairs. I sipped my drink. It didn't taste too bad, mainly of coke. Hopefully one drink wouldn't make me drunk.

'Come on,' Melody shouted in my ear, and pulled my arm. She drank the whiskey in one gulp and put the empty glass on a table. She ignored Dan who was trying to speak to her and made towards the stairs dragging me with her. Barty and Dan followed after us.

'Midnight, two thirty and four thirty,' Barty managed to scream into my ear. I felt relieved.

'How much?' I asked him as we pushed our way up the stairs.

Upstairs was worse, there were even more people pressed into a smaller place. It was too dark to see much and the music was so loud I wanted to put my hands over my ears to protect them. I could feel the vibrations jumping in my chest. The floor bounced with the weight of people dancing. I couldn't see the band just the backs of the people standing in front of me. Melody started to push her way through the crowd towards the front but I didn't dare go with her and Dan and Barty stayed by me, near the door. Maybe they could see the band from where we were standing but I had no chance. My face was inches from the baggy woollen jumper of the man in front of me. He smelt so bad I wanted to gag and I had to breathe through my mouth. Gradually I got pushed further and further towards the back of the room as more people came up the stairs and flung themselves towards the front. I lost contact with Dan and Barty and finally was squashed against the back wall where some people were standing on chairs and dancing.

I didn't understand how anyone could enjoy this. A boy barged into me and my drink jumped out of my glass and onto the jeans of the man standing next to me. He scowled at me.

'Sorry,' I said but it wasn't my fault. It was really hard to keep your balance with the pushing and shoving. There was every chance I would be killed. The floor was wet from spilt drinks and if I slipped I'd be trampled flatter than a flower in a flower press. Another wave of people came up the stairs and I stumbled back into a chair.

'Here,' a male voice shouted in my ear and a hand grabbed the back of my dress and hauled me up like I was one of those soft furry toys in an arcade machine grabbed by a crane hook. I found myself standing on a wooden chair next to a man with a bald head and a lot of stubble. Having saved my life he took no further notice of me. His whole attention was on the band that I could finally see on a tiny stage at the far end of the room. Three skinny boys with guitars and a drummer were making this deafening noise. In front of the stage some people were jumping up and down and thrashing their arms about. In amongst them I could see Melody doing a strange jerky dance that fitted with the music. She was right in the middle of the group of scary looking men that we'd followed upstairs. There was no way I'd get her to leave now but at least, if what Barty said was right, we'd be ok getting home. The music was rough and scraped against my ears. Listening to them I couldn't even imagine the sound of birdsong. This was concrete mixers, electric hammers and chain saws. This was every power tool in your Dad's shed switched on at once. But as getting out was impossible I had no choice but to listen.

Gradually I started to get it. The scream in the music was the same as the one I had trapped inside me. I thought it was only me who had an inner scream but maybe other people did too. My legs were aching from standing up, I felt limp.

I wondered if I was the youngest person in the room. Most of the men, I guessed, were in their twenties or thirties. If only Mick hadn't turned out to be a total waster. I even looked for Barty but I couldn't see him anywhere.

Melody was having a great time down at the front - it was alright for her. One of the men had lifted her up on his shoulders and she was drinking from his bottle. She'd only been in London for a couple of hours and already she was at the centre of things. If I'd come to London with Vivienne, we could have stayed around Trafalgar Square and just messed about and had fun.

I drifted into a sort of trance as if I was asleep standing up. I let the noise swirl through me. The music made you want to thrash about like Melody and the others at the front were doing, but after that video, no one was ever going to see me dance again. In the tight dress I was wearing everyone would be laughing at the size of my bottom.

When the band finished people began stamping down the stairs. The moment the room emptied a little, I pushed my way through to Melody. She was sitting on the edge of the stage drinking beer from a can and talking to the guitarist, a handsome dark haired guy in a battered leather flying jacket. He must have been at least twenty-five.

'We should go now Mel, or we'll miss the last tube,' I said interrupting them.

She smiled at me.

'This is Pen, she's my guardian Angel.' The man took no notice of me he was targeted on Melody.

'Are you an angel?' he asked her.

'What do you think?' Melody pouted, her mouth slightly open, and he laughed.

'Mel, the tube,' I pleaded.

'Relax Angel, I told you not to worry, Jay says we can crash at his place.' She beamed at me and I could tell she was really drunk.

44

We didn't have to walk far, round the back of the pub was a narrow lane that led past a primary school playground and into a council estate. There were huge rectangular blocks of flats, red brick and ten storeys high, where thousands of people must have lived. On the other side of the estate was a long road of Victorian terraced houses. They were big three floor jobs with iron railings outside and steps up to the front door. Some of them had been done up and looked really posh. At the far end of the street on the right, was a house with chip board over the front windows and an old mattress dumped in the garden. The concrete door posts either side of the steps had half crumbled balls on top of them.

Jay, the guitarist, explained that he and some mates were squatting a deserted house. In principle I approved of squats. We'd done a project on them in Religious Studies as one of our ethical debates. There were pictures of ruined houses that had been painted and repaired and made into lovely homes. But there were also photographs of horrid dives with no power or running water and where people used buckets as toilets. I didn't want to spend the night in a squat with people I didn't know, especially not if it turned out to be the toilet bucket sort, the whole idea was creepy in the extreme.

The front door was open and I could hear rock music playing inside. Melody went in with Jay and I had no choice but to tag along behind her. I felt like a faithful dog entering unknown and dangerous territory, hackles raised.

One bare electric light bulb was trying to light a long thin hallway with a flight of stairs going up to the other floors. At least they had electricity. Jay led the way to a large room at the back of the house where a real fire was burning in a marble fireplace. The house must have been quite grand once upon a time but now it was reduced to bare floor boards and peeling wall paper. There were a couple of battered settees. The sweet musky fug I recognised from Chas's car overpowered the underlying hints of damp, beer and possibly urine. In essence it smelt bad, not gagging bad but not far off.

A sound system in the corner was the source of the music and two men who must have been in their late twenties, maybe older, sat on chairs pulled near to the fireplace, drinking beer and smoking. They looked up when we came in and stared at Melody and I. Jay didn't bother to introduce us. He helped himself to a beer bottle from a box next to the sound system. He threw one to Melody and another to me. I caught it even though I didn't drink beer. He launched himself onto one of the sofas and indicated to Melody that she sit next to him.

They didn't invite me so not knowing what else to do I curled up in the corner of the other settee. Inside me the frightened bird had frozen. I'd never been anywhere as alarming as this room. I felt completely abandoned by Melody. I made myself as small as I could. Jay opened their beers and forgot to pass me the opener. I put my bottle down on the floor as I didn't want it anyway. One of the men by the fire kept staring at me and I was worried that he was going to come over. I turned my head away from him. I wanted to get eye contact with Melody to signal how freaked out I was but she had her back to me.

The only light in the room came from the fire and shadows ran across the walls in swooping waves. The thick smoke in the room made me want to sneeze. Jay was playing with the chains round Melody's neck using them to pull her towards him so they came face to face, noses touching. They kissed in a loud slurping way that made me uncomfortable. There didn't seem to be anywhere safe to look so I focused on the fireplace. At least it was warm near the fire.

I loved real fires, particularly bonfires - watching the flames against the black sky, with sparks spiralling up to the stars. There was a huge log on this fire that must have been a bit wet because every so often it hissed and spat. What looked like the remains of a fence were piled to the right of the fireplace and the man sitting that side threw in jagged sections when the flames started to dwindle.

I didn't know how I'd got myself into a place

like this. If I'd had my phone I would have given in and called Dad. Melody seemed to have forgotten about me. She and Jay were whispering to each other. Was she going to start going out with Jay now? Where were Melody and I going to sleep?

All I had to hold onto for comfort was the fire. I concentrated on one flame and let the rest of the room disappear into darkness. The flame flickered and faltered, stretched tall then grew a waist and shrank down, twisting and turning as it crouched. The centre of the blade was blue with a black arch and the point was yellow. I'd always thought of fire as orangey-red but only the glowing embers were actually red. The big log shimmered in tiny sequinned sections. That log would once have been a beautiful tree, like the ones in our garden, with roots stretching deep into the earth and branches reaching up into the clouds, home to birds and squirrels. Now it was giving up its life for me. Thank you tree for giving me your energy, I wish I could save you from the flames but I can't. You can't go back to your old life, feeling the wind rustle in your leaves, tasting clean fresh air. You've got to burn into ash, into nothing, into darkness.

45

I must have nodded off. For a moment, as I came back into consciousness I thought I was still in the VW beetle snuggled up next to Mick. Opening my eyes and seeing the fireplace I remembered where I was. The fire had dwindled down to embers and the two men sitting there had gone, or rather, one had gone. The other was now on the sofa next to me. He had one arm around my shoulder. I didn't even know his name but he was pushing his other hand through my jacket. His fingers stroked my breast through the sweater dress and he squeezed my nipple. I froze for an instant and then pushed away his hand struggling to sit up and wriggle out of his arms. He took hold of my hand and held it against his jeans. My palm was pressed along something like a tree branch but more elastic and warm. When I realised what it must be I wrenched my hand away from his hold.

'Calm down Tiger,' he laughed, 'no need to be scared.'

I jumped off the sofa and kicked him as hard as I could.

'Ow, 'he said clutching at his knee. Turning round I saw that Jay was crouched over Melody undoing his belt. She was lying on the sofa with her t-shirt round her neck and her jeans unzipped, she looked completely drunk and half asleep. I leapt across the room and grabbed a handful of Jay's hair and pulled him off her. He was completely unprepared for the attack and yelped, rolling off the settee onto the floor clutching his head. In my fist I had a clump of black hair. I grabbed hold of Melody's arm and pulled her onto her feet.

'Come on Mel, let's go.' I dragged her towards the door.

'Little bitch,' I heard Jay swearing. I didn't look back to see if he was following. I had my arm round Melody's waist pushing her into the hall. We had to get away before they came after us.

'What's going on?' Melody was pulling away from me. I got her through the front door and headed down the steps but she didn't follow.

'What's going on?' Melody had stopped on the top step. She was swaying.

'Come on we've got to get out of here.'

'What are you playing at?' she sounded cross.

'They were trying to rape us. You don't realise, you're drunk. Come on lets go.' I went back up the steps and reached out my hand to help her down. She bashed it away.

'Leave me alone,' she turned round.

'Where are you going?' I screamed after her. 'Don't go back in there, don't.'

She twisted back to look at me.

'It's only sex Pen, it's no big deal.'

The shock of her words hit me in the stomach and I almost crumpled. Melody was squinting at me as if she was having trouble focusing her eyes.

'I just hope you haven't messed things up,' she sounded angry as she walked away from me.

'Mel don't - come with me,' I pleaded. 'I'll look

after you.'

She turned back.

'You couldn't look after a kitten,' she said. 'Grow up Angel.' She went back through the front door and I was left standing on the steps on my own.

Panic flew up inside me like a flock of pigeons. I thought I might black out. I reached for something to hold onto and found the broken concrete post and steadied myself. Keep calm Pen, you've got to keep calm. But what was I going to do? I couldn't go back inside. They might make me have sex and I just couldn't, not for the first time with someone I didn't even know.

I looked down the long street, the end of the road disappeared into darkness and shadows. There was no one around to ask for help. A few houses still had lights on but I couldn't go and knock on a door could I? They'd be in bed? I had no idea where I was and I didn't know if I could find my way back to the main road. How could I manage on my own in a place I'd never been to before? Every choice I had was horrible. I couldn't stay out here by myself. How had I got myself into such a terrible mess?

Maybe I should go back into the house and

apologise. Say I was sorry that I'd overreacted. As long as they didn't make me have sex. They'd be angry but I didn't have a choice. I had to go back.

I tiptoed up the steps into the house. I waited in the corridor outside the door to the living room trying to find the courage to go in. What could I say? I felt such an twat. I could hear them talking.

'What was that about?' Jay asked.

'She freaked out, silly cow,' Melody said.

'Vicious little cat isn't she? Where's she gone?'

'Who knows? She's turned into a right drag.'

'Will she be alright?'

'She'll run back home to Mummy,' Melody laughed.

Well maybe I would go home to Mummy! At least I had a Mummy. She may have hit me, she may be utterly useless and self-obsessed and full of fear but she wouldn't want me to be raped. She'd care about that!

I ran out of the house and down the steps and kept running. Anger surged through my body so that I could actually feel the heat of it. Fury made me brave. I sped down the street keeping my eyes straight ahead. If I could find my way back to the main road then there were loads of cabs. I'd get one to the Station and then I'd catch the train home. That's what I was going to do, go home and sort things out.

When I reached the end of Jay's street I turned left and kept going. I didn't know if it was the right direction or not but I was just letting my body decide where we went. When I saw the council estate ahead I realised I was going the right way. Running through that estate was awful but I kept my head down and went as fast as I could. Fear kept me running. I'm sure I broke an Olympic record flying through there. In a few minutes I was out the other side and back at the road with the pub. I hadn't met anyone else on the streets.

The pub was in total darkness now, not a light anywhere. I had to stop and catch my breath. Huge gulps ripped up my throat. I bent over and held onto my knees. The road was empty too, no people, no moving cars. I guessed it must have been two or even three in the morning by then. I tried to remember which way we'd walked to get here with Dan and Barty. I crossed over the road and turned up a side street with parked cars on both sides of the road. I needed to walk for a bit because I couldn't keep running. I didn't have any breath left.

I kept thinking there were attackers hiding between the parked cars. They seem to stand up in the distance and only disappear when I came near. I couldn't get the thought of that man's penis out of my head. I rubbed my hand down my coat. I felt like he'd left germs on me. I turned down a side street but it was a no through road so that wasn't right. I went back and tried the next road. I was just guessing. Why had I thrown my phone away? I couldn't call anyone.

Eventually I found my way back to the main road where we'd stopped at the café. But that was empty too. I thought in London a main road would keep busy all night. Panicky sensations were jumping in my tummy but I squeezed them down. I turned in the direction of the square where Chas had dropped us off and started to run again. There'd been loads of cabs parked near there. Chas had said his parent's flat was nearby. Maybe I could find the Beetle. I tried to remember what the number plate was. A big lorry lumbered past, then another one, there were a few cars going by. The street lights on this main road were the tall double ones so this road was brighter than the smaller streets. The rows of locked up shops were really spooky and I was sure that the empty market stalls were full of lurking rapists. Three cars and a lorry drove by. Maybe a cab would come soon.

I slowed down to a fast walk. My breath was ragged and I tried to recover. I breathed in deeply, like I did with Mum when she got an attack. I tried to count to three as I breathed in. Please, please, please, God, don't leave me here on my own, help me to get back home to Birmingham.

It was as if my prayers were answered, because out of nowhere a black cab came zooming along the road. I waved but it didn't see me so I ran out into the road straight in front of it. I thought it was going to crash into me because the driver didn't slow down at all, just tried to swerve around me. I kept running towards him and he was forced to slam on his brakes. There was a loud tyre screech as the cab slid to a stop. I ran round to the driver's side and hammered on the window.

'What the hell do you think you're doing? I could 'ave killed you.' The taxi driver was yelling at me through the window, his face maroon coloured and screwed up tight.

'Can you take me to Euston Station please.' I held onto the open window.

'I'm finished for the night. Lights off, can't you see.'

'Please, please, I've got money.'

He started to wind up the window.

'I'll give you twenty pounds, thirty pounds,' I screamed before my fingers got caught in the top. He stopped winding.

'Show me,' he said.

I reached into my inside pocket and my purse was still there, thank goodness, for a moment I thought it might have fallen out. I started to unravel the string.

'I haven't got all night,' he said.

My fingers were shaking and the more I hurried the worse it got.

'There,' I pulled out the bundle of notes but in the light from the street lamps there was a rolled up napkin.

'I don't understand, I,' there was nothing else inside the purse, just the paper napkin, 'someone must have stolen it.'

'Haven't heard that before,' the driver whizzed

his window up fast and pulled away. I clung to the side of the car holding onto the door handle.

'I'm telling the truth, please I don't know what to do.' But he accelerated and I couldn't keep up.

I sat down on the kerbside under a street light and turned my purse inside out. Eighty pounds gone, nothing left, not even enough to make a phone call. The napkin was one of those half napkins that came out of the dispensers they'd had at the egg and chips' café. That was the last time I'd used my purse. I'd left my jacket on the seat when I went to the loo. Somebody must have stolen it then. Dan was sitting by my jacket when I came back, but then why stay and buy us drinks, why put the napkin inside, why not just take the whole purse? A horrible thought seeped into my brain and made me feel sick. I remembered Melody taking the money out of Gary's till. She was the only one who'd seen the money in there. Somehow, because of the napkin, I knew it was the truth. Melody had taken my money.

46

I crouched over the side of the road and thought I was going to vomit. My hands were flat on the black tarmac and the cold, wet, gritty feel of the surface crept into my palms and up my arms and into my heart. I wanted the street to open up and eat me.

The sound of a car engine coming by fast on my side of the road jerked my head up. A green and silver car screamed past me. The driver was hunched over the wheel like a racing driver but he stared at me as he shot by.

I was shivering. I didn't know what to do. Maybe keep moving to keep warm. My mouth was dry and I wished I had some water to drink. I got up and started walking with no idea where I was going. Far off was a hum like the sound of the sea, only sadder; traffic noise. Somewhere nearby there must be a busy road. Several lorries drove towards me on the other side of the road and their headlights dazzled my eyes. I felt confused and dizzy. I was like a zombie walking with no purpose, just staggering along. Another car passed on the other side, going quite slowly. It was similar to the fast one, sporty looking, long and low with silvery green paint work. I recognised the driver and realised it was the same car. He disappeared past again.

I looked for somewhere to hide but there were only shop fronts. I started to walk faster. Head lights came from behind me, the same car again, and this time moving very slowly, driving close to the pavement, crawling along beside me. I kept walking.

'You ok?' The driver called through the passenger seat window. I sped up but the car kept pace. He had dark hair and a big rectangular head and reminded me a bit of Dad. He looked concerned.

'Isn't it a bit early to be out on your own pet?'

I didn't answer and edged away from the roadside, moving closer to the shops and kept walking.

'Hop in and I'll give you a lift, it's not safe round

here.'

I ignored him.

'There's a gang of lout's further up this road, I've just past them. Let me help you.' He sounded worried. I looked at him again. He didn't seem creepy or anything. He was probably someone's Dad. I stared up the road trying to pierce the darkness. Was there really a gang up there?

'Come on,' he said and that decided me. He was in too much of a hurry. I started to jog.

'Don't be stupid,' he shouted after me. 'It isn't safe.' The car accelerated and then pulled in up ahead. The driver got out, he was much taller than Dad, and stood on the pavement in front of me.

'I don't want to hurt you. Let me help, the car's warm.' Tobacco and beer floated through the air towards me. My heart was jumping in my throat so I could hardly breathe.

'Leave me alone. Go away!' My voice went squeaky. He smiled then and came towards me.

'You don't mean that do you, pet?' As he grabbed for my arm, I leapt to one side. There was an explosion of energy in my thighs like I'd never felt before, not even at the Tartan Fling workshop. I burst across the road just in front of a giant lorry that braked and blared its horn. Escaping death by a millimetre, I ran back down the main road on the other side in the opposite direction and took the first turning on the left. I kept running, took the next side road and didn't stop, keeping to the shadows. I didn't know whether he was following because I didn't look back. I ran until my breath started to falter and I couldn't run anymore. I heard a voice behind me. There was an alley way between two houses without a gate on it and I dived into the darkness.

47

I dived straight into a row of bins. The clashing noise reverberated down the passage. Please don't let him have heard. I squeezed past the bins and crouched down with my back against the brick wall of the alley. There was no way anyone could find me unless they'd seen me turn in here. The bins smelt of mouldy vegetables and worse. I had to breathe through my mouth. I could hear rustling and scuffling which I was sure must be rats but I was much more frightened of the man.

I could hear shouting but couldn't work out how far away he was. There were several voices, so maybe it wasn't the car driver, maybe it was the gang of louts. Please, please, let them not have seen me, let them go past. Shouting and laughing came from the pavement nearby. The voices sounded like young men's. How many were there? Tamasin had once shown me a webpage of pornographic films. In one of them a girl was gang raped by a group of bikers. For months every time I tried to sleep the scene would come into my head.

I heard a bottle smash. I didn't know if it'd been thrown or deliberately broken to attack me with. My muscles were jittering with the effort of balancing in a squatting position. The men were parallel with my alley and their voices sounded as if they were right next to my ear.

'How far to your place?'

'Another mile'

There were at least three of them, I thought, maybe more.

'I'll catch you up.'

One of them turned into my alley and bumped into the bins just like I had.

'Shit,' he kicked the bins but then seemed to freeze. I was trembling all over trying to stay still in the stupid crouched position. My knee caps felt as if they'd pop out and my thighs couldn't hold me up any longer so I slid silently down the wall and sat on the floor hugging my knees up by my chin to make myself as tiny as possible. I heard the sound of pouring water and there was an overwhelming smell of urine. My eyes had grown accustomed to the darkness. I could see a banana skin flattened on the concrete floor like a star fish and next to that an empty silver foil dish from a Chinese take away. Looking up, the man's head and shoulders loomed above me just a few feet away. There must have been a downward slope because a stream of urine ran down the passage and hit my boot. More liquid came rushing my way. I had to sit there and let the man's warm piss soak into my dress. A minute later he was gone. Still I didn't move, I waited until I couldn't hear them anymore, then I sat up out of the wee. The back of my dress was sodden and his piss had soaked through my tights onto my legs and bottom.

I couldn't bear it. Nobody in the whole universe knew where I was and nobody cared. I'd totally run out of 'brave', I might as well be dead. I might as well run back to the main road and throw myself under a lorry. That horrible taxi driver had said he'd nearly killed me, well the next lorry could. Then at least this night would be over.

But I couldn't find my way back to the main road. I'd come such a twisting route, escaping from the car man, and was so scared that I had no idea which way I'd come. All the streets looked the same, row after row of terraced houses. This was a residential area and every car was parked. I couldn't hear any traffic noise. There wasn't a single moving vehicle to throw myself under.

I was so useless I couldn't even kill myself. I tried every direction but couldn't find one that led back to the main road. Eventually I found myself on a curving street with a few trees. There was a bench by a bus stop so I gave up and sat down in my wet dress. I was lost, totally, completely, utterly lost.

A blackbird started singing. I knew it was a blackbird because we had a pair in the garden at home. When I went out night dancing, they welcomed me home. As I listened to the blackbird's song I looked up above me and saw there were stars, the same stars that shone over Knighlow Road. Miles above me was the night sky, the same sky that I knew and loved.

The blackbird had found me in the loneliest

place I'd ever been. It was as if I still had one friend left. Maybe the black bird was singing for me. Focusing everything on his voice I heard him sing the word 'dance', that one word very softly, 'dance' he called to me, 'dance'.

I found myself standing up, my dress sticking to my legs, and I started to do the funny move I'd developed in Jock Briggs workshop, the tiny soft fluttery sequence. Everything around me stopped, the breeze in the trees calmed, the buzz of the electric lights waited, not a cat or a rat made a sound. There was total silence. I did my move again.

Out of the stillness came a huge whooshing sound as the night came rushing towards me. A feeling, like the warmest, strongest love you could ever imagine came out of the blackness, and wrapped around me. I swear to you with my whole heart - I actually felt love surround me. The night came to save me. Not the brutal nasty London night, but my night, the out there above us night, the night I loved and trusted.

I started doing a little jive step, that Dad had taught me when we used to dance together as a family, when we were happy. Twist left, twist right, circle round, twist left, twist right, circle round, in time to the blackbird singing. The 'I want to die' pain was still there, right in the centre of my chest like red hot embers, burning a hole. If I killed myself this pain wouldn't die with me it would transfer to people who cared about me, like Thomas, and Vivienne, maybe Mum and Dad. If I stayed alive and was able to bear this pain, let it burn inside me – then I'd burn up some of the world's sadness. I wouldn't be totally useless because I'd have made the world a tiny bit less sad.

This was the thought that flamed up and gave me courage. I would burn and go on. I thought of holding out my leg in *develope* for Wendy, my ballet teacher, and how it hurt so much I couldn't bear it, but she'd say - thirty seconds more - and I always managed to hold on. I did a leaping twirl. Ok, so I looked like a pig, but there was no one here to watch me. The night didn't care about the size of my bottom but the size of my heart. I'd dance to feel the blood surging through my body. I'd do a 'burning the pain' dance. I ran and leapt, then stopped and swerved my body in a bent over jack knife. When I was dancing everything felt better. I didn't know where I was going or what I was going to do – all I thought was keep dancing, don't stop moving.

I didn't look at anything, not to see if there was anyone around, or to check out the shops or any landmarks I was passing, I just kept listening to the blackbird's song. His voice kept me going as the notes reached out through the darkness, echoing along the empty street. The scent of lilac drifted into my nose and I followed.

I found myself by a small round park full of trees with a bandstand. Bird song filled the air. They were going crazy. I couldn't see the birds but their notes were clear, like stepping stones floating over the void. I would hop on their notes and every hop would be a sign of hope. Hop hope, hop hope, hop hope, I circled the park skipping. Keep hopping, keep hoping, that's how you learn to fly, the birds told me. In the orchestra of the night the birds sing the lullabies, like mothers, watching over their babies. They were watching over me, teaching me their dance. Somehow they'd sing me home.

I came to the corner of a small quaint street marked with a 'No Through Road' sign. I stared at the street name. Surely there could only be one road in the whole of London with that name. *The Cottages* was such an inappropriate name for a London Street. The thing was, I knew where I was, I'd even looked the street up on Google maps. Twenty seven, The Cottages, London EC1 – I'd learnt the address by heart. This was where Tartan Fling's studio was. The birds had led me to the only person I knew who lived in London.

48

It wasn't really a street more like a courtyard with cobbles on the floor and a square of little terraced houses painted different colours. In the middle were two old- fashioned street lamps that created soft amber circles on the stones. The moment I walked into the courtyard some of my fear evaporated. This little cul-de-sac felt safe. A few of the houses had porch lights and terracotta flower pots on either side of their front doors. This wasn't the sort of place where rapists would hang out.

Number twenty seven was at the far end with a strange wooden double door and bricks that had been painted white. It was a different shape to the other houses, longer and only two storeys high. Maybe the building had been used as a stable at one time. There weren't any windows on the ground floor so I peered through the crack in the door but I couldn't see anything. The upper level had a panel of long windows but there were no lights on inside. I didn't know if Jock lived here or if this was just where they rehearsed. But he'd be here sometime. I just had to wait. Maybe this was where I was meant to end up.

Sitting on the doorstep of Jock's studio, with my back against the wooden doors, I watched the opening of the cul-de-sac. There was an old floor plank propped up against the studio wall, with a rusty nail sticking out of one side. Holding the other end in both hands I practised swinging the plank. The rough wood scratched into my palms but I could move it with enough force to do some serious damage. I took my weapon back to the step and sat down. If anyone came into the courtyard to attack me I was ready for them.

The dancing had warmed me up. Funny how dancing made me feel so much better. I could think properly again. I'd been so stupid not seeing through Melody. She'd lied to me about staying at Chas's parents' place and she'd stolen my money. Vivienne had been totally right about her. Had Melody ever really liked me or had she always been using me?

Vivienne had been right about Tamasin too. I bet it was Tamasin who'd filmed me on her fancy phone. She wanted to stop me dancing, I could see that now. Vivienne had warned me that Tamasin was jealous of me. She didn't like me getting attention. If I'd listened to Vivienne I wouldn't be in this mess. She'd been on my side all along. But I'd been jealous of her; jealous because she had a boyfriend, especially one like Louis, and because her parents loved her so much. I was such an idiot. I'd got everyone the wrong way round. Vivienne was the person I should have chosen to have on the lifeboat rope with me, not Melody.

I started to cry as I thought about how horrible I'd been to Vivienne and then about Thomas and how upset he'd be about me running away. He had a tough enough time as it was, being frightened of going to school, Dad never taking any notice of him. Instead of helping my sweet little brother I'd made things worse. I was a terrible, awful, person but if I ever made it home I'd find a way to make it up to Thomas and to Vivienne.

Tears streamed down my neck, like a gushing

fountain, much worse than Vivienne when she'd run away. They could have hooked me up to the water board and stopped the next drought. Salty water flowed down my front then froze against my skin. Sitting still I realised how cold I was. The sweater dress, especially where it was soaked in urine, had turned into an ice block. My teeth started to chatter because I was shaking so much. I clutched my jacket tightly round me and wished I had some cardboard boxes to make a shelter like homeless people did. But there wasn't anything I could see to use. Voices at the end of the road jolted me to my feet clutching the wooden plank. Two men walked past the end of the road but didn't notice me. I put down the plank. I'd have to keep dancing to stay warm. I started my routine, the one I'd done for the dance show, only now I was changing the moves making them wiser and sadder.

As I danced a plan started to form. Jock Briggs had said I could do work experience with them. He hadn't said I was too fat to dance. He'd said he liked my energy. I'd wait here for him and I'd ask him to take me on as a dancer.

49

I must have closed my eyes for a moment because I was being shaken awake. My eyelids were so heavy that they didn't want to open but I knew somehow they had to. There was a pale brown face, with eyes the colour of polished conkers, staring at me. I leapt up reaching for the plank with the nail but it had gone. The man in front of me was holding it. He was wearing a brightly coloured woollen hat.

'If you touch me I'll kill you,' I screamed and he dropped the plank and put his hands up, as if I'd held a gun on him. His head and shoulders drooped and the brown eyes looked sad.

'I'm not going to hurt you,' he said and his voice was gentle and Scottish.

Oh my God, I'd blown it. Here was Jock Briggs and I'd threatened to kill him. I slumped back down onto the doorstep.

'Sorry, I'm sorry, I was asleep.'

The sky was turning pink and the air was woven with the loudest birdsong you'd ever heard. Dawn. I'd made it through the night. The courtyard was filled with sunlight but I started to shiver.

Jock crouched down in front of me sitting on his heels in a squat. He was looking at the cobbles. Struck by a shaft of early morning sun they gleamed golden. We both stared down at them and watched a beetle crawl between two of the stones, as if making its way along an ancient path. The creature's back sparked translucent green and blue. We watched him disappear underneath one of the cobbles.

'The thing is,' Jock was speaking, 'I have to get in that door before I can make us both a cup of tea.'

I leapt up then and almost knocked him over.

It was now or never, 'I'm Pen, Pen Flowers, you probably don't remember but I did your workshop in Birmingham, and you said I should stay in touch and that I could do work experience with you. So here I am.' I was speaking too fast and my heart was hammering. I tried to appear calm but my body was shaking uncontrollably and my teeth were chattering again. 'I wondered if you could give me a job.' Jock had unlocked the door and was waving me inside.

'I remember,' was all he said. I walked in front of him into shadow and the smell of oil and petrol. From the open door a tunnel of thick yellow light burrowed through the darkness. Jock reached for a switch and two strip lights stuttered on, blinding me for a second and then filling a large empty room with harsh white light. The walls were bare brick with workbenches and tools and bikes propped up against them. There was a pile of lumpy stuff under tarpaulins in the far corner.

'This is the workshop, the studio's upstairs.' He led the way to wooden steps attached to the far side of the wall. 'You're lucky I'm here. I don't often come in on a Saturday. I'm expecting a lorry with the sets from our tour.'

I followed him up the stairs into a small room with a kitchen unit down one side and a little table with chairs and a battered settee on the other. He filled up a kettle and switched it on.

'There's a toilet through there if you need it,' he pointed to a green door. 'I've just got to make a phone call.' Jock went back downstairs. Peeking through an open door on the opposite side of the room I caught a glimpse of white floorboards.

I did need the loo, urgently, because I'd realised how awful I smelt. What must Jock think of me? No wonder he made the suggestion. The tiny square of mirror over the wash basin showed me that I looked as bad as I smelt. There was soap and a towel so I did my best. I rubbed down the back of my dress but it didn't do much good. My new hairstyle stuck out at odd angles. The fringe had gone wonky; that cool angular punk girl hadn't survived the night. I tried wetting my hair to get it to lie flat but it just started to kink up even more.

When I came back into the kitchen Jock was already there.

'Sit down,' he indicated one of the chairs at the table. When I did he draped a blanket round my shoulders and put a cup of tea in front of me, 'that should warm you up.'

I needed to give him some kind of explanation.

'I got a lift with a friend you see, we got here early.'

He smiled at me. 'People usually phone and make an appointment.'

'It was a last minute thing, if you're busy I..,'

'Drink your tea - I put two sugars in,' he was standing looking out of the window into the courtyard. 'Worth getting up early just for the light isn't it?'

I nodded and he carried on speaking.

'There's a Sufi poet called Rumi; heard of him?'

I shook my head.

'"The breezes at dawn have secrets to tell you, don't go back to sleep."' Jock spoke the words in a hushed whisper then laughed. He didn't look at me just kept staring out of the window and I was glad.

The hot tea was a life saver. I cradled the mug in both hands so that the warmth would stop them shaking. Heat ran through me with each mouthful and I began to feel a bit steadier. Jock sat down on the chair opposite me and drank his tea.

'So you want to be a dancer, is that right?'

I nodded.

'When I was your age I wanted to be a footballer,

and I wasn't bad. I was on the youth squad for Celtic. My Dad was heartbroken when I changed to dancing.'

He was making an effort to talk to me but I couldn't think of anything to say. We finished our tea in silence.

'Would you like something to eat?'

I shook my head. I couldn't eat not with my tummy twisted into knots.

'Can I show you my dance?' I blurted out.

'You want to dance now? You're sure you're up to it?'

I nodded like an idiot. Stop nodding, for goodness sake Pen. He'll think you're special needs!

'Please, have you got Stravinsky's Rites of Spring, that's my music?'

'I can find it,' Jock was looking me over, 'at least dancing will warm you up.'

He led the way through the open door into the studio. At first I was blinded by the brightness and had to close my eyes. The sunlight glowed red on the back of my eyelids. I turned into the warmth and let out a sigh. The in-my-bones coldness was starting to thaw. Moving my back to the windows I opened my eyes. The room was painted white; floor, ceiling, walls, all white, apart from a giant mirror running along the back wall. Light poured in through the squared glass windows hit the mirror and bounced back. The room was swirling with sunlight and I felt giddy.

In the mirror I was a black blob. I turned away and took off my jacket, boots and socks. My feet, sticking out from my black dance tights, were white with blotchy red marks from being inside my boots for so long. They looked like two little animals scrunched up after a winter's hibernation. In the far corner there was a music deck and Jock was searching for my music on his tablet. I made a few stretches. There was a sharp pain in one shoulder spreading up through my neck from sleeping in an odd position. I felt hollow as if I'd been cored like an apple. My music was playing.

'Which track?' Jock asked.

'It's the opening piece,' I couldn't look at his face I felt too shy. I was a bug that had crawled into heaven.

'This right?'

I nodded. He stopped the music and picking up a broom propped against the wall, started to sweep the floor. He moved methodically across the room with long slow strokes that made a swooshing sound. I carried on stretching and leant down to watch him secretly, through my open legs. He looked small and neat in the big room and stepped so lightly that I couldn't hear his feet. Every part of his body seemed relaxed as if there were no snags or pulls and he was free to flow gently into the space. My own body felt too heavy and tight to dance. Who was I trying to kid? I didn't want to make a fool of myself in front of this graceful man.

The sweeping sound stopped.

'Are you ready? I'll sit over here if that's ok?' His voice edged into silence in the same way that he moved across the room - leaving it undisturbed. He sat down on the floor next to the sound system with his legs crossed and his back against the wall. I stood about three feet in front of him with the mirror to my left and the windows to my right. I turned slightly towards the right wanting to block my reflection from my eye line. My feet had returned to a more normal colour and I spread them on the floor, took a deep breath, and then knelt down. I gave Jock a nod to begin the music before curling into my starting position. The bassoon solo drifted through the room.

I really was new born that morning because the girl who rose up slowly from her knees wasn't any Pen Flowers that had ever been before. Certainly not the one, who once upon a time long, long ago, had gone mad in dance class. Everything that had happened to me over the night was in my body. I'd changed the moves but now they were shifting again as I shed some of the night's loneliness and fear in the bright morning.

I had no choice but to dance out of my raw flayed heart, laying every bit of me on the floor for Jock to see. I danced the way the birds had taught me to dance last night, small and fluttering, but burning inside. As if all I could do was leap and hope that by some miracle I managed to fly.

I finished lying on the floor looking up at the white ceiling. If I'd died at that moment I'd have rocketed straight to heaven. But my heart kept on beating, very energetically, and after a bit I sat up. Jock was sitting on the floor watching me. He didn't say anything but stood up, tucking his feet underneath him and rising in one smooth movement without using his hands. I wished I could do that.

He switched on the music and came and knelt beside me.

'Teach me, 'he said, as the music started again.

I didn't understand.

'Teach me the dance.'

How could I refuse? It was incredible how quickly he picked it up, as if just from watching once he'd memorised everything. We went through the moves side by side and it was fun until he began to change things. I glared at him. This was my dance he should copy me. Only then I understood, he wasn't really changing the dance, he was adapting the moves so that our bodies reacted together, transforming the piece from a solo into a duet. When I realised what he was doing I stopped resisting him and joined in and then it was amazing. I was smiling so much my face hurt. I wanted to go on dancing forever.

'Again?' He asked as the track finished.

'Oh yes,' I gasped for breath. I was unbelievably tired but I never wanted to stop.

'Ready?'

This time we faced the mirror and I could see

how the dance looked with two people. Dancing with Jock was spell binding, he was so strong and graceful. It was as if his magic had spread over me and I could dance like him. He caught every shape I'd invented and made it into something bigger, funnier, lovelier, or more frightening. I started hearing new things in the music, the way the different instruments had different jobs to do and could be used to trigger alternative shapes and sequences. As the music built towards the final climax, where I usually sank to the floor and turned on my back, Jock put his back against mine. We started to spin, back to back, leaning our weight against each other. Then suddenly, I don't even know how he did it, but he'd swung me onto his back and up to his shoulder and over his head. He was holding me above him and we were gliding slowly round. I wasn't on the floor looking up at the stars any more. I was flying through the sky, spinning like the earth itself.

The music stopped and he lowered me to the ground. We were both breathing hard.

'That is a beautiful dance,' he said, 'the song of the night.'

I stared.

'How did you know?' I hadn't told anyone, not even Mrs Hadley, what the dance was really about.

'I felt it,' he said and banged his fist against his chest, 'I felt the night flow through me.'

I started to cry again then. As if I hadn't done enough crying already. I don't know why I was blubbing apart from the fact that someone had heard what I was trying to say. Jock laughed and patted my back.

'More tea, I think, and maybe toast.'

Back in the kitchen he made more tea and a pile of hot buttered toast and told me to rest on the settee.

'You look done in,' he said.

'Didn't get much sleep last night,' I admitted, 'but I don't want to get in your way.' I wanted to ask about a job, whether I could be one of his dancers, but I couldn't seem to make the effort. I was afraid he'd say no.

'I'll be downstairs in the workshop, if you need me,' he said.

I must have fallen asleep again because next thing I knew I heard the sound of a van arriving outside and my tea had gone cold. I was sitting on the settee covered in a blanket. I could hear voices in the workshop below. The truck with the sets must have arrived. I should go down and help them unload to show Jock what a good worker I could be. But it was so lovely being warm and cosy after last night that I couldn't get myself to move.

Someone was running with heavy steps up the stairs, it didn't sound like Jock.

50

Vivienne Cooper burst through the door.

'Pen, oh Pen,' she flung herself at me enveloping me in a great bear hug, 'I'm so glad you're safe.'

How could Vivienne Cooper possibly be in the kitchen of Jock's London studio? But I knew I wasn't dreaming because she was squeezing me so tightly I thought one of my ribs would break. Not that I minded because I was extremely pleased to see her. Never had I seen a more beautiful sight. Why had I'd ever thought Vivienne was ugly. She had the kindest, warmest, friendliest face in the whole world. I was hugging her right back.

'Pen, I can't breathe,' she said and I realised that I was the one doing the squeezing and let her go.

'I don't understand - how did you know where I was? How did you get here?'

'Dad's downstairs with the van. The police found out that you'd gone to London with Mel. If you'd gone to London I guessed it would be to see Jock Briggs. Mrs Hadley got his number from her friend and we called him last night. When you turned up this morning he phoned us.' Vivienne was sitting next to me on the sofa holding my hand. To her it must have seemed simple, I'd come to London to see Jock.

'Everyone's been incredibly worried about you. I'm so pleased you're alright,' she squeezed my hand. 'We've come to take you home.'

I pulled away from her. Of course I wanted to go home. I wanted to go home more than I'd ever wanted anything in the world. I never ever intended spending a night on the streets again as long as I lived. But going home for me was, was, well impossible. From nowhere this loud sobbing burst out of my mouth. I was crying just like Mum did when she'd totally lost control.

Vivienne reached out for me and held me against her big soft body. There was a sharp pain in my chest like my heart had broken in half. Vivienne was the only thing I had to hold onto, the only way I could hold myself together.

'I can't go home Viv, it's hopeless, you don't know what happened with Tamasin, I hit her, I'm going to be expelled. And Mum and Dad are furious with me, it's too horrible, I just can't face it. I'm not brave at all. I've made a stupid mess of everything.' My body was shuddering but Vivienne kept holding onto me, stroking my back until I calmed down. Gradually, I managed to get my breath even but the tears still poured from my eyes.

'Well, actually, you haven't,' Vivienne's tone was matter of fact, 'messed up everything, because Jock said that considering you'd been out on the streets all night, your dancing was remarkable.'

That stopped me crying. I sat up and looked at her.

'Did he say that? When?'

'Just now, downstairs, to me and Dad, he said you were tough, and that was good because you needed to be tough to make it as a dancer. I think he likes you.'

I turned this bit of information over.

'What about Mum and Dad, are they really angry with me?'

'They've been going crazy with worry. Your Dad wanted to come and get you but the police thought it would be better if I did. My Dad's promised your parents he'll take you straight back. We've put a mattress in the back of the van – it's really cosy, you'll see.' She pulled me up on my feet and pushed me towards the door. 'When did you get your hair done? The colour's amazing.'

'What about school, have I been expelled?' I was hanging back.

'Of course you haven't – stop being such a drama queen.'

'You can talk,' I said but she was already disappearing down the stairs.

Jock handed me a square of paper.

'Write your address and phone number on that Pen, and your email if you've got one, and I'll be in touch.'

I couldn't look him in the eye, I felt so foolish.

'Thank you for watching me dance,' I managed

to say.

'That was a dance I'll remember for a long time,' he took the piece of paper off me and lifted his eyes to mine. 'I don't generally go in for advice Pen, but there was a second century monk called Vasubhandu, who said you should live life as if your head's on fire. You blaze away Pen, and don't let anyone, not your friends, not your family, nor your enemies, put your flame out.' He squeezed my shoulder gently and I reached across and hugged him.

'So can I join your company?' I blurted out. Jock smiled and shook his head. 'When I'm older I mean, if I work really hard.'

'We'll see, stay in touch, you might change your mind, remember I wanted to be a footballer.'

'Never, ever,' I said.

51

Going home in the van was an odd way to travel. Mr Cooper's window cleaning ladders were tied to the sides, and they rattled and clanked every time we hit a bump in the road. Plus there was a strong smell of wet rags. Vivienne and I sat on the mattress and ate the packed lunch Viv had brought; sandwiches and crisps and even some of Mrs Cooper's chocolate cake. Never before had it tasted quite as good. Then we snuggled down to lie on our backs. All you could see from out of the van windows was the sky zooming by. Odd bits of tree and building and lamp post stuck out so that you could hardly recognise them. I thought about the car journey down to London wedged between Mick and Yogi. I still found it hard to believe that Vivienne had found me. I propped myself up on my elbow and turned to face her.

'I went with Mel to see a band, you know. I only ended up at Jock's because everything went wrong. How did you know I'd be there?'

'Well I didn't, but given that you like couldn't stop talking about Jock- it was a good guess.'

I felt my cheeks go hot. I remembered what I'd shouted at Vivienne on the library stairs, about her going on about Louis. Vivienne went quiet as if she was thinking about that too. The pause went on for too long. I took a big breath.

'Look I'm sorry about what I said about you being obsessed by Louis, I was jealous. I thought you wouldn't need me anymore.'

'Yeh well, I was like really angry with you. Of course I wanted to talk about Louis, I'd had to keep him secret for so long. But I should've guessed how vulnerable you'd feel, with what was going on at school and everything.'

'And I should've understood how important it was for you to finally be open about Louis.'

There was another big pause. I felt as shy as if

I'd only just met Vivienne.

The van braked sharply and swerved and I was thrown against her, banging my head on her chin.

'Wanker, use your indicators,' Mr Cooper was shouting at another driver.

'Ouch,' I rubbed my head and looked at Vivienne, 'how's your chin?'

'Bit sore. Friends then?' Vivienne asked.

'Absolutely,' I said.

She reached out and squeezed my hand. We lay for a while listening to the noise of the car engine.

'There is one thing Pen, I hope you don't mind me saying it,' Vivienne sounded nervous. I braced myself, knowing I was going to hear some awful truth about myself that would make me feel ashamed.

'You smell really dreadful.'

52

I was jolted awake by the van stopping. I was still in a fuzzy, sleep-drenched daze when the back doors opened and Mum's head appeared, followed by her body as she clambered into the van and grabbed hold of me.

'Pen, Pen,' she kept saying, her eyes never leaving my face as she hugged me to her. Somehow Mum was outside the house, in the road, and worrying about me! I thought I was still dreaming.

'Sweetheart, you're here, you're home.' She couldn't stop cuddling me and stroking my hair and face. Then Thomas arrived, leaping over the mattress, nearly blinding Vivienne, who had to dodge his flying dive.

'Don't run away again, Pen, not ever,' he told

me. Even Dad was there, standing by the van doors helping Vivienne to jump down.

'Everyone out,' he said, 'let's get Pen inside,' laughing at the commotion and no sign of his 'I'm deeply disappointed in you' face.

'The Prodigal daughter has returned,' he announced as I emerged from the van. He lifted me up and was swinging me around like he used to when I was a kid. 'With purple hair!' And he didn't even go off on one.

Everyone seemed happy to have me back. Mum apologised for hitting me and even Dad said he was sorry that he'd been angry and hadn't listened. They were ready to listen now and I wanted to tell them everything. The truth poured out of me - about Tamasin and Sadie and the porno picture and school songs and the birthday trip. I went online on our computer and showed them the video of me dancing with all the horrible comments so that they understood. They were really shocked especially about Tamasin. Dad said he'd make an appointment to see the Headmistress on Monday.

I couldn't wait to get my disgusting clothes off.

Sinking into a hot bath was the best sensation ever. Knowing that Mum and Dad were going to help me sort out things at school felt such a relief. I wasn't on my own anymore. I threw Mel's stinking sweater dress into the bin and vowed that I would never smell that bad again.

On Monday the Head called a meeting with me and my parents and Tamasin and hers. It wasn't anywhere near as bad as I'd feared. I didn't get expelled, Tamasin apologised for posting the video. Her Mum said they'd removed the original post but when I said it was still online she admitted that there was nothing they could do to remove it entirely once it was public. I was going to have to live with that. Tamasin looked guilty but maybe she was putting on a show for her parents who seemed to be on my side. I apologised for hitting her but I wasn't going to rush back to being her friend. No way.

I found out later that Sadie, because she was already on a warning, had been moved out of our class into 10c. If there was any more trouble she was the one going to be expelled not me. Vivienne did alright – she came out as a heroine for finding me in London and got a Kings' Award for Special Service and a hundred house points as reward.

On the last day of term I was doing some practise in the dance studio when Mrs Hadley interrupted.

'Penny, good news,' she was wearing a new daffodil yellow track suit.

Dazzled by her glory I stopped dancing and walked over.

'I've just had Jock Briggs on the phone,' she said. 'He wants you to do some training with Tartan Fling in the summer holidays after your GCSE's.'

'No!' I screamed.

'Oh yes,' Mrs Hadley confirmed.

I couldn't stop myself I threw myself into the sunshine blaze of her sweatshirt and hugged her.

It wasn't until I'd been back home for a week, when I'd thought everything was sorted, that Mum and Dad dropped the bomb. They were splitting up and Dad was moving out.

53

'Happy Birthday dear Penelope,' Mum, Dad and Thomas burst out singing as the waitress arrived at our table with a giant Tropical Paradise Ice Cream Sundae decorated with palm trees and umbrellas and incandescent with sparklers.

'Wow,' Thomas's smile was a mile wide, 'that's better than a City goal.' Dad had taken him to the home match last Saturday and ever since then everything was footie related. We were in Captain America's for my birthday dinner. Dad had given me a new smart phone and Mum had got me my first real leather ballet pumps. It was weird but since Dad had moved out they'd started being nicer to each other.

'Everyone dig in,' Dad said. There were four

spoons with long handles.

We actually saw more of Dad because when he came round or took us out he spent time with us rather than burying himself in jazz music or history pamphlets.

'Look there's different creatures. I've got a shark, what can you find Thomas?' Mum was better than she'd been for ages. A lady from the Mental Health team came round twice a week to help her. She was even managing to walk Thomas to the end of the road to encourage him to go to school in the mornings. Since London I was more understanding about what she was dealing with. I was proud of her for doing so well. She was getting stronger without Dad around which I would never have expected.

After the meal the family went home and I met up with Vivienne and Louis at The Institute to see a band from Handsworth that Louis knew. They were awesome and we were all dancing. I was going for it like a wild woman when someone tapped me on my shoulder.

'Pen,' Mick was smiling nervously. My first reaction was to blank him.

'I didn't know how to get hold of you,' he said quickly, 'the number Mel had didn't work.' I didn't say anything. 'We came back to get you. But you'd gone, we couldn't find you anywhere.' The music was loud and he had to shout for me to hear. I kept getting knocked by the people leaping about near me.

'Come outside so we can talk,' Mick said. I hesitated. Vivienne was by my side, her face next to mine.

'I'm going outside,' I told her, 'I'll be back in a minute.'

'You've got your phone?' she asked. I nodded. Anyone would think Mick was going to kidnap me.

After the manic dancing the fresh night air felt good. A thin layer of sweat cooled and tightened on my skin. The sky was clear and moonlight silvered the street. You could hear the thump of the music inside, but muffled and distant. Other people were standing in clumps, some smoking, a couple were making out against the wall. Mick walked a few yards up the road, until we were away from everyone else. We faced each other but standing apart and avoiding eye contact. I remembered our kiss by the Trafalgar Square fountain.

'I've been trying to get hold of you,' he said. 'When Mel said she didn't know what had happened to you, we all freaked out, even Chas.'

'When did you see Mel?'

'At the gig, the next night, she stayed over at Chas's parents' flat and then drove home with us. So you were ok? You got back by yourself?'

I couldn't believe it. Melody Jones had actually managed to get what she wanted and had wangled her way into Chas's parents' flat.

'What did Mel say?'

'You ran off. She thought you'd got the train back.'

I couldn't speak. Melody was unbelievable. How did she think I could get a train when she'd stolen my money? I could have been murdered for all she knew.

'She was here earlier,' Mick reached out and touched my hand. 'I've been hoping I'd bump into you. Can I have your number?' he asked.

I wasn't sure. I felt flustered. Had he really tried to come and find me in London? He looked anxious now.

'Give me your number,' I decided. That didn't mean I'd forgiven him but I might think about giving him another chance.

We went back inside and I carried on dancing with Vivienne. I knew Mick was watching me. Wriggling, squirming feelings were cavorting about in my tummy. I was churned up by everything he'd told me and wasn't sure. Did I want to see him again or not?

When the band finished, Louis walked us to the bus stop to get the night bus home. Vivienne was sleeping over at my house and I was desperate to talk to her about Mick and see what she thought.

All the pubs were emptying out onto the streets and crowds of people were milling about shouting and laughing. I was glad we were with Louis. As we passed the Bull Ring a giant moon floated into view, hanging low in the sky so that New Street was as light as daylight almost.

'What about that moon? I've never seen one so big,' I said, being a bit of a nightscape expert. It was like a space ship had landed behind the Rotunda. This was a perfect night for dancing on the streets.

'My Dad calls that a bomber's moon,' Louis said. His Granddad had been in the RAF during the Second World War.

People were queuing up to get into the clubs. Outside *The Ocean* there was some kind of commotion going on. A woman was yelling. Louis crossed us over to the other side of the road. He was good at keeping out of trouble.

Two bouncers in black suits held a young woman by the arms. They marched her away from the club's entrance and pushed her into the street. She staggered back struggling to keep her balance but steadied herself and then put her head down and charged back at them, screaming as she ran.

'Isn't that...' Vivienne started to speak. The giant moon gave the night a mysterious glow, everything seemed to be slowed down and back lit. The bouncers blocked the woman's charge before she hit them. Taking her by the shoulders this time, they threw her roughly back onto the street again. She zigzagged for a few steps then fell. There was a loud crack as she hit the ground then she lay motionless, her hair glowing brilliant copper against the pale grey line of the road.

There was the sound of a police siren in the distance.

'Pen,' I heard Vivienne shout as I ran into the street.

'Are you ok?' I crouched down on the road and put my arm underneath her. 'Can you sit up?'

Melody Jones opened her eyes and raised her head from the road.

'Oh hello Angel,' I had one arm round her waist and was supporting her with my body. She held her head.

'Oww,' she said struggling to get up. Vivienne had joined me on the road and she went to her other side. Together we got her to her feet.

'Should we take her to the hospital do you think?' I asked Vivienne.

'Hairy arsed, shrunken dicked, gorillas,' Melody was shouting at the bouncers.

'I think she's ok,' Vivienne said as Melody spat on the road in front of the club. Melody turned to smile at me.

'Let's go dancing Angel,' she shook off Vivienne and hooked her arm into mine. She was drunk, of course, but even so, I couldn't believe that she was behaving like my dearest friend. She seemed to have no memory of how she'd behaved the last time she'd seen me.

'I'm going home with Vivienne,' I said untangling my arm.

Melody shrugged and stepped away, swaying and still holding her head.

'Maybe you should come with us?' I suggested.

'No way,' she walked unsteadily back towards *The Ocean,* shouting over her shoulder, 'see you, Angel.'

Avoiding the bouncers, she made her way to the back of the queue.

'Get us in, will you, love,' I heard her say as she clutched onto a man's arm.

Vivienne and I stood in the middle of the road amazed, until a car horn blared at us and we had to move. Then Louis was shouting that our bus was coming, so we ran for it.

Maybe it was meeting Melody again, or more likely it was the moon's fault, but after Vivienne had gone to sleep, I lay awake staring at the strips of blue light slanting across my bedroom wall and gave in to the call of the night.

I didn't climb out of the window but crept downstairs and put the front door on the latch, not intending to go far. The moon was spectacular, a great white circle of stillness and calm. I stood in the middle of the road letting the light flow into me, fill me to the brim.

Life was tough. It was messy and complicated but I had lots to be grateful for. Mum was getting better, Vivienne was the greatest friend anyone could ever want and maybe Mick wasn't as awful as I'd thought. But best of all, I was going to be doing work experience with Tartan Fling in the summer holidays. I leapt into the air; thank you Night for caring for me, for looking over me, for guiding me home.

I swooped up Knightlow Road stretching out my wings and feeling the explosive power in my thighs. Whatever felt special, whatever burnt inside, that's what you had to be true to. I wasn't going to let anyone stop me dancing. Flame on, Pen Flowers, I declared, making high scissor kicks down the centre of the street, flame on and let's get blazing. Live like your head's on fire.

Coming soon
Love Like Your Heart's On Fire

Pen Flowers reckons that falling in love is a Big Mistake. All around her emotional chaos seethes. Her parents have separated and her newly dating Mum is behaving like a teenager. Even her best friend, Vivienne, is a mess for love, falling appart when her relationship with Louis ends.

No way is Pen going to let any man ruin her life. But her heart has other ideas.

When Pen's heart explodes her plans are blasted into a zillion pieces. Will she be able to keep the promise she made herself or will love lead her to throw away her dream of being a dancer?

Acknowledgements

This book has taken a long while to be born and a great many people have helped with the birthing. My thanks to Ian Nettleton for getting me started, Jane Rogers for guiding me through early drafts and most of all to Yvvette Edwards for believing in me as a writer and helping me to become a better one.

To my young readers Ella and Mia Sharrock, and Zara Hunter, thank you, I couldn't have done this without your insights.

Big thanks to first readers Sara Willett, Ruth Harper and Lora Stimson for their encouragement and to Deborah Arnander, Johnny Fincham, Elizabeth Jolly and Sarah Passingham for their long term support.

I'd like to thank the National Centre for Writers' Escalator Programme, the Arts Council of England and The Literary Consultancy Free Reads Scheme for their professional and financial assistance.

Working with my editor, Sam Ruddock, the warmest hearted and most sensitive publisher any writer could desire, has been a total joy. My lifelong gratitude to Sam.

Finally, thanks to my mother and brother for their love and patience, to Sara for her understanding, laughter and company on this roller coaster adventure, and to AFW whose quiet steady love has made everything possible.